Albany County Public Library
Sources of Materials
FY12

- County Sales Tax
- City Sales Tax
- Foundation
- Friends
- Cash Gifts from Public
- Replacement Fees
- Donated Items

THE
SECRET HISTORY
OF
COSTAGUANA

ALSO BY JUAN GABRIEL VÁSQUEZ

The Informers

THE
SECRET HISTORY
OF
COSTAGUANA

Juan Gabriel Vásquez

translated from the Spanish by Anne McLean

RIVERHEAD BOOKS

a member of Penguin Group (USA) Inc.

New York

2011

RIVERHEAD BOOKS
Published by the Penguin Group
Penguin Group (USA) Inc., 375 Hudson Street, New York, New York 10014, USA •
Penguin Group (Canada), 90 Eglinton Avenue East, Suite 700, Toronto, Ontario M4P 2Y3,
Canada (a division of Pearson Penguin Canada Inc.) • Penguin Books Ltd, 80 Strand, London
WC2R 0RL, England • Penguin Ireland, 25 St Stephen's Green, Dublin 2, Ireland (a division
of Penguin Books Ltd) • Penguin Group (Australia), 250 Camberwell Road, Camberwell,
Victoria 3124, Australia (a division of Pearson Australia Group Pty Ltd) • Penguin Books
India Pvt Ltd, 11 Community Centre, Panchsheel Park, New Delhi–110 017, India •
Penguin Group (NZ), 67 Apollo Drive, Rosedale, North Shore 0632, New Zealand
(a division of Pearson New Zealand Ltd) • Penguin Books (South Africa) (Pty) Ltd,
24 Sturdee Avenue, Rosebank, Johannesburg 2196, South Africa

Penguin Books Ltd, Registered Offices: 80 Strand, London WC2R 0RL, England

First published in the United States 2011
Copyright © 2007 by Juan Gabriel Vásquez
English translation © 2010 by Anne McLean

Library of Congress Cataloging-in-Publication Data

Vásquez, Juan Gabriel, date.
[Historia secreta de Costaguana. English.]
The secret history of Costaguana / Juan Gabriel Vásquez ; translated from the Spanish by Anne McLean.
p.   cm.
ISBN 978-1-59448-803-0
1. Colombians—England—London—Fiction.   2. Conrad, Joseph, 1857–1924—Fiction.
3. Conrad, Joseph, 1857–1924. Nostromo—Fiction.   4. Novelists, English—20th century—Fiction.
5. Fiction—Authorship—Fiction.   6. Colombia—Fiction.   I. McLean, Anne, date.   II. Title.
PQ8180.32.A797H5713   2011   2011005706
863.7—dc22

Printed in the United States of America
1   3   5   7   9   10   8   6   4   2

Book design by Michelle McMillian

For Martina and Carlota,
who brought their own book with them
when they arrived

Contents

I want to talk to you of the work I am engaged on now.
I hardly dare avow my audacity—but I am placing it in
South America in a Republic I call Costaguana.

—Joseph Conrad
Letter to Robert Cunninghame Graham

PART ONE

There is never any God in a country where men will not help themselves.

Joseph Conrad, *Nostromo*

I

Upside-down Frogs,
Chinamen, and Civil Wars

Let's just come right out and say it: the man has died. No, that won't do. I'll be more precise: the Novelist (with a capital *N*) has died. You all know who I mean. Don't you? Well, I'll try again: the Great English Novelist has died. The Great English Novelist—Polish by birth, sailor before he became a writer—has died. The Great English-language Novelist—Polish by birth, sailor before he became a writer, who went from failed suicide to living classic, from common gunrunner to Jewel of the British Crown—has died. Ladies and gentlemen: Joseph Conrad has died. I receive the news familiarly, as one might receive an old friend, then realize, not without some sadness, that I've spent my whole life waiting for it.

I begin writing this with all the London broadsheets (their microscopic print, their uneven, narrow columns) spread out over my green leather desktop. Through the press, which has played such diverse roles over the course of my life—threatening to ruin it at times, and at others granting what little luster it has—I am informed of the heart attack and its circumstances: the visit from Nurse Vinten, the shout heard from downstairs, the body falling out of the chair. Through enterprising journalism I attend the funeral in Canterbury; through the impertinences of reporters I watch them lower the body and place the stone, that headstone beset with errors (a *K* out of place, a vowel wrong in one of the names). Today, August 7, 1924, while in my distant Colombia they are celebrating one hundred and five years since the Battle of Boyacá, here in England they mourn, without pomp and ceremony, the passing of the Great Novelist. While in Colombia they commemorate the victory of the armies of independence over the forces of the Spanish Empire, here, in this ground of another empire, the man has been buried forever, the man who robbed me . . .

But no.

Not yet.

It's still too soon.

It's too soon to explain the forms and qualities of that theft; it's too soon to explain what merchandise was stolen, what motives the thief had, what damage the victim suffered. I hear the questions clamoring from the stalls: What can a famous novelist have in common with a poor, anonymous, exiled Colombian? Readers: have patience. You don't want to know everything at the beginning; do not investigate, do not ask, for this narrator, like a benevolent father, will gradually provide the necessary information as the tale proceeds. . . . In other words, leave it all in my hands. I'll decide when and how to tell what I want to tell, when to hide, when to reveal, when to lose myself in the nooks and crannies of my memory for the mere pleasure of doing so. Here I shall tell you of implausible murders and unpredictable hangings, elegant declarations of war and slovenly peace accords, of fires and floods and intriguing ships and conspiratorial trains; but somehow all that I tell you will be aimed at explaining and explaining to myself, link by link, the chain of events that provoked the encounter for which my life was destined.

For that's how it is: the disagreeable business of destiny has its share of responsibility in all this. Conrad and I, who were born countless meridians apart, our lives marked by the difference of the hemispheres, had a common future that would have been obvious from the first moment, even to the most skeptical person. When this happens, when the paths of two men born in distant places are destined to cross, a map can be drawn a posteriori. Most often the encounter is singular: Franz Ferdinand encounters Gavrilo Princip in Sarajevo and is shot dead along with his wife, the nineteenth century, and all those European certainties; General Rafael Uribe Uribe encounters two peasants, Galarza and Carvajal, in Bogotá and shortly thereafter dies near the Plaza de Bolívar, with an ax embedded in his skull and the weight of several civil wars on his shoulders. Conrad and I met only once, but long ago we had been on the verge of doing so. Twenty-seven years passed between the two events. The aborted encounter, which was on the verge of taking place but which never happened, occurred in 1876, in the Colombian province of Panama; the other meeting—the actual one, the fateful one—happened at the end of November 1903. And it happened here: in the chaotic, imperial, and decadent city of London. Here, in the city where I write and where death predictably awaits me, city of gray skies and the smell of coal in which I arrived for reasons not easy, yet obligatory, to explain.

I came to London, like so many people have come to so many places, fleeing from the history that was my lot, or rather, from the history of the country that was my lot. In other words, I came to London because here history had ceased some time ago: nothing happened in these lands anymore, everything had already been invented and done; they'd already had all the ideas, all the empires had arisen and they'd fought all the wars, and I would be forever safe from the disasters that Great Moments can impress onto Small Lives. Coming here was, therefore, a legitimate act of self-defense; the jury that judges me will have to take that into consideration.

For I, too, shall be accused in this book; I, too, shall sit on the time-worn bench, although the patient reader will have to cover more than a few pages to discover of what I accuse myself. I, who came in flight from Big History, now go back a whole century to the core of my little story, and shall attempt to investigate the roots of my disgrace. During that night, the night of our encounter, Conrad listened to me tell my story; and now, dear readers—readers who shall judge me, Readers of the Jury—it's your turn. For the success of my tale rests on this supposition: you will have to know all that Conrad knew.

(But there is someone else . . . Eloísa, you, too, will have to get to know these reminiscences, these confessions. You, too, will have to deliver, when the time comes, your own pardon or your own guilty verdict.)

My story begins in February 1820, five months after Simón Bolívar made his victorious entrance into the capital of my recently liberated country. Every story has a father, and this one begins with the birth of mine: Don Miguel Felipe Rodrigo Lazaro del Niño Jesús Altamirano. Miguel Altamirano, known to his friends as the Last Renaissance Man, was born in the schizophrenic city of Santa Fe de Bogotá, which from here on in will be called either Santa Fe or Bogotá or even That Shit Hole; while my grandmother tugged hard on the midwife's hair and let out screams that frightened the slaves, a few steps away the law was approved by which Bolívar, in his capacity as father of the nation, chose the name for that country fresh out of the oven, and the country was solemnly baptized. So the Republic of Colombia—schizophrenic country that will later be called New Granada or the United States of Colombia or even That Shit Hole—was a babe in arms, and the corpses of the executed Spaniards were still fresh; but there is no historical event that marks or distinguishes my father's birth, except for the superfluous ceremony of that baptism.

My father was—as I have already said—the Last Renaissance Man. I cannot say he was of blue blood, because that hue was no longer acceptable in the new republic, but what flowed through his veins was magenta, shall we say, or maybe purple. His tutor, a frail and sickly man who had been educated in Madrid, educated my father in turn with the *Quixote* and Garcilaso; but the young Altamirano, who by the age of twelve was already a consummate rebel (as well as a terrible literary critic), strove to reject the literature of the Spaniards, the Voice of the Occupation, and in the end succeeded in doing so. He learned English to read Thomas Malory, and one of his first published poems, a hyperromantic and mawkish creation comparing Lord Byron to Simón Bolívar, appeared under the signature Lancelot of the Lake. My father discovered later that Byron had in fact wanted to come and fight with Bolívar, and it was only chance that finally took him to Greece; and what he henceforth felt for Romantics, from England and anywhere else, began to replace little by little the devotions and loyalties his elders had left him as his birthright.

Not that this was difficult, for by the age of twenty the Latin American Byron was already orphaned. His mother had been killed by smallpox; his father (in a much more elegant way) by Christianity. My grandfather, an illustrious colonel who had fought against the dragoons of many Spanish regiments, was stationed in the southern provinces when the progressive government decreed the closure of four convents, and saw the first riots in defense of religion at bayonet point. One of those Catholic, apostolic, and Roman bayonets, one of those steel points engaged on the crusade for the faith, stabbed him months later; the news of his death arrived in Bogotá at the same time as the city was preparing to repel an attack by those same Catholic revolutionaries. But Bogotá or Santa Fe was, like the rest of the country, divided, and my father would never forget it: leaning out of a window at the university, he saw the people of Santa Fe in procession carrying a figure of Christ dressed in a general's uniform, heard the shouts of "Death to the Jews," and marveled at the thought that they referred to his stabbed father, and then returned to the classroom routine, in time to observe his fellow students stabbing with sharp, pointed instruments cadavers recently arrived from the battlefields. For there was nothing at that time, absolutely nothing, the Latin American Byron liked more than being a first-hand witness to the fascinating advances of medical science.

He had enrolled in the Faculty of Law, in obedience to my grandfather's wishes, but after a while devoted only the first part of his days to the legal codes. Like a Don Juan divided between two lovers, my father went from the ordeal of waking at five in the morning to listen to lectures on codified crimes and methods of acquiring dominion to the hidden or secret or parallel life he began after lunch. My father had purchased, for the exorbitant price of half a *real*, a hat with a doctor's rosette, so as not to be detected by the university police, and each day, until five in the afternoon, he hid out in the Faculty of Medicine and spent hours watching young men like himself, young men of his age and no more intelligent, carry out bold explorations into unknown regions of the human body. My father wanted to see how his friend Ricardo Rueda was able to deliver single-handedly the twins clandestinely born to an Andalusian gypsy, as well as to operate on the appendix of the nephew of Don José Ignacio de Márquez, professor of Roman law. And while this went on, a few blocks from the university other procedures were being carried out that were not surgical but whose consequences were no less serious, for in the velvet-covered armchairs of a ministry sat two men with a quill pen signing the Mallarino-Bidlack Treaty. In accordance with article XXXV, the country that was now called New Granada granted to the United States the exclusive right of transit across the Isthmus of the province of Panama, and the United States undertook, among other things, to maintain strict neutrality in questions of internal politics. And here begins the disorder, here begins . . .

But no.

Not yet.

I'll reveal more on the subject in a few pages.

The Last Renaissance Man earned a law degree, he did, but I hasten to say that he never practiced: he was too busy with the absorbing vocation of Enlightenment and Progress. By the age of thirty he had not been linked to a single young lady, but his file as founder of Benthamist/revolutionary/socialist/Girondist newspapers expanded scandalously. There was no bishop he had not insulted; there was no respectable family who had not forbidden his entrance into their home or his courting of their daughters. (At La Merced College, a recently founded school for the most distinguished señoritas, his name was anathema.) Little by little my father specialized in the delicate art of earning disfavor and doors slammed in his face, and Santa Fe society joined willingly in the great slamming. My father did not worry: at that time the country he lived in had become unrecognizable—its borders had changed or were threatening to change, it had a different name, its political constitution was as *mobile* as a *donna*—and the government for which my grandfather had died had turned, for this reader of Lamartine and Saint-Simon, into the most reactionary of afflictions.

Enter Miguel Altamirano, activist, idealist, optimist; Miguel Altamirano, more than liberal, radical, anticlerical. During the elections of 1849, my father was one of those who purchased the material for the banners that hung all over Bogotá with the slogan VIVA LÓPEZ, TERROR OF THE CONSERVATIVES; he was one of those who gathered outside Congress to intimidate (successfully) the men who were going to elect a new president; once López, candidate of the young revolutionaries, was elected, he was one of those who demanded from the columns of the newspaper of the moment—I don't remember which one it was at the time, whether *The Martyr* or *The Struggle*—the expulsion of the Jesuits. Reaction of the reactionary society: eighty little girls dressed in white with flowers in their hands assembled in front of the Palace to oppose the measure; in his newspaper, my father called them "Instruments of Obscurantism." Two hundred ladies of unquestionable lineage repeated the demonstration, and my father distributed a pamphlet entitled *Hell Hath No Fury Like a Jesuit Scorned*. The priests of that New Granada, deprived of authority and privileges, hardened their positions as the months went by, and the sensation of harassment increased. My father, in response, joined the Estrella del Tequendama Masonic lodge: the secret meetings gave him a sense of conspiring (ergo of being alive), and the fact that the elders exempted him from the initiation trials made him think that Freemasonry was a sort of natural habitat. Through his efforts the temple managed to catechize two young priests; his patrons recognized these achievements with advanced promotions. And at some point in that brief process, my father, young soldier in search of battles, found one that appeared minor at first glance, almost trivial, but which would, albeit indirectly, change his life.

In September 1852, while it seemed to rain for forty days and forty nights all over New Granada, my father heard from an old friend from the Faculty of Medicine, liberal like him but less quarrelsome, of the Most Recent Outrage Against the God of Progress: Father Eustorgio Valenzuela, who had declared himself the spiritual guardian of the University of Bogotá, had unofficially banned the use of human cadavers for pedagogical, anatomical, and academic purposes. Surgical apprentices could practice on frogs or mice or rabbits, said the priest, but the human body, creation of divine hand and will, sacred receptacle of the soul, was inviolable and should be respected.

"Medieval!" shouted my father from some printed page or other. "Rancid Papist!" But to no avail: Father Valenzuela's network of loyalties was solid, and soon the parishioners from neighboring towns, Chía and Bosa and Zipaquirá, did what they could to prevent the students from the sinful capital having recourse to other morgues. The university's civil authorities came under pressure from the heads of (good) families, and before anyone realized, they had yielded before the blackmail. Upon the university dissection tables crowded the open frogs—the white, porous bellies slit by the scalpel in a violet line—and in the kitchen half the chickens were destined for the stew pot and the other half for the operating room. The Embargo on Bodies became a topic of conversation in the salons and in a matter of weeks was taking up significant space in the newspapers. My father declared the foundation of the New Materialism, and in several manifestos quoted conversations with different authorities: "On the dissection table," said one, "the tip of my scalpel has never encountered a soul." Others, more daring (and often anonymous): "The Holy Trinity is something else now: the Holy Spirit has been replaced by Laplace." The followers, whether voluntary or not, of Father Valenzuela founded in their turn the Old Spiritualism, and produced their own share of witnesses and publicity phrases. They were able to release one accurate and convincing fact: Pascal and Newton had been faithful and practicing Christians. They were able to release a slogan, cheap but no less effective for it: TWO CUPS OF SCIENCE LEAD TO ATHEISM, BUT THREE CUPS LEAD TO FAITH. And thus the matter progressed (or rather did not).

The city watched the vultures squabble. The corpses of cholera victims, which had been leaving the San Juan de Dios Hospital, sporadically, for the last year, were viewed with the avarice of merchants by the radical students, but also by Father Valenzuela's crusading followers. When one of the patients admitted with fever and vomiting became too thirsty or too cold, word began to circulate and the political forces to prepare themselves: Father Valenzuela came to perform the last rites, and in the midst of them obliged the patient (with bluish skin, eyes sunk deep into the head) to sign a testament containing the unambiguous clause "I die in Christ; I deny my body to science." My father published an article accusing the priests of denying the patients divine absolution unless they signed those prefabricated testaments; and the priests replied accusing the Materialists of denying those same patients not absolution but tartar emetic. And in the midst of those foul debates, no one stopped to wonder how the illness had managed to climb to 2,600 meters above sea level or whence it had arrived.

Then fate intervened, as tends to happen in history and will happen often in mine, and did so disguised as a foreigner, as a man-from-elsewhere. (Which increased the fears of the Spiritualists. Enclosed as they were on an inaccessible plateau, ten days' travel away from the Caribbean coast—which in winter could be double—Father Valenzuela's followers had ensconced themselves in the condition of blinkered horses, and all that came from outside seemed to them worthy of meticulous suspicion.) During those days my father was seen meeting a man who was not from the city. They were seen coming out of the Observatory, or going together to the Commission for Cleanliness and Sanitation, or even entering my grandparents' house to hold secret conversations among the nettles of the patio, far from the servants. But the servants, two widowed freedwomen and their adolescent children, had arts my father could not have anticipated, and so the street, and then the block, and then the neighborhood, began to find out that the man was tongue-tied when he spoke (by Beelzebub, said Valenzuela), that he was the owner of a train, and that he had come to sell to the University of Bogotá as many dead Chinamen as it wanted to buy.

"If the local dead are forbidden," my father was heard to say, "then foreign dead will have to be used. If Christian dead are forbidden, we'll have to avail ourselves of others."

And that seemed to confirm the worst suspicions of the Old Spiritualism.

Among the suspicious was Presbyter Echavarría, of the Santo Tomás Church, a younger man than Valenzuela and more, yes, much more energetic.

And the foreigner?

The man from elsewhere?

Some words on that character or, rather, some clarifications. He was not actually tongue-tied but spoke Spanish with a Boston accent; he was not the owner of a train but the representative of the Panama Railroad Company, and he did not come to sell dead Chinamen to the university but rather . . . Well, all right: he did come to sell dead Chinamen to the university, or at least that was one of his various missions as ambassador in the capital. Need I state the obvious? His mission was a success. My father and the Materialists had found themselves with their backs against the wall, or rather the opposing side had pushed them there; they were desperate, of course, because this was more than a debate in the press: it was a fundamental battle in the long struggle of Light against Darkness. The appearance of the man from the Company— Clarence was his name, and he was the son of Protestants—was providential. The arrangement did not come about immediately: a number of letters, a number of authorizations, a number of incentives (Valenzuela said bribes) were needed, but in July, there arrived from Honda, and before that from Barranquilla, and before that from the brand-new city of Colón, founded only a few months earlier, fifteen barrels full of ice. In each one came a Chinese coolie doubled over and recently deceased from dysentery or malaria, or even cholera, which in Bogotá was now a thing of the past. Many other nameless cadavers were leaving Panama for many other destinations, and this would continue to happen until the railway works came out the other side of the swamp they were in at the time, until they reached some land where it would be possible to build a cemetery able to withstand the ravages of the climate until Judgment Day.

And the dead Chinamen had a story to tell. Calm yourself, Eloísa dear: this is not one of those books where the dead speak, or where beautiful women ascend to the sky, or priests rise above the ground after drinking a steaming potion. But I hope I'll be granted some license, and I hope it'll not be just this once. The university paid an undisclosed sum for the dead Chinamen, but according to some it was not more than three pesos per corpse; in other words, a seamstress could buy herself a cadaver with three months' work. Soon young surgeons were able to sink their scalpels into the yellow skin; and lying there, cold and pale, launched on a race against their own rate of decomposition, the Chinese workers began to speak of the Panama railroad. They said things that everyone now knows, but which in those days were fresh pieces of news for the great majority of the thirty thousand inhabitants of the capital. The scene now begins to move northward (in space) and recede a few years (in time). And thus, without any other tricks than my own sovereignty over this tale, we arrive at Coloma, California. The year is 1848. More precisely, it is January 24. The carpenter James Marshall has traveled the long and winding trail from New Jersey to conquer the world's frontier and build a saw mill there. While excavating, he notices that something sparkles in the earth.

And the world goes mad. All of a sudden, the east coast of the United States realizes that the Route to the Gold goes through that obscure isthmus, province of that obscure country that is always changing its name, that mass of murderous jungle whose particular blessing is being the narrowest point of Central America. A year has not yet passed and the *Falcon* steamship is approaching the Panamanian Limón Bay, solemnly entering the mouth of the Panamanian Chagres River, carrying hundreds of Gringos who clatter pans and rifles and pickaxes every time they move like mobile orchestras and ask loudly where the hell the Pacific is. Some guess; of these, there are those who arrive at their destination. But others fall by the wayside, killed by fever—not gold fever, but the other one—beside the dead mules, dead men and mules back to back in the green river mud, defeated by the heat of those swamps where the trees do not permit the light to pass through. This is how it is: this corrected version of El Dorado, this Gold Trail in the process of being opened, is a place where the sun does not exist, where the heat wilts bodies, where one waves a finger through the air and the finger ends up soaking wet as if it had just come out of the river. This place is hell, but it is a watery hell. And meanwhile the gold calls, and some way must be found to cross hell. I take in the whole country in a single glance: at the same time as my father is calling for the expulsion of the Jesuits in Bogotá, in the Panamanian jungle step by step, sleeper by sleeper, dead worker by dead worker, the miracle of the railroad begins to make its way.

And the fifteen Chinese coolies who later rest on the long dissection tables at the University of Bogotá, after having taught a distracted trainee the location of the liver and the length of the large intestine, those fifteen Chinamen who now begin to develop black stains on their backs (if they are faceup) or on their chests (if they're facedown), those fifteen Chinamen say in chorus and with pride: We were there. We cleared a way through the jungle, we dug in those swamps, we laid the iron and the sleepers. One of those fifteen Chinamen tells his story to my father, and my father, leaning over the rigor mortis while he examines out of pure Renaissance-man curiosity what is there under a rib, listens with more attention than he thinks. And what is under that rib? My father asks for forceps, and after a while the forceps emerge from the body carrying a splinter of bamboo. And now the talkative and impertinent Chinaman begins to tell my father of the patience with which he had sharpened the stick, of the skillful decency with which he had stuck it into the muddy earth, of the force with which he had thrown himself onto the sharpened point.

A suicide? my father asks (let's admit it is not a very intelligent question). No, replies the Chinaman, he had not killed himself, the sadness had killed him, and before the sadness the malaria. . . . Watching his ill workmates hang themselves with the ropes used in the construction of the railway or steal the foreman's pistol to shoot themselves with had killed him, seeing that in those swamps it was not possible to construct a decent cemetery had killed him, and knowing the jungle's victims would end up scattered around the world in barrels of ice had killed him. I, says the Chinaman, his skin now almost blue, his stench almost unbearable, I, who in life have built the Panama Railroad, in death shall help to finance it, as will the other nine thousand nine hundred and ninety-eight dead workers, Chinese, blacks, and Irish, who are visiting the universities and hospitals of the world right now. Oh, how a body travels . . .

All this the dead Chinaman tells my father.

But what my father hears is slightly different.

My father does not hear a story of personal tragedies, does not see the dead Chinaman as the nameless worker of no fixed address for whom no grave is possible. He sees him as a martyr, and sees the history of the railway as a true epic. The train versus the jungle, man versus nature . . . The dead Chinaman is an emissary from the future, an outpost of Progress. The Chinaman tells him that the passenger infected with cholera, directly responsible for the two thousand deaths in Cartagena and hundreds in Bogotá, was on board that ship, the *Falcon*; but my father admires the passenger who had left everything to pursue the promise of gold through the murderous jungle. The Chinaman tells my father about the saloons and brothels proliferating in Panama since the foreigners began to arrive; for my father, each drunken worker is an Arthurian knight, each whore an Amazon. The seventy thousand railway sleepers are seventy thousand prophecies of the vanguard. The iron line that crosses the Isthmus is the navel of the world. The dead Chinaman is no longer simply an emissary from the future: he is a herald angel, thinks my father, and he has come to make him see, amid the fallen leaves of his sad life in Bogotá, the vague but luminous promise of a better life.

Speaking for the defense: It was not out of madness that my father cut the dead Chinaman's hand off. It was not out of madness—my father had never felt saner in his life—that he had it cleaned by one of the Chapinero butchers and put it out in the sun (the scant Bogotá sun) to dry. He had it mounted with bronze screws on a small pedestal that looked like marble, and kept it on one of the shelves of his library, between a tattered edition of Engels's *The Peasant War in Germany* and a miniature oil painting of my grandmother with a large ornamental comb in her hair, by an artist of the Gregorio Vásquez school. The index finger, slightly outstretched, points with each of its bare phalanges toward the path my father would have to take.

Friends who visited my father during this time said yes, it was true that the carpal and the metacarpal bones pointed toward the Isthmus of Panama the way a Muslim bows in the direction of Mecca. And I, in spite of how much I might want to launch my tale in the direction indicated by the desiccated finger, must first concentrate on other incidents in the life of my father, who stepped out one fine day of that year of Our Lord 1845 to discover through the word on the street that he had been excommunicated. So much time had passed since the Battle of the Bodies that it took him a while to associate one matter with the other. One Sunday, while my father was receiving the title of Venerable pro Tempore in the Masonic lodge, Presbyter Echavarría mentioned him by name from the accusing pulpit of Santo Tomás Church. Miguel Altamirano had the blood of innocents on his hands. Miguel Altamirano dealt in souls of the dead and was in league with the Devil. Miguel Altamirano, declared Father Echavarría before his audience of faithful and fanatics, was a formal enemy of God and the Church.

My father, as suited the circumstances and as precedents suggested, took the matter as a joke. A few meters from the ostentatious front door of the church was the humbler and particularly nonsanctum door to the printer's; the same Sunday, late that night, my father delivered his column for *El Comunero*.

(Or was it *El Temporal*? These precisions are perhaps superfluous, but no less tormenting for me not to be able to keep track of the leaflets and newspapers published by my father. *La Opinión*? *El Granadino*? *La Opinión Granadina*? or *El Comunero Temporal*? It is futile. Readers of the Jury, please forgive my poor memory.)

Anyway, whichever newspaper it was, my father delivered his column. The following is not a literal reproduction, but merely what my memory has preserved, though I believe it corresponds quite accurately to the spirit of those words. "A certain backward cleric, one of those who have transformed faith into superstition and Christian rites into sectarian paganism, has assumed the right to excommunicate me, going over the head of the prelate's judgment and, most of all, that of common sense," he wrote for all of Bogotá society to read. "The undersigned, in his capacity as Doctor of Earthly Laws, Spokesman of Public Opinion, and Defender of Civilized Values, has received comprehensive and sufficient authority from the community he represents, which has decided to pay the cleric back in kind. And thus Presbyter Echavarría, whom God does not hold in his Glory, is hereby excommunicated from the communion of civilized men. From the Santo Tomás pulpit, he has expelled us from his communion; we, from the pulpit of Gutenberg, expel him from ours. Let it be solemnly enacted."

The rest of the week went by without incident. But the following Saturday, my father and his radical comrades had gathered at the Café Le Boulevardier, near the cloister of the University of Bogotá, with the members of a Spanish theater company who were on a Latin American tour. The work they had staged, a sort of *Le Bourgeois gentilhomme* where the gentleman was replaced by a seminarian assaulted by doubts, had already been denounced by the Archbishop, and that was good enough for *El Comunero* or *El Granadino*. My father, as editor (as well) of the Varieties section, had proposed an extensive interview with the actors; that evening, once the interview was over—the reporter put away his notebook and his Waterloo pen that a friend had brought him from London—and between one brandy and the next, they spoke of the Echavarría affair. The actors made their own speculations about the Sunday Mass and had started wagering whole *reales* on the contents of the next day's sermon when it suddenly began to rain heavily, and the people in the street flocked like chickens: under the eaves, into the doorways, completely blocking the entrance to the café. The place filled with the smell of damp ponchos; beneath trousers and boots that dripped water the café floor became slippery. Then a soprano voice ordered my father to stand, to give up his seat.

My father had never seen Presbyter Echavarría: the news of his excommunication had reached him by way of third parties, and the dispute, until that moment, had gone no further than the confines of the printed page. Looking up, he found himself facing a long, perfectly dry cassock and a closed black umbrella, its tip in a puddle of water shiny and silver like mercury, the handle easily supporting the weight of effeminate hands. The soprano spoke again: "The chair, heretic." I must believe what my father would tell me years later: that if he did not respond it was not out of insolence, but that the vaudevillian situation—the priest entering a café, the dry priest where all were wet, the priest whose womanly voice undermined his imperious manner—surprised him so much that he didn't know how to do so. Echavarría interpreted the silence as disdain and returned to the attack:

"The chair, heathen."

"Come again?"

"The chair, blasphemer. The chair, murderous Jew."

Then he hit my father lightly on the knee with the tip of his umbrella, once, maybe twice; and at that moment all hell broke loose.

Like a jack-in-the-box, my father swatted away the umbrella (the palm of his hand was left wet and a little red) and stood up. Echavarría let some reaction out from between incensed teeth, "But how dare you," or words to that effect. As he said it, my father, who had perhaps experienced a fleeting second of good sense, was already turning around to collect his jacket and leave without a glance at his companions, and did not see the moment when the priest went to slap him; nor did he see—this he would say many times, begging to be believed—his own hand, closing of its own accord and landing with all the strength of his pivoting shoulders, on the indignant and pursed little mouth, on the hairless and powdered lip of Presbyter Echavarría. The chin emitted a hollow crunch, the cassock swept backward, as if floating, the boots beneath the cassock slipped in the puddle, and the umbrella fell to the floor a brief second before its owner.

"You should have seen," my father told me much later, facing the sea, brandy in hand. "At that moment the silence was louder than the downpour."

The actors stood up. My father's radical comrades stood up. And this I have thought every time I remember this story: if my father had been alone, or if he had not been in a place frequented by university men, he would have found himself confronted by a furious crowd ready to skewer him on the spot for the affront; but in spite of the odd isolated and anonymous insult emerging from the crowd, in spite of the lethal looks from the two strangers who helped Echavarría to his feet, who recovered his umbrella for him, who brushed off his cassock (with an extra pat or two on the ministerial buttocks), nothing happened. Echavarría left the Boulevardier hurling insults that no one had ever heard a clergyman in Santa Fe de Bogotá say, and threats worthy of a sailor from Marseille, but there ended the latest run-in. My father reached up to touch his face, confirmed that his cheek was hot, said good night to his companions, and walked home in the rain. Two days later, in the early morning before first light, someone knocked on his door. The servant opened the door and saw no one. The reason was obvious: the knocks were not those of someone coming to call, but those of a hammer nailing up a notice.

The anonymous tract did not carry an imprint, but in other respects its contents were quite clear: all the faithful who read those lines were exhorted not to speak to the heretic Miguel Altamirano, to refuse him bread, water, and shelter; it declared that the heretic Miguel Altamirano was considered to be possessed by demons; and it proclaimed that killing him without qualms, as one would a dog, would be a virtuous act, worthy of divine favor.

My father tore it off the door, went back inside, looked for the key to the storage room under the stairs, and took out one of the two pistols that had arrived in my grandfather's trunk. On his way out he took care, thinking to eliminate any revealing traces, to pull off all the scraps of paper still stuck to the wood of the door under the nail; but then he realized the precaution was useless, because he came upon the same notice ten or fifteen times in the short walk from his house to the printing press that turned out *La Opinión*. More than that, along the way he also came upon accusing fingers and voices, the powerful prosecution of the Catholics who now, without any actual proceedings taking place, had declared him their enemy. My father, accustomed to attracting attention, was not quite so used to attracting malevolence. The public prosecutors appeared on the wooden balconies (crosses dangling over their chests), and the fact that they did not dare to shout at him was not a relief to my father, but rather confirmation that darker fates than mere public disgrace awaited. He walked into the printer's with the crumpled notice in his hand, asking the brothers Acosta, the owners of the press, if they could identify the machines responsible: to no avail. He spent the afternoon in the Commerce Club, tried to find out what his comrades thought, and heard that the radical societies had already reached a decision: they would respond with blood and fire, burning down the church and killing every cleric, if Miguel Altamirano was to suffer any attack.

He felt less alone, but he also felt that the city was about to suffer a catastrophe. And so that night he made his way to Santo Tomás Church to look for Father Echavarría, walking beneath yellow street lamps that lit up the gleaming white walls of the houses, thinking that two men who had exchanged insults can, just as easily, exchange apologies; but the church was deserted.

Or almost.

Because in one of the last pews was a shape, or what my father, blinded as he entered by the sudden darkness, for the time the retina with all its rods and cones takes to accommodate to the new conditions, had taken for a shape. After strolling up one of the aisles toward the chancel, after going behind—into areas where he was an intruder—and looking for the door to the presbytery and descending the two worn stone steps and stretching out a prudent and polite knuckle to knock a couple of times, my father selected a random pew, one that had a view of the gilding on the altar, and sat down to wait, although he really did not know what words he could use to convince that fanatic.

And then he heard someone say: "That's him."

He turned around and saw that the shape was dividing into two. From one side, a cassocked figure that was not Father Echavarría already had his back to him and was leaving the church; from the other, a man in a poncho and hat, a sort of giant bell with legs, began to walk up the center aisle toward the chancel. My father imagined that, beneath the straw hat, in that black space where human features would soon emerge, the eyes of the man were scrutinizing him. My father looked around. From an oil painting he was being watched by a bearded man who was sticking his index finger (well covered with flesh and skin, unlike the one on his Chinaman's dead hand) into Christ's open wound. In another painting was a man with wings and a woman who kept her page in a book with

another finger just as fleshed out: my father recognized the Annunciation, but the angel was not Chinese. No one seemed prepared to get him
out of this fix; the man in the poncho, meanwhile, approached silently,
as if sliding over a sheet of oil. My father saw he was wearing rope-soled
shoes, saw the rolled-up trousers, and saw, hanging beneath the edge of
the poncho, the dirty point of a knife.

Neither of the two spoke. My father knew he could not kill the man
there, not because at the age of thirty-four he had never killed anybody
(there is always a first time, and my father handled a pistol as well as anyone), but because to do so without witnesses would be like condemning
himself in advance. He needed people to see: to see the provocation, the
attack, the legitimate defense. He stood up, went out to the side aisle of
the nave, and began to take big steps toward the front door; instead of
following him, the man in the poncho returned down the central aisle,
and pew by pew they walked, tracing parallel lines, while my father
was thinking what to do when they ran out of pews. He counted them
quickly: six pews, now five, now four.

Three pews.

Now two.

Now one.

My father put his hand in his pocket and cocked the pistol. As
they both neared the church door, as the parallel lines converged, the
man swept his poncho out of the way and pulled back the hand that
held the knife. My father raised the cocked pistol, pointed at the center of the man's chest, thought of the sad consequences of what he was
about to do, thought of the passersby who would invade the church
as soon as they heard the shot, thought of the court that would condemn him for voluntary homicide on the basis of testimony from those
passersby, thought of my grandfather stabbed by the bayonet and the

Chinaman stabbed by the bamboo stake, thought of the firing squad that would shoot him against a rough wall, and said to himself that he was not made for the court or the gallows, that it would be a question of honor to kill his attacker but that the next bullet would be for his own chest.

Then he fired.

"Then I fired," my father would tell me.

But he did not hear the shot from his own pistol, or rather it seemed that his shot produced such an echo as had never before been heard, a reverberation unprecedented in the world, because at that moment, from the Plaza Bolívar, arrived the thunder of other explosions from many other guns. It was just past midnight, the date was April 17, and the honorable General José María Melo had just led a military coup and declared himself dictator of that poor confused republic.

That's how it is: the Angel of History saved my father, even though, as will be seen, he did so in a transitory way, simply by swapping one of his enemies for another. My father fired, but no one heard his shot. When he went outside, all the doors were closed and all the balconies deserted; the air smelled of gunpowder and horse shit, and in the distance there were now shouts and heels on cobblestones to be heard and, of course, insistent gunfire. "I knew that very instant. They were the sounds that announced a civil war," my father would tell me in an oracular tone. . . . He liked to assume those poses, and many times over the course of our life together (which was not long) he put his hand on my shoulder and looked at me, arching a solemn eyebrow, to tell me that he had predicted this, that he had guessed that. He told me of some event he had witnessed indirectly and then said, "You could see it coming a mile off." Or rather, "I don't know how they failed to realize." Yes, that was my father: the man who, after a certain age, beaten senseless by Great Events—saved on a few occasions, damned on most—ends up developing that curious defense mechanism of predicting things many years after they'd happened.

But allow me a brief aside, another digression. Because I have always believed that on that night the history of my country demonstrated that it at least has a sense of humor. I have spoken of the Great Incident. I take out the magnifying glass and examine it more closely. What do I see? To what does my father owe his improbable impunity? Briefly: One night in January, General Melo drunkenly leaves a military banquet, and when he gets to the Plaza Santander, where his barracks are, runs into a corporal called Quirós, a poor unkempt lad walking the streets at that hour without a pass. The General gives him a good dressing-down, the Corporal forgets himself and responds with insolence, and General Melo sees no better punishment than drawing his sword then and there and cutting his throat in one slash. Great scandal in Bogotá society; great condemnations of militarism and violence. The public prosecutor accuses; the judge is on the point of issuing an arrest warrant against the accused. Melo thinks, with impeccable reasoning: the best defense is not just a good offense, it's dictatorship. He had the army of war veterans under his command, and he put it to use in his service. Who could blame him?

Well now, I admit, this is no more than a cheap joke, typical gossip—our national sport—but caveat emptor, and I tell it anyway. It is true that in some versions Corporal Quirós arrives late back to the barracks after finding himself involved in a street brawl and is already injured when he runs into Melo; in others, Quirós finds out about the accusations against the General and from his death bed absolves him of all responsibility. (Isn't that version pretty? It has all that master-and-disciple, mentor-and-protégé mystery. It is gentlemanly, and my father was no doubt fond of it.) But beyond these various explanations, one single thing is irrefutable: General Melo, with his cowlick and double-chinned Mona Lisa face, was the instrument that history used to split its sides laughing at the fate of our young republics, those badly finished inventions for which no patent could be taken out. My father had killed someone, but that fact would pass into nonexistence when another man, to avoid his own indictment as a common criminal, decided to take by force those things of which every Colombian speaks with pride: Liberty, Democracy, and the Institutions. And the Angel of History, sitting in the stalls in his Phrygian cap, burst out laughing so hard he fell off his seat.

Readers of the Jury: I do not know who first compared history to the theater (that distinction does not belong to me), but one thing is sure: that lucid soul was not aware of the tragicomic nature of our Colombian scenario, created by mediocre dramatists, fabricated by sloppy set designers, produced by unscrupulous impresarios. Colombia is a play in five acts that someone tried to write in classical verse but that came out composed of the most vulgar prose, performed by actors with exaggerated gestures and terrible diction. . . . Well, I return now to that small theater (I shall do so often) and return to my scene: doors and balconies barred, the streets near the Palace of Government transformed into a ghost town. No one heard the shot that thundered between the cold stone walls, no one saw my father leave Santo Tomás Church, no one saw him slip like a shadow through the streets to his home, no one saw him arrive so late that night with a still-warm pistol in his pocket. The small incident had been obliterated by the Big Event: the minuscule death of some anonymous resident of the Egipto neighborhood, by the Superlative Deaths that are the patrimony of Our Lady War. But I have said before that my father did nothing but change enemies, and that's how it was: once his ecclesiastic pursuer was eliminated, my father found himself pursued by the military. In the new Bogotá of Melo and his allies, radicals like my father were feared for their formidable capacity for disorder—they had not specialized in revolutions and political riots in vain—and twenty-four hours hadn't yet passed since the man in the poncho, or rather his corpse, had collapsed in Santo Tomás Church, when arrests began all over the city. The radicals, university students or members of Congress, received armed and not particularly pleasant visits from Melo's men; the cells filled up; several leaders were already fearing for their lives.

My father did not hear this news from his comrades. A lieutenant of the seditious army arrived at his house in the middle of the night and woke him up by banging his rifle butt against the window frame. "I thought my life had ended in that instant," my father would tell me much later. But that was not the case: across the Lieutenant's face, a grimace drifted between pride and guilt. My father, resigned, opened the door, but the man did not enter. Before dawn, the Lieutenant told him, a squad of soldiers would be coming to arrest him.

"And how do you know?" my father asked.

"I know because it's my squad," said the Lieutenant, "and I have issued the order."

And he took his leave with a Masonic salute.

Only then did my father recognize him: he was a member of the Estrella del Tequendama lodge.

So after throwing together a few basic necessities, including the murderous pistol and the bony hand, my father sought refuge at the brothers Acosta's press. He found that several of his fellows had had the same idea: the new opposition was already beginning to organize to return the country to democracy. Death to the tyrant, they shouted (or rather whispered prudently, because there was no sense in alerting the patrols). The fact is that there, that night, among printers and bookbinders, who only went through the motions of seeming impartial, among those lead characters, who looked so peaceful but could stir up entire revolutions when set, surrounded by hundreds or perhaps thousands of wooden drawers that seemed to contain all the protests, threats, manifestos and countermanifestos, accusations and denunciations and vindications of the political world, several radical leaders had gathered to leave the occupied capital together and plan with the armies of other provinces the campaign to recover it. They received my father as if the most natural thing in the world would be to entrust him with the captaincy of a regiment and told him of their plans. My father joined them, in part because the company made him feel safe, in part for the emotion of camaraderie that always seizes idealists; but at the back of his mind he had already made a decision, and his intention remained the same from the beginning of the journey.

Here I speed up. For as I have at times devoted several pages to the events of a single day, at this moment my tale demands I cover in a few lines what happened in several months. Accompanied by a servant, protected by the darkness of the savannah night and well armed, the defenders of the institutions left Bogotá. They climbed the Guadalupe Hill to deserted plateaux where even the *frailejón* plants froze to death, descending into the tropical lowlands on stubborn, hungry mules they had purchased along the way; they arrived at the Magdalena River, and after eight hours in an unstable dugout they entered Honda and declared it the headquarters of the resistance. During the months that followed, my father recruited men, stockpiled weapons and organized squads, marched as one of General Franco's volunteers and returned defeated from Zipaquirá, listened to General Herrera predict his own death and then saw the prophecy fulfilled, tried to organize an alternative government in Ibagué and failed in the attempt, ordered the convocation of the

Congress the dictator had dispersed, singlehandedly raised a battalion of young *bogotáno* or *santafereño* exiles and incorporated it into General Lopez's army, received over the course of the final days the belated but victorious news that arrived from Bosa and Las Cruces and Los Egidos, heard that on December 3 the nine thousand men of the army entered Santa Fe de Bogotá, and then, while his comrades were celebrating the news by eating trout *a la diabla* and drinking more brandy than my father had ever seen, thought he would celebrate with them, drink his own brandy and finish his trout, and then tell them the truth: he would not take part in the march of triumph, he would not enter the recovered city.

Yes, he would explain: he wasn't interested in returning, because the city, although now regained for democracy, was still lost to him. He would never return to live in it, he'd tell them, for his life there seemed finished, as if it belonged to another man. In Bogotá he had killed, in Bogotá he had hidden, nothing remained for him in Bogotá. But they wouldn't understand, of course, and those who did understand would refuse to believe him or try to convince him otherwise with phrases like *the city of your forefathers* or *of your struggles* or *the city where you were born*, and he would have to show them, as irrefutable and incontrovertible proof of his new destiny, the hand of the dead Chinaman, the index finger that always points, as if by magic, toward the province of Panama.

II

The Revelations of
Antonia de Narváez

At nine in the morning on December 17, while in Bogotá General Melo's life was spared, in the river port of Honda my father boarded an English steamer called the *Isabel*, belonging to the John Dixon Powles Company, which plied the route from the interior to the Caribbean on a regular basis. Eight days later, having spent Christmas Eve on board, he arrived in Colón, the Panamanian port not yet three years old but already a member of the Schizophrenic Places Club. The founders had elected to baptize the city with the Spanish surname of Don Christopher Columbus, the disoriented Genoese sailor who by pure chance bumped into a Caribbean island and nevertheless passed into history as the discoverer of the continent; but the Gringos who were constructing the railroad did not read the ordinance, or perhaps they read it but didn't understand it—their Spanish, surely, was not as good as they thought—and ended up conferring their own name upon the city: Aspinwall. Whereupon Colón became Colón for Colombians and Aspinwall for the Gringos, and Colón-Aspinwall for the rest of the world (the spirit of conciliation has never been lacking in Latin America). And it was in this embryonic, ambiguous city, this city with no past, that Miguel Altamirano arrived.

But before telling of his arrival and all that happened in consequence, I should like and must speak of a couple without whose assistance, I can assure you, I would not be what I am. And I say this, as you'll see, literally.

Sometime around 1835, the engineer William Beckman (New Orleans, 1801–Honda, 1855) had gone up the Magdalena River on a private, profit-seeking mission, and months later founded a company of boats and barges for the commercial exploitation of the region. He soon became a daily spectacle for the ports' inhabitants: blond, almost albino, Beckman filled a big dugout with ten tons of merchandise, covered the wooden cases with ox hides and slept on top of them, beneath a little canopy of palm leaves on which his skin and therefore his life depended, and went up and down the river like that, from Honda to Buenavista, from Nare to Puerto Berrio. After five years of considerable success, during which he had come to dominate the coffee and cacao trade between the provinces along the river, Beckman (true to his adventurer's nature, after all) decided to invest his not terribly abundant riches in the risky venture of Don Francisco Montoya, who was then in England commissioning a steamer adapted to the Magdalena River. The *Union*, built in the Royal Shipyards, came up the river in January 1842 as far as La Dorada, six leagues from Honda, and was received by mayors and military officers with honors a minister would envy. She was filled with cases of tobacco—"Enough to get all of the United Kingdom addicted," Beckman would comment recalling those years—and sailed without incident to the mouth of the Miel River . . . where that English steamer, just like all the rest of the characters in this book, had her encounter with the ever impertinent (tedious, meddlesome) Angel of

History. Beckman wasn't even aware that the civil war of the day ("Is it another or the same one?" he asked) had come that far; but he had to bow to the evidence, for in a matter of hours the *Union* had become embroiled in combat with boats of vague political allegiances, a cannonball had broken the boilers, and dozens of tons of tobacco, as well as all the engineer's capital, sank without ever knowing the reasons for the attack.

I said they sank. Not exactly: the *Union* almost reached the riverbank after the cannon blast, and did not sink entirely. For years, her two chimneys were visible to passengers on the river, breaking the yellow waters like lost Easter Island statues, like sophisticated wooden menhirs. My father definitely saw them; I saw them when my turn came . . . and Engineer Beckman saw them and would continue to see them with some frequency, for he never returned to New Orleans. By the time of the semi-sinking, he had already fallen in love, had already asked for that hand—which for him did not indicate travels, but stillness—and would marry in the days immediately following his bankruptcy, offering his bride a cheap honeymoon on the opposite bank of the river. Great disappointment on the part of the young lady's (good) family, *bogotános* of limited means and boundless aspirations, social climbers who would have put any Rastignac to shame, who customarily spent long periods in their hacienda in Honda and had thought themselves so fortunate when that rich Gringo had laid those pale-browed blue eyes on the rebellious daughter of the house. And who was the lucky girl? A twenty-year-old called Antonia de Narváez, amateur toreador in the Santo Patrón running of the bulls, occasional gambler, and steadfast cynic.

What do we know of Antonia de Narváez? That she had wanted to travel to Paris, but not to meet Flora Tristán, which she thought would be a waste of time, but to read de Sade in the original. That she had made herself briefly famous in the salons of the capital for publicly disparaging the memory of

Policarpa Salavarrieta ("Dying for the country is for people with nothing better to do," she'd said). That she had used what little influence her family had to get inside the Palace of Government, which conceded her a permit and threw her out after ten minutes, when she asked the Bishop where the famous bed was, the one where Manuela Sáenz, the most celebrated mistress in Colombian history, had screwed the Liberator.

Readers of the Jury: I can hear your perplexity from here, and am prepared to alleviate it. Would you tolerate a brief review of that fundamental historic moment? Doña Manuela Sáenz, from Quito originally, had left her legitimate (and oh-so-boring) husband, a certain James or Jaime Thorne; in 1822, the Liberator Simón Bolívar makes his triumphant entrance into Quito; shortly thereafter, ditto with Manuela. We are dealing with an extraordinary woman: she is skillful on horseback and handles weapons magnificently; as Bolívar is able to see for himself during the exploits of independence, Manuela rides as well as she shoots. Pessimistic in view of social condemnation, Bolívar writes to her: "Nothing in the world can unite us under the auspices of innocence and honor." Manuela responds by arriving unannounced at his house and showing him, with a few thrusts of her hips, just what she thinks of those auspices. And on September 25, 1828, while the Liberator and his *Libertadora* take multiple mutual liberties in the presidential bed of that incipient Colombia, a group of envious conspirators—generals no longer young whose wives neither ride nor shoot—decide that this coitus shall be interruptus: they attempt to assassinate Bolívar. With Manuela's help, Simón leaps out of the window and escapes to hide under a bridge. So then, that was the notorious bed Antonia de Narváez wanted to see as if it were a relic, which, to be honest, perhaps it was.

And in December 1854, the night my father celebrates with trout and brandy the victory of the democratic armies over the dictatorship of Melo, Antonia de Narváez tells this anecdote. As simple as that. She remembers the anecdote of the bed, and she tells it.

By that time, Antonia had been married to Mr. William Beckman for twelve years; that is, as many years as her husband was older than his wife. After the *Union* disaster, Beckman had accepted a portion of his in-laws' property—three or four acres on the riverbank—and had built a house with whitewashed walls and seven rooms in which to receive occasional travelers, including the crew of the odd North American steamer, who, after so many ports where no one had understood them, longed to hear their language again if only for a single night. The house was surrounded by banana trees and fields of cassava; but its most important source of income, what kept food on the couple's table, came from one of the best patronized firewood suppliers on the Magdalena. That was how Antonia de Narváez de Beckman filled her days, a woman who in other lands and in another life would have been burned at the stake or maybe made a fortune writing erotic novels under a pseud-onym: giving room and board to the river's travelers and wood to the boilers of its steamships. Oh, yes, she also filled them by listening to the unbearable songs her husband, lover of the local landscape, came up with while accompanying himself on a wretched banjo:

> *In the wilds of fair Colombia, near the equinoctial line,*
> *Where the summer lasts forever and the sultry sun doth shine,*
> *There is a charming valley where the grass is always green,*
> *Through which flow the rapid waters of the Muddy Magdalene.*

My father also knew this song, my father also found out from it that Colombia is a place neighboring the equator where the summer is eternal (the author, obviously, never got as far as Bogotá). But we were talking about my father. Miguel Altamirano never told me if he'd learned the song the very night of the victory, but that night the inevitable happened: brandy, banjo, ballad. The Beckman house, natural habitat of foreigners, a meeting place for people passing through, played host that night as drunken soldiers went down to Caracolí beach and assembled, with the acquiescence (and the shirts, and the trousers) of the place's owner, a straw-stuffed effigy of the defeated dictator. I don't know how many times I've imagined the hours that followed. The soldiers begin to collapse on the damp sand of the river, overcome by the local *chicha*— the brandy was reserved for officers, a matter of hierarchy—the hosts and two or three high-ranking guests, among whom was my father, extinguish the bonfire in which the remains of the dictator lie scorched and return to the drawing room. The servants prepare a cold *agua de panela*; the conversation begins to turn to the respective past lives in Bogotá of those present. And at that moment, while Manuela Sáenz lies ill in a remote Peruvian city, Antonia de Narváez laughingly tells of the day she went to look at the bed where Manuela Sáenz loved Bolívar. And then it is as if my father has just seen her for the first time, as if she, being seen, were seeing my father for the first time. The idealist and the cynic had shared alcohol and food all evening, but when speaking of the Liberator's lover, they notice each other's existence for the first time. One of the two recalled the lyric then circulating in the young Republic:

> *Bolívar, sword displayed:*
> *"Manuela, here stands my blade."*
> *"Simón, I will chase it,*
> *And moistly I'll encase it."*

And that was like the sealing wax on a secret letter. I cannot be sure whether Antonia and my father blushed when realizing the (obscene) symbolic charge the figures of Manuela and Simón had taken on for them; nor do I want to go to the trouble of imagining it, so I'll not subject you, Readers of the Jury, to the qualities and forms this sort of dance entailed, the complete match that can happen between two people without their backsides even for an instant lifting up off their seats. But in those final hours, before each retired to his or her room, across the solid walnut table flew ingenious comments (from the male), tinkling laughter (from the other), exchanges of witticisms that are the human version of dogs sniffing each other's tails. For Mr. Beckman, who had not yet read *Dangerous Liaisons*, those civilized mating rituals went unnoticed.

And all over a simple anecdote about Manuela Sáenz.

That night and the nights that follow, my father, with that capacity progressives have to find great personalities and praiseworthy causes where there are neither the former nor the latter, thinks on what he has seen: a woman who is intelligent and sharp and even a little racy, a woman who deserves a better fate. But my father is human, in spite of all that has been suggested, and also thinks of the physical and potentially tangible side of the matter: a woman with black eyebrows, shapely but thick like . . . Her face adorned by those gold earrings that had belonged to . . . And all that set off by a cotton shawl that covered a chest firm like . . . The reader will have noticed by now: my father was not a born narrator, like myself, and we cannot ask too much agility of him when it comes to finding the best simile for a pair of eyebrows or breasts, or remembering the origins of some humble family jewels; but it pleases me that my father never forgot that simple white shawl Antonia always wore at night. The temperatures in Honda, so violent during the day, plummet when darkness comes, and bring colds and rheumatism to the unwary. A white shawl is one of the ways the locals defend themselves from the cruel unforeseen tropical eventualities: indigestion, yellow fever, malignant fever, a simple temperature. It's rare for the locals to find themselves affected by these ailments (residence creates immunities); but for someone from Bogotá it is normal, almost a daily occurrence, and the guest houses, in these places where finding a doctor can take days, tend to be prepared to treat less severe cases. And one night, while in the rest of Honda Christians were finishing their novena prayers, my father, who had not yet read *The Imaginary Invalid*, thinks his head feels heavy.

And here, to our (not very great) surprise, the versions contradict each other. According to my father, he had left the Beckman guest house two nights before, because the *Isabel* had already arrived in port and the provisioning stopover—wood, coffee, fresh fish—was lasting longer than expected due to some damage to the boilers. According to Antonia de Narváez, the damage to the boilers never existed, my father was still a guest, and that afternoon he hired two porters to carry his things onto the *Isabel*, but he had not yet spent his first night aboard the English steamer. According to my father, it was ten at night when he paid a boy in red trousers, a fisherman's son, to go to the Gringo's guest house and tell the lady there was a feverish man on board. According to Antonia de Narváez, the porters were the ones who told her, exchanging mocking glances and still playing with the half a *real* they'd received as a tip. The two versions come to agree, at least, on one fact, which in any case has left verifiable consequences and the denial of which, from a historic point of view, would be futile.

Armed with a doctor's bag, Antonia de Narváez boarded the *Isabel* and from among the two hundred and seven cabins found the feverish man without asking; when she went in she found him lying on a canvas cot, not on the comfortable main bed, and covered with a blanket. She felt his forehead and did not notice a temperature of any kind; nevertheless, she took a bottle of quinine out of her medical bag and told my father that yes, he did have a bit of a temperature, that he should take five grains with his morning coffee. My father asked her whether a sponge bath with rubbing alcohol wasn't advisable in these cases. Antonia de Narváez agreed, took two more bottles out of her bag, rolled up her sleeves, and asked the patient to remove his shirt, and for my father the penetrating smell of surgical spirit would remain forever associated with the moment when Antonia de Narváez, her hands still wet, pulled back the blanket, untied the white shawl around her neck, and with a slightly lewd movement, lifted her petticoats and straddled him atop his woolen underwear.

It was December 16 and the clock struck eleven; exactly forty-nine and a half years had passed—it's a shame that the symmetries so dear to history couldn't have given us a nice round half-century—since the city of Honda, which once had been a spoiled daughter of the Spaniards and key point of colonial commerce, was destroyed by an earthquake at eleven at night on June 16, 1805. The ruins still existed that night: a short distance from the *Isabel* were the arches of the convents, the stone corners that once were whole walls; and now I can imagine, because no rule of credibility forbids me, that the violent jolts of the camp bed might have evoked those ruins for the lovers. I know, I know: Credibility might be keeping mum, but Good Taste leaps up to reproach me for such a concession to sentimentality. But we'll do without her opinion for an instant: everyone's entitled to one moment of kitsch in this life, and this is mine . . . because starting from this instant, I am physically present in my tale. Although to say *physically* might be a bit of hyperbole.

Aboard the *Isabel*, my father and Antonia de Narváez reproduce, in 1854, the tremors of 1805; aboard Antonia de Narváez, biology, treacherous biology, begins to do its stuff with heats and fluids; and in his room, abed and protected by a muslin mosquito net, Mr. Beckman, who has not yet read *Madame Bovary*, sighs with contentment, harboring not the slightest suspicion, closes his eyes to listen to the silence of the river, and almost by accident begins to sing softly to himself:

> *The forest on your banks by the flood and earthquake torn*
> *Is madly on your bosom to the mighty Ocean borne.*
> *May you still roll for ages and your grass be always green*
> *And your waters aye be cool and sweet, oh Muddy Magdalene.*

Oh, the forests on the riverbank, the cool, sweet waters . . . Today, while I write not far from the Thames, I measure the distance between the two rivers, and marvel that this is the distance of my life. I have ended my days, dear Eloísa, in English lands. And now I feel I have a right to ask: Is it not very appropriate that an English steamer should have been the scene of my conception? The circle closes, the snake bites his own tail, all those clichés.

The preceding I write for the benefit of my more subtle readers, those who appreciate the art of allusion and suggestion. For the cruder among you, I write simply: yes, you have understood. Antonia de Narváez was my mother.

Yes, yes, yes: you have understood.

I, José Altamirano, am a bastard son.

After their encounter on the camp bed of the *Isabel*, after the faked fever and authentic orgasms, my father and Antonia de Narváez began a very brief correspondence, the most important instances of which I must now present as part of my argument (i.e., reasoning used to convince another) and also my argument (i.e., subject matter of a book). But I must do so by first clarifying certain points. This labor of family archaeology I've carried out—I can already hear the objections I've heard all my life: mine was not really a family, I have no right to this respectable noun—is based, on occasion, on tangible documents; and that is why, Readers of the Jury, you have and will have in some passages of the narration the uncomfortable responsibilities of a judge.

Journalism is the court of our days. And therefore: I declare that the following documents are perfectly genuine. It's true that I am Colombian, and that all Colombians are liars, but I must declare the following (and here I place my right hand on the Bible or the book that serves in its place): what I am about to write is the truth, the whole truth, and nothing but the truth. No one will object if here and there I gloss certain passages, which, out of context, might be obscure. But I have not inserted a single word, nor altered any emphasis, nor changed any meaning. So help me God.

Letter from Miguel Altamirano to Antonia de Narváez, Barran-quilla, undated

You will mock me, but I cannot stop thinking of you. And sympathizing with you, for you will have had to return to the one you do not love, while I move inexorably away from the one I adore.* Are my words excessive, my feelings illegitimate? . . . We disembarked yesterday; today we are crossing the sandy plain that separates us from Salgar, where the steamer that will take us to our destination awaits. The sight of the Great Atlantic Ocean, route of my future, supplies much welcome calm. . . . I am traveling with a likable foreigner, ignorant of our language but very willing to learn it.

---

* The reader would do well to refer to the letter from Simón Bolívar to Manuela Sáenz (April 20, 1825). The two texts are curiously similar. Were the words lodged in his unconscious, or did my father seek to establish a complicity at once carnal and literary with Antonia de Narváez? Was he sure that Antonia de Narváez would catch the allusion? Impossible to know.

He has opened his travel diary and shown me cuttings from the *Panama Star* that describe, I believe, the advances of the railroad. In reply, I have tried to make him understand that the very same iron track, able to conquer the dense jungle palm by palm, was also the object of my most profound admiration; I do not know, however, if I managed to convey that to him.

Letter from Antonia de Narváez to Miguel Altamirano, place not specified, Christmas Day

Your words are excessive and your feelings illegitimate. Ours, sir, was an encounter the reasons for which I have not yet ascertained and furthermore refuse to explore; I regret nothing, but why pretend interest in what is nothing more than an accident? It does not seem that our destiny is to find each other; I assure you, in any case, that I shall do what is in my power to keep that from occurring. . . . My life is here, my good sir, and here I must stay, just as I must stay at my husband's side. I cannot accept your claim, in an act of incredible arrogance, to know where my heart lies. I find myself obliged to remind you that, in spite of the ineffable event, you, Don Miguel, do not know me. Are my words cruel? Take them as you please.

Letter from Miguel Altamirano to Antonia de Narváez, Colón, January 29, 1855

At last it has happened: the Railroad has been inaugurated, and it was my privilege to witness such a great step forward toward Progress. The ceremony, in my modest opinion, was not as lavish as the event warranted; but the whole town came out to celebrate, the unofficial representatives of all Humanity, and in these streets one hears all the languages man's genius has created.* . . . In the crowd, veritable Ark of human races, I was surprised to recognize a certain Melo-supporting lieutenant, whose name is not worth writing down. He was banished to Panama as punishment for participating in the coup, yes, the very one that my humble services contributed to toppling. When he told me, I confess, I was flabbergasted. Panama, punishment for rebels? The Isthmus, Residence of the Future, a place to banish enemies of democracy? Little could I find to contradict him. I had to bow to the evidence; what I consider a prize, one of the greatest my worthless life has granted me, is for my own government a disaster just short of the gallows. . . . Your words, dear lady, are daggers that pierce my heart. Spurn me, but do not repudiate me; insult me, but do not ignore me. I am, since that night, your deferential servant, and I do not close the door to our re-encounter. . . . The Isthmus's climate is marvelous. The skies are clear, the air sweet. Its reputation, I can now say, is a tremendous injustice.

Letter from Miguel Altamirano to Antonia de Narváez, Colón, April 1, 1855

The climate is lethal. It never stops raining, the houses flood; the rivers burst their banks and people sleep in the treetops; above

---

* In my father's correspondence, as in the newspaper he'd run later and from which I'll quote the odd fragment, if I can bring myself to, these excited references to anything that suggests the clash of cultures, the melting pot of civilizations, appear frequently. I am surprised, in fact, that in this letter he does not speak of his enthusiasm for the Creole spoken in Panama, which in other documents appears as "unique language of civilized man," "instrument of peace between peoples," and even, in moments of particular grandiloquence, "victor over Babel."

puddles of still water swarm clouds of mosquitoes that look like locusts from ancient Babylon; the train carriages have to be cared for as if they were babes in arms for fear they'll be devoured by the humidity. Plague reigns over the Isthmus, and sick men wander the city, some begging for a glass of water to bring down the fever, others dragging themselves to the hospital doors, under the illusion that a miracle will save their lives. . . . A few days ago we recovered the corpse of Lieutenant Campillo; now it is justifiable to commit his name to paper, though not for that any less painful.* . . . I must assume that your reply has gone astray; the reverse would be inadmissible. Dear lady, there is a conspiracy of fate that prevents my forgetting, for I am constantly crossing paths with messengers of memory. The lives of the locals begin each morning with the sacred ritual of coffee and quinine, which protects them from the phantoms of fever; and I myself have adopted the customs of those I visit, for I judge them healthy. So what can I do if every tiny grain brings me the flavor of our night? What can I do?

Letter from Antonia de Narváez to Miguel Altamirano, Honda, May 10, 1855

Do not write to me, sir, and do not seek me. I consider this exchange closed and what was between us forgotten. My husband

---

* My father avoids going into details of the Lieutenant's death. It's possible he mentioned the events leading up to it in another letter, and that this letter did not arrive. Lieutenant Campillo's fate is quite well known: he lost his mind, went off alone into the Darien Jungle and did not return. There was speculation at the time that he was trying to return clandestinely to Bogotá. Since he had no friends, his absence was a long time in alarming anyone. In March an expedition went out in search of him; the body was in an advanced state of decomposition, and the actual cause of death was never ascertained.

has died; know this, Don Miguel Altamirano, from this day on I am dead to you.*

Letter from Miguel Altamirano to Antonia de Narváez, Colón, July 29, 1855

With my face disfigured by incredulity, I read over your terse message. Do you really expect me to obey your orders? By issuing them, do you seek to put my feelings to the test? You leave me, my dear lady, in an impossible situation, for complying with your directive would be to destroy my love, and not doing so would be to go against you. . . . You have no reason to doubt my words; the death of Mr. William Beckman, honorable man and favored guest of our nation, has deeply saddened me. You are excessively sparing with your words, my dear, and I do not know if it would be rash to inquire into the circumstances of the tragedy on the same page as I transmit my most sincere condolences to you. . . . I do so desire to see you again . . . but I cannot dare request your presence, and at times I think that perhaps it is this that has offended you. If this is the case, I beg you to understand me: here there are no women or children. So insalubrious is this land, that men prefer solitude during the course of their stay. They know, because experience has shown it to be so, that bringing their family with them is to condemn them to death as efficiently as running a machete through their chests.† These men, who have come to

---

* This letter does not contain anything else of interest. To be precise: this letter does not contain anything else.

† My father does not say so, but the foreigner who traveled with him on board the *Isabel* died around that time. His surname was Jennings; I haven't found his first name anywhere. Jennings committed the error of bringing

cross from one ocean to another toward gold mines in the land of California, are in search of instant riches, it's true, and they are willing to stake their own lives on it; but not those of their loved ones, for to whom would they return with their pockets filled with gold dust? No, my dear lady; if we are to see one another again, it will be in a more pleasant spot. That is why I await your summons; a word, a single one, and I shall be at your side. Until that moment, until you concede me the grace of your company,

I remain yours,

Miguel Altamirano

Eloísa dear: this letter received no reply.

Nor did the next.

Nor did the next.

And thus ended the correspondence, at least as far as this tale is concerned, between the two individuals who with time and certain circumstances I have grown accustomed to calling my parents. The reader of the preceding pages will look in vain for a reference to Antonia de Narváez's pregnancy, not to mention to the birth of her son. The letters I have not copied also take meticulous care to hide the first nauseas, the protruding belly, and, of course, the details of the birth. So Miguel Altamirano would wait a long time before finding out that his sperm had got its way, that a son of his had been born in the country's interior.

My date of birth was always a small domestic mystery. My mother

---

his young and pregnant wife, who survived no more than six months. After the death of her husband, Mrs. Jennings, already infected with the fever as well, was hired as a barmaid in an infamous casino, and there she was seen serving drinks to gold prospectors with arms so pale it was impossible to distinguish them from her blouse, her chest and hips so scrawny from the disease they did not even provoke passes from any drunken gamblers.

celebrated my birthday indiscriminately on July 20, August 7, and September 12; I, as a simple matter of dignity, have never celebrated it. As for places, I can say the following: unlike the majority of human beings, I know that of my conception but not that of my birth. Antonia de Narváez once told me, and then regretted having done so, that I was born in Santa Fe de Bogotá, in a gigantic bed covered in uncured hides and beside a chair whose back was carved with a certain noble coat of arms. On sad days, my mother rescinded that version: I had been born in the middle of the Muddy Magdalene, on a barge that sailed from Honda to La Dorada, between bundles of tobacco and oarsmen frightened at the spectacle of that deranged white woman and her open legs. But, in light of all the evidence, that birth most likely took place on the solid riverbank ground of the predictable city of Honda and, to be precise, in that very room of the Beckman guest house where the owner, the good-natured man who would have been my stepfather, put a shotgun in his mouth and pulled the trigger upon learning that what was in that swollen belly was not his.

I have always thought admirable the coldness with which my mother says in her letter, "My husband has died," when in reality she is referring to a horrid suicide that tormented her for decades and for which she would never stop feeling in part guilty. Long before his miserable cuckolded tropical fate, Beckman had asked—you know how these adventurers' last requests are—to be buried in the Muddy Magdalene; and early one morning his body was taken out by a lighter to the middle of the river and thrown overboard so he could sink into the adjective-riddled waters of that unbearable song. As the years went by he became the protagonist of my childhood nightmares: a mummy wrapped in canvas who came up onto the beach, leaking water through the hole in the back of his head and half devoured by the *bocachico* fish, to punish

me for lying to my elders or for killing birds with stones, for swearing or
for that time I tore the wings off a fly and told it to fuck off on foot. The
white figure of the suicide Beckman, my putative and dead father, was
my worst nocturnal threat until I was able to read, for the first of many
times, the story of a certain Captain Ahab.

(The mind generates associations that the pen cannot accept. Now,
while I write, I remember one of the last things my mother told me.
Shortly before dying in Paita, Manuela Sáenz received a visit from a
half-mad Gringo who was passing through Peru. The Gringo, without even removing his wide-brimmed hat, told her he was writing a
novel about whales. Were there whales to be seen around there? Manuela Sáenz didn't know what to say. She died on November 23, 1856,
thinking not of Simón Bolívar but of the white whales of a failed
novelist.)

So without precise coordinates, deprived of places and dates, I began
to exist. The imprecision extended to my name; and to keep from boring the reader again with the narrative cliché of identity problems,
the facile *what's-in-a-name*, I'll simply say that I was baptized—yes,
with a splash of holy water and everything: my mother might be a
convinced iconoclast, but she didn't want her only son ending up in
limbo on her account—as José Beckman, son of the crazy Gringo who
killed himself out of homesickness before the arrival of his descendant,
and a little while later, after a confession or two from my tormented
mother, I became José de Narváez, son of an unknown father. All
that, of course, before arriving at the surname that belonged to me by
blood.

The thing is that I began, finally, to exist; I begin to exist in these
pages, and my tale will be told in the first person from now on.

I'm the one doing the telling. I'm the one who counts. I am that I am. Me. Me. Me.

Now, having presented the written correspondence that took place between my parents, I must concern myself with another quite different form of correspondence: that between twin souls, yes, that doppelgänger correspondence. I hear murmurs in the audience. Intelligent readers, readers who are always one step ahead of the narrator, you will already be intuiting what's coming here; you're already guessing that a shadow is beginning to be cast over my life, the shadow of Joseph Conrad.

And so it is: because now that time has passed and I can see events clearly, arrange them on the map of my life, I am aware of the traversing lines, the subtle parallels that have kept us connected since my birth. Here is the proof: it doesn't matter how determined I am to tell the story of my life; doing so, inevitably, is telling the others. By virtue of physical affinities, according to experts, twins who have been separated at birth spend their lives feeling the pains and anxieties that overwhelm the other, even if they've never laid eyes on each other and even if an ocean separates them. On the level of metaphysical affinities, which are exactly what interest me, it takes on a different complexion but also happens. Yes, there is no doubt that this happens, too. Conrad and Altamirano, two incarnations of the same Joe, two versions of the same fate, bear witness to the fact.

No more philosophy! No more abstractions, demand the skeptics. Examples! We want examples! All right then, my pockets are full of them, and nothing seems easier to me than pulling out a few to sate the journalistic thirst of certain nonconformist spirits. . . . I can tell you that in December 1857 a child is born in Poland, he is baptized Józef Teodor Konrad Korzeniowski, and his father dedicates a poem to him: "To my son born in the 85th year of the Muscovite Oppression." In Colombia, a little boy, also called José, receives a box of pastels as a Christmas present and spends several days drawing soldiers without body armor humiliating the Spanish oppressors. While I, at the age of six, was writing my first compositions for a tutor from Bogotá (one of them about a bumblebee that flew over the river), Józef Teodor Konrad Korzeniowski, who was not yet four, wrote to his father: "I don't like it much when the mosquitoes bite."

More examples, Readers of the Jury?

In 1863, I was listening to the grown-ups talking about the Liberal revolution and its result, the secular and socialist Rionegro Constitution; in the same year, Józef Teodor Konrad Korzeniowski was also witness to a revolution in the adult world around him, that of the Polish nationalists against the Russian Tsar, a revolution that sent many of his relatives to prison, exile, or in front of a firing squad. While I, at the age of fifteen, began to ask questions about the identity of my father—in other words, began to bring him to life—Józef Teodor Konrad Korzeniowski watched as his gave way little by little to tuberculosis—in other words, to death. By 1871 or '72, Józef Teodor Konrad Korzeniowski had already begun to announce his desire to leave Poland and become a sailor, although he had never in his life seen the sea. And it must have been around then, when I was sixteen or seventeen, that I began to threaten to leave my mother home and the city of Honda, to disappear forever from her sight, unless . . . If she didn't want to lose me forever, it would be best . . .

That's how it was: I went directly from peaceful doubt to savage inquisition. What happened in my head was very simple. My usual doubts, with which I'd maintained a cordial and diplomatic relationship as a child, a sort of nonaggression pact, suddenly began to rebel against all peace initiatives and to launch offensives whose objective, invariably, was my poor blackmailed mother. Who? I asked. When? Why?

Who? (Stubborn tone.)

How? (Irreverent tone.)

Where? (Frankly aggressive tone.)

Our negotiations went on for months; summit meetings took place in the kitchen of the Beckman guest house, among the saucepans and burned oil and the penetrating smell of fried *mojarra*, while my mother barked orders at Rosita, the household cook. Antonia de Narváez never committed the vulgarity of telling me my father had died, of turning him into a hero of the civil war—a position to which every Colombian can aspire sooner or later—or a victim of some poetic accident, a fall off a fine horse, a duel over lost honor. No, I always knew the man existed somewhere, and my mother summed up and sentenced the matter with a platitude: "The thing is that somewhere isn't here." It took me an entire afternoon, the length of time it takes to cook the stew for dinner, to find out where that somewhere was. Then, for the first time, that word that had been so hard for me as a child (*itsmess*, I used to say, my tongue tangled up, in geography classes) acquired a certain reality for me, became tangible. There, in that twisted and deformed arm that stuck out of the territory of my country, in that inaccessible appendix out of God's hands and separate from the rest of the nation by a jungle whose fevers killed with just the mention of its name, that little hell where there were more illnesses than settlers, and where the only hint of human life was a primitive train that helped fortune hunters get from New York to California in less time than it would take them to cross their own country, there, in Panama, lived my father.

Panama. For my mother, as for most Colombians—who tend to act just like their governments, to harbor the same irrationalities, feel the same dislikes—Panama was a place as real as Calcutta or Berdichev or Kinshasa, a word that marks a map and little more. The railroad had brought the Panamanians out of oblivion, true, but only in a momentary and painfully brief way. A satellite: that was Panama. And the political regime didn't help much. The country was around about fifty years old, more or less, and here began to act its age. The midlife crisis, that mysterious age when men take lovers who could be their daughters and women heat up for no reason, affected the country in its own way: New Granada became federal. Like a poet or a cabaret artist, it took a new pseudonym: the United States of Colombia. Well then, Panama was one of those states, and it floated in the orbit of the Great Lady in Crisis more due to the mere pull of gravity than anything else. Which was an elegant way of saying that powerful Colombians, the moneyed merchants of Honda or Mompós, the politicians of Santa Fe or the military officers all over the country, didn't give a damn about the State of Panama, much less about the state of Panama.

And in that place lived my father.

What?

Why?

Who with?

For a couple of years as long as centuries, during those eternal cooking sessions that resulted in an extremely complicated roast of veal or a simple rice soup with *agua de panela*, I gradually perfected my interrogator's technique, and Antonia de Narváez softened like potatoes in a stew before the insistence of my questions. Thus I heard her speak of *La Opinión Comunera* or *El Granadino Temporal*; thus I found out about the sinking of the *Union*, and I even paid good money so an oarsman would take me out on a lighter to see the smokestacks; thus I found out about the encounter on the *Isabel*, and my mother's tale had the taste of quinine and the smell of rubbing alcohol. Another round of questions. What had happened in the two decades since then? What else did she know of him? Had there been no further contact in all these years? What was my father doing in 1860, while General Mosquera declared himself Supreme Director of War and the entire country was submerged—yes, Eloísa dear: once more—in the blood of the two parties? What was he doing, with whom was he dining, what was he talking about, while Liberal soldiers arrived at the Beckman guest house one week and Conservatives the next, while my mother fed one lot and tended the wounds of the others like a perfect Florence Nightingale of the Tropical Lowlands? What did he think and write in the following years, during which his radical, atheist, and rationalist comrades made friends with the power my father had pursued since his youth? His ideals prevailed, the clergy (blight of our time) had been stripped of their useless and unproductive hectares, and the illustrious Archbishop (director in chief of the blight) was duly incarcerated. Had my father's pen not left a trace of that in the press? How was that possible?

I began to confront a dreadful possibility: my father, who had barely begun to be born for me, could already be dead. And Antonia de Narváez must have seen me looking desperate, must have feared I would don an absurd, Hamlet-like mourning for a father I'd never known, and wanted to spare me those unwarranted laments. Compassionate, or maybe blackmailed, or maybe both at once, my mother confessed that, every year, round about December 16, she received a couple of pages with which Miguel Altamirano kept her up to date with his life. None of the letters received a reply, she continued to confess (I was shocked to see she felt not the slightest guilt). Antonia de Narváez had burned them all, even the latest one, but not before reading them the way one reads a serial by Dumas or Dickens: taking an interest in the fate of the protagonist, yes, but always aware that neither the pathetic moron David Copperfield nor the poor, weepy Lady of the Camellias existed in reality, that their happiness or their disgraces, as moving as they might be to us, have no effect whatsoever on the lives of flesh-and-blood people.

"Well then, tell me," I said.

And she told me.

She told me that, a few months after his arrival in Colón, Miguel Altamirano found that his reputation as an incendiary writer and champion of Progress preceded him and, almost before he realized, found himself contracted by the *Panama Star*, the same newspaper the ill-fated Mr. Jennings had been reading on board the *Isabel*. She told me the mission my father was charged with was very simple: he had to wander around the city, visit the offices of the Panama Railroad Company, even board the train as often as he liked to cross the Isthmus to Panama City, and then write about what a great marvel the railway was and the vast benefits it had brought and would continue to bring to the foreign investors as well as to the local inhabitants. She told me my father knew perfectly well that they were using him as a propagandist, but the good of the cause, from his point of view, justified it all; and with time he gradually realized, also, that years after the inauguration of the railway the streets still remained unpaved, and their only decoration continued to be dead animals and rotting garbage. I repeat: he realized. But none of that affected his unshakable faith, as if the simple image of the train going from one side to the other erased those elements of the landscape. That symptom, mentioned in passing like a simple character trait, would acquire extraordinary importance years later.

All this my mother told me.

And kept telling me.

She told me that in a matter of five years my father had become a sort of pampered son of Panamanian society: the Company's shareholders feted him like an ambassador, senators from Bogotá took him to lunch to ask his advice, and every official of the state government, each and every member of that rancid isthmian aristocracy, from the Herreras to the Arosemenas, from the Arangos to the Menocals, aspired to have him as husband to their daughter. She told me, finally, that what Miguel Altamirano was paid for his columns was barely sufficient for his confirmed bachelor's lifestyle, but that didn't prevent him from spending his mornings offering his services free of charge caring for the sick in the Colón hospital. "The hospital is the largest building in the city," my mother with her good memory recalled my father writing in one of his lost letters. "That gives an idea of the salubriousness of the environment. But all progress toward the future has its down sides, my dear, and this one was not to be the exception."

But that was not all that Antonia de Narváez told me. Like any novelist, my mother had left the most important thing until the end.

Miguel Altamirano was with Blas Arosemena the February morning when the *Nipsic*, a steam sloop carrying North American marines and Panamanian *macheteros*, picked him up in Colón and took him to Caledonia Bay. Don Blas had arrived at his house the previous night and said to him: "Pack for several days. Tomorrow we're going on an expedition." Miguel Altamirano obeyed, and four days later he was entering the Darien Jungle, accompanied by ninety-seven men, and for a week he walked behind them in the perpetual twilight of the rain forest, and saw the shirtless men who blazed the trail with clean machete blows, while others, the white men in their straw hats and blue-flannel shirts, wrote in their notebooks about everything they saw: the depth of the Chucunaque River when they tried to wade across it, but also the affection that scorpions felt for canvas shoes; the geological constitution of a ravine, but also the taste of roast monkey washed down with whiskey. A Gringo called Jeremy, veteran of the War of Secession, lent my father his rifle, because no man should be unarmed in these places, and told him that the rifle had fought in Chickamauga, where the forests were no less dense than here and the visibility shorter than the distance an arrow flies. My father, victim of his adventurer's instincts, was fascinated.

One of those nights they camped beside a rock polished by the Indians and covered with burgundy-colored hieroglyphics—the same Indians who, armed with poison-tipped arrows, with faces marked by such seriousness as my father had never seen, had guided them for a good part of the route. My father was standing up, observing in stunned silence the figure of a man with both arms raised facing a jaguar or maybe a puma; and then, as he listened to the arguments that would arise between a Confederate lieutenant and a small, bespectacled botanist, he felt all of a sudden that this crossing justified his life. "The enthusiasm kept me awake," he wrote to Antonia de Narváez. Although Antonia de Narváez was of the opinion that it wasn't the enthusiasm but rather the gnats, I felt I came to understand my father at that moment. On that page, lost long ago in my mother's purges, surely written in haste and still under the influence of the expedition, Miguel Altamirano had found the profound meaning of his existence. "They want to part the land as Moses parted the sea. They want to separate the continent in two and realize the distant dreams of Balboa and Humboldt. Common sense and all the explorations undertaken dictate that the idea of a canal between the two oceans is impossible. Dear Lady, I make this promise to you with all the solemnity of which I am capable: I shall not die without having seen that canal."

Readers of the Jury: you know, as does the whole British Empire, the famous anecdote we've so often been told by the world-famous Joseph Conrad about the origins of his passion for Africa. Do you remember? The scene has an exquisite romanticism, but it won't be me who satirizes that aspect of his tale. Joseph Conrad is still a child, he is still Józef Teodor Konrad Korzeniowski, and the map of Africa is a blank space whose contents—its rivers, its mountains—are completely unknown; a place of bright obscurity, a true deposit of mysteries. The boy Korzeniowski puts a finger on the empty map and says, "I shall go there." So then, what the map of Africa was to the boy Korzeniowski, the image of my father in Panama was to me. My father crossing the Darien Jungle, along with a group of madmen who wondered if they could build a canal there; my father sitting in the Colón hospital beside a patient with dysentery. The letters that Antonia de Narváez had brought back to life by memory, no doubt making mistakes with precise details, chronologies, and the odd proper name, had become in my head a space comparable to the Africa of my friend Korzeniowski: a continent without contents. My mother's narration had drawn a border around Miguel Altamirano's life; but what that border confined became, as the months and years went by, my very own heart of darkness. Readers of the Jury: I, José Altamirano, was twenty-one years old when I put a finger on my own blank map and pronounced, excited and trembling, my own *I shall go there.*

At the end of August 1876, a few leagues from the door of my house, I boarded the American steamship *Selfridge*, without saying good-bye to Antonia de Narváez, and followed the same route my father had covered after scattering his sperm. Sixteen years had passed since the last Colombian civil war, in which the Liberals had killed more, not because their army was better or braver, but because it was their turn. The regular massacre of compatriots is our version of the changing of the guard: it's done every so often, generally following the same criteria as children at play ("It's my turn to govern," "No, it's my turn"); and it happened that the moment of my departure for Panama coincided with another changing of the guard, as usual under the stage directions of the Angel of History. I sailed a Magdalena colonized or dominated by the alternating traffic of the two warring parties, or by barges filled not with cacao or tobacco, but with dead soldiers whose putrid stench was stronger than the smoke coming out of the funnels. And I came out onto the Caribbean Sea at Barranquilla, and sighted the Cerro de la Popa from the deck and also the city walls of Cartagena, and I probably had some innocent thought (I may have wondered, for example, if my father had seen the same view, and what he'd thought upon seeing it).

But I could not have imagined that a ship sailing under a French flag had just passed through this walled port, en route from Marseille with stops in Saint-Pierre, Puerto Cabello, Santa Marta, and Sabanilla, and now heading for the city some of its passengers knew as Aspinwall and others as Colón. I sailed across the wake of the *Saint-Antoine* but didn't know it; and when I arrived that night in Colón, I also didn't know my steamer had passed less than two leagues from that sailing ship comfortably anchored in Limón Bay. Other things I didn't know: that the *Saint-Antoine* was making that trip clandestinely and would not keep a record of it in the logbook; that its cargo was not what was declared either but seven thousand contraband rifles for the Conservative revolutionaries; and that one of the smugglers was a young man two years my junior, a steward with a nominal salary, of noble birth, Catholic beliefs, and timid appearance, whose surname was unpronounceable to the rest of the crew and whose head was already beginning, clandestinely, to archive what he saw and heard, to conserve anecdotes, to classify characters. Because his head (although the young man did not yet know it) was the head of a storyteller. Do I need to tell you what is so obvious? It was a certain Korzeniowski, by the name of Józef, by the name of Teodor, by the name of Konrad.

III

Joseph Conrad
Asks for Help

Yes, my dear Joseph, yes: I was there, in Colón, while you were. . . .
I was not a witness, but that, given the nature of our almost telepathic
relationship, of the invisible threads that kept us on the same wave-
length, was not necessary. Why does that seem so implausible to you,
my dear Joseph? Don't you know, as I do, that our encounter was pro-
grammed by the Angel of History, the great *metteur-en-scène*, the expert
puppeteer? Don't you know that no one escapes his destiny, and didn't
you write it several times in several places? Don't you know our relationship already forms part of history, and history is renowned for never
bowing to the irksome obligation of plausibility?

But now I must go back in time. I warn you now that further on
I'll move ahead again, and then back again, and so on alternately,
successively, and stubbornly. (I'll get fed up with this temporal navi-
gation, but I don't have too many options. How to remember without getting worn down by the past? To put it another way: How does

a body manage to endure the weight of his memory?) Anyway, I'm going back.

Shortly before docking, young Korzeniowski avails himself of a moment of calm, he leans on the rail of the *Saint-Antoine* and allows his gaze to wander at random over the landscape. It is his third voyage to the Caribbean, but never before has he passed by the Gulf of Urabá, never has he seen the coastlines of the Isthmus. After passing the gulf, approaching Limón Bay, Korzeniowski distinguishes three uninhabited islands, three caymans half submerged in the water, enjoying the sun and pursuing any ray that pierces the veil of clouds at this time of year. Later he'll ask and will be told: yes, the three islands, yes, they have names. They'll tell him: the archipelago of the Mulatas. They'll tell him: Great Mulata, Little Mulata, and Isla Hermosa. Or that, at least, is what he will remember years later, in London, when he tries to revive the details of that voyage. . . . And then he'll wonder if his own memory has been faithful to him, if it hasn't failed him, whether he really saw a ragged old palm tree on Little Mulata, whether someone actually told him there was a freshwater spring on Great Mulata issuing from the side of a ravine. The *Saint-Antoine* continues its approach to Limón Bay; night falls, and Korzeniowski senses that the play of light on the sea is starting to deceive his eyes, for Isla Hermosa appears to be little more than a flat, gray rock, smoking (or is it a mirage?) from the heat accumulated during the day. Then night swallows the earth, and eyes have appeared on the coast: the bonfires of the Cuna Indians are the only things visible from the ship, beacons that do not guide or help but confuse and frighten.

I, too, saw the Cunas' fires lighting up the night, of course, but let me say in a good loud voice: I saw nothing else. No islands, no palm trees, much less any steaming rocks. Because that night, the night of my arrival in Colón hours after young Korzeniowski arrived, a dense fog had fallen over the bay that only abated to give way to the most extraordinary downpour I had ever chanced to see up to that moment. The deck of the ship was lashed with harsh gusts of rain, and I swear I feared at some point, in my ignorance, that it would extinguish the boilers. As if that weren't enough, there were so many ships taking up the few moorings in Colón, that the *Selfridge* could not dock, and we spent that night on board. Let us begin, readers, to put to rest a few tropical myths: it is not true that there are no mosquitoes far from land. Those of the Panama coast are able, to judge by what I saw that night, to cross entire bays to force incautious passengers to take shelter under their nets. In five words: it was an unbearable night.

Dawn broke at last, at last the clouds of mosquitoes and the real clouds scattered, and the passengers and crew of the *Selfridge* spent the day on deck, taking the sun just like caimans or the Mulatas, waiting for the good news that they could dock. But night fell again, and the clouds returned, the real ones and the others; and the docks of Colón remained as full as a sailors' brothel. The resurrection occurred on the third day. The sky had cleared miraculously, and in the cool night air (that luxury article) the *Selfridge* managed to find a bed in the brothel. Passengers and crew burst ashore like a downpour, and I set foot for the first time on the land of my maledictions.

I came to Colón because I was told that here I would find my father, the well-known Miguel Altamirano; but as soon as my smelly feet, my damp, stiff boots, stepped into the Schizophrenic City, all the nobility of the classic theme—all those stories of Oedipus and Laius, Telemachus and Odysseus—went very quickly to hell. It won't be me who tries to disguise the truth at this stage in life: walking into the commotion of the city, the Father Quest turned into the last of my priorities. I confess, yes, I confess I was distracted. I allowed Colón to distract me.

My first impression was of a city too small for the chaos it harbored. The serpent of the railway line rested about ten meters from the waters of the bay, and seemed ready to slide into them and sink forever at the slightest tremor of the earth. The stevedores shouted unintelligibly and without that seeming to matter to them: the Babel my father had evoked, far from being overcome, remained alive and kicking on the docks that separated the railroad from the shore. I thought: This is the world. Hotels that didn't receive guests but went out hunting for them; American saloons where men drank whiskey, played poker, and talked with bullets; Jamaican slums; Chinese butcher shops; in the middle of everything, the private house of an old railway employee. I was twenty-one years old, dear reader, and the long, black braid of the Chinese man who sold meat over the counter and liquor under it, or Maggs & Oates pawnshop and its display window on the main street with the most gigantic jewels I'd ever seen, or the West Indian cobblers' shops where they danced soca were for me like notifications of a disorderly and magnificent world, allusions to countless sins, welcome letters from Gomorrah.

That night I did something for the first time that I would repeat many years later and on another continent: arrive in an unknown city and look for a hotel at night. I confess: I didn't look too closely at where I was staying, and I wasn't intimidated by the fact that the owner/receptionist held a Winchester as he pushed the visitors' book toward me. Sleepwalking, I went outside again, made my way between mules and carts and carts with mules to a two-storey saloon. Above the wooden sign—GENERAL GRANT, it read—waved the stars and stripes. I leaned on the bar, ordered what the man next to me had ordered, but before the mustached bartender had poured my whiskey, I had already turned around: the saloon and its customers were a better spectacle.

I saw two Gringos having a knife fight with three Panamanians. I saw a whore they called Francisca—hips that had already opened for one or more children, worn-out tits, a certain bitterness in her expression, and a comb out of place in her hair—and imagined that she'd committed the error of accompanying her husband on his Panama adventure and that in a matter of months the poor little man had gone to swell the statistics of the Colón hospital. I saw a group of sailors, bare-chested thugs in unbuttoned, dark, knitted shirts, who surrounded her and solicited her in their language, insistently but not impolitely, and I saw or noticed that the woman enjoyed that unusual and now exotic moment when a man treated her with something resembling respect. I saw a cart driver come in and start asking for help to move a dead mule off the railway tracks; I saw a group of Americans look him over, from under their broad-brimmed hats, before rolling up the bright sleeves of their shirts and going out to help.

I saw all that.

But there was something I didn't see. And the things we don't see tend to be the ones that affect us most. (This epigram has been sponsored by the Angel of History.)

I didn't see a small man, a mouse who looked like a notary, approach the bar and ask for the attention of the drinkers. I didn't hear him explain in laborious English that he had purchased two tickets for the next morning's train to Panama City, that during the course of the day his young son had died of cholera, and that now he wanted to recoup the fifty dollars he'd spent on the tickets to prevent the child's being tossed into a pauper's grave. I didn't see that the Captain of the French sailors approached him and asked him to repeat all that he'd just said, to make sure he'd understood, and I did not see the moment that one of his subordinates, a broad-chested man of about forty, rummaged through a leather bag, came over to the Captain, and put the money for the tickets, in U.S. dollars tied with a velvet ribbon, in his hand. The transaction didn't last longer than a drink of whiskey (I, concerned with my own, didn't see it). But in that short space of time something had happened beside me, almost touching me, something . . . Let's look for the appropriate figure: Did the wing of destiny brush my face? The ghost of encounters to come? No, I'll explain it as it happened, without meddling tropes. Readers, pity me, or mock me if you wish: I did not see the scene, the scene passed me by, and, logically, I didn't know it had happened. I didn't know one of those men was called Escarras and that he was Captain of the *Saint-Antoine*. This might not seem much; the problem is that I also didn't know that his right-hand man, the broad-chested forty-year-old, was called Dominic Cervoni, or that one of his companions that night of binges and business, a young steward who distractedly observed the scene, was called Józef Korzeniowski, or that many years later that distracted young man—when he was no longer called Korzeniowski, but Conrad—would use the sailor—calling him not Cervoni, but Nostromo—to the ends for which he'd become famous . . . "A one-eyed giant would not have had the ghost of a chance against Dominic Cervoni, of Corsica, not Ithaca," a mature and prematurely nostalgic novelist would write years later. Conrad admired Cervoni as any disciple admires any master; Cervoni, for his part, had voluntarily taken on the role of godfather of adventure for the disoriented young Pole. That was the relationship that united them: Cervoni in charge of the sentimental education of that apprentice sailor and amateur smuggler. But that night I did not know that Cervoni was Cervoni, or that Conrad was Conrad.

I'm the man who didn't see.

I'm the man who didn't know.

I'm the man who wasn't there.

Yes, that's me: the anti-witness.

The list of things I didn't see and didn't know either is much longer: I could fill several pages and label them: IMPORTANT THINGS THAT HAP-PENED TO ME WITHOUT MY REALIZING. I didn't know that after buying the tickets Captain Escarras and his crew returned to the *Saint-Antoine* for a few hours' rest. I didn't know that before dawn Cervoni would load four rowboats and, along with six other oarsmen (Korzeniowski among them), would return to the port more or less at the same time as I was leaving the General Grant, not drunk but a little queasy. While I spent a couple of hours wandering the heaving streets of Colón-Aspinwall-Gomorrah, Dominic Cervoni directed the maneuvers of the four boats up to the railway-loading piers, where a group of *cargadores* awaited him in the shadows; and while I was returning to the hotel, preparing to get up early and begin my Father Quest, the stevedores moved the contents of those stealthy nocturnal transports, carried them under the arches of the depot, packed them into the freight cars of the train to Panama City (and in doing so heard the clatter of the barrels and the thud of the wood, without asking what, or for whom, or where), and covered them with tarpaulins, so they wouldn't be ruined by one of those sudden downpours, trademark of life in the Isthmus.

All this passed me by, almost without touching me. It's a flimsy con-solation to think that, even though I wasn't present, I could have been (as if that would authenticate me). If a few hours later, instead of sleep-ing the sleep of the dead in the uncomfortable folding bed in my room, I had looked out from the hotel balcony, I would have seen Korzeniowski and Cervoni, the Ulysses of Corsica and the Telemachus of Berdichev, climb aboard the last carriage of the train with the tickets purchased the evening before from the poor little mouse in the saloon. If I had stood on the balcony until eight that morning, I would have seen the ticket collectors lean out between the carriages—their hats pulled down firmly on their heads—to announce the departure punctually, and I would have smelled the smoke of the locomotive and heard the screech from its smokestack. The train would have pulled out right under my nose, taking Cervoni and Korzeniowski, among other passengers, and, in the freight cars, the one thousand two hundred and ninety-three breech-loading, bolt-action Chassepot rifles, which had crossed the Atlantic Ocean aboard the *Saint-Antoine* and which had, themselves, a good story to tell.

Yes, Readers of the Jury, in my democratic tale things also have a voice, and will also be allowed to take the floor. (Oh, the tricks a poor narrator must resort to in order to tell what he doesn't know, to fill his uncertainties with something interesting. . . .) Well, I wonder: if, instead of snoring in my room, *ad portas* of a terrible headache, I had gone down to the station and mixed with the travelers, and I had meddled in the freight car and interrogated one of the Chassepots, any one of them, one chosen at random for the objectives of my limitless curiosity, what story would it have told me? In a certain Conradian novel whose name I do not care to remember, a certain rather affected character, a certain Frenchified Creole, asks: "What do I know of military rifles?" And I, now, put myself on the other side with a much more interesting (forgive my modesty) question: What do rifles know of us?

The Chassepot brought by Korzeniowski to Colombian lands was manufactured in the Toulon armories in 1866. In 1870 it was taken as army-issue weapon to the Battle of Wissembourg and used, under the

orders of General Douay, by soldier Pierre-Henri Desfourgues, who dex-
terously aimed it at Boris Seeler (1849) and Karl Heinz Waldraff (1851).
Pierre-Henri Desfourgues was wounded by a Dreyse and removed from
the front; in the hospital, he received the news that Mademoiselle
Henriette Arnaud (1850), his fiancée, was breaking their engagement
to marry Monsieur Jacques-Philippe Lambert (1821), presumably for
financial reasons. Pierre-Henri Desfourgues cried for twenty-seven
consecutive nights, at the end of which he introduced the barrel of the
Chassepot (11 millimeters) into his own mouth, till it touched his uvula
(7 millimeters) with the sight (4 millimeters), and squeezed the trigger
(10 millimeters).

The Chassepot was inherited by Alphonse Desfourgues, Pierre-
Henri's first cousin, who turned up armed with it for the defense of
Mars-la-Tour. Alphonse shot it sixteen times during the course of the
battle; not once did he hit a target. The Chassepot was then taken from
him (in a rude way, apparently) by Captain Julien Roba (1839), who
from the Metz Fortress successfully shot cavalrymen Friedrich Strecket,
Ivo Schmitt, and Dieter Dorrestein (all 1848). Emboldened, Captain
Roba joined the vanguard and withstood five hours of the attack of
two Prussian regiments. He died after taking a bullet from a Snider-
Enfield. No one has been able to explain what a Snider-Enfield was
doing in the hands of a Prussian of the 7th Armored Division (Georg
Schlink, 1844).

During the Battle of Gravelotte, the Chassepot changed hands one
hundred and forty-five times and fired five hundred and ninety-nine
bullets, of which two hundred and thirty-one missed, one hundred and
ninety-seven killed, and one hundred and seventy-one caused injuries.
Between the hours of 2:10 and 7:30 p.m. it lay abandoned in a trench
in Saint-Privat. Jean-Marie Ray (1847), under the orders of General

Canrobert, had replaced a dead gunner on a *mitrailleuse* and died in his turn. Recovered after the battle, the Chassepot had the luck to fight in Sedan, under Napoleon III; like Napoleon III it was defeated and taken prisoner. Difference: while Napoleon went into exile in England, the Chassepot served Konrad Deresser (1829), artillery captain of the Prussian 11th Regiment, during the siege of Paris. In Deresser's hands, it was present in the Hall of Mirrors of the Palace of Versailles and witnessed the proclamation of the German Empire; hanging over Deresser's back, it was present in the Louis XIV Salon and witnessed the suggestive glances of Madame Isabelle Lafourie; at Deresser's feet, it was present in the woods behind the Palace, and witnessed the way the Captain's pelvis responded to those glances. Days later, Deresser moved to Paris as part of the German occupation; Madame Lafourie, in her capacity as occupied territory, became a regular creditor of his favors (January 29, February 12, February 13, March 2, March 15 at 6:30 and at 6:55 p.m., April 1). April 2: Monsieur Lafourie enters a room on rue de l'Arcade by surprise and by force. April 3: Konrad Deresser receives Monsieur Lafourie's seconds. April 4: The Chassepot waits on the side, while Monsieur Lafourie and Captain Deresser each take a Galand revolver (1868, made in Belgium). Both Galands fire, but only Deresser is hit by a bullet (10.4 millimeters) and falls the full span of his height (1,750 millimeters). On April 5, 1871, Monsieur Lafourie sells the defeated man's Chassepot on the black market. Which is far from an honorable way to behave.

For five years, two months, and twenty-one days, the Chassepot disappears. But at the end of June 1876 it is acquired, along with another one thousand two hundred and ninety-two rifles, veterans like itself of the Franco-Prussian War, by Frédéric Fontaigne. Fontaigne—it is a secret to no one—works as member of staff in charge of various matters for a firm called Déléstang & Fils, owner of a fleet of sailing ships based in Marseille, as well as playing the straw man for Monsieur Déléstang, aristocrat and amateur banker, fanatic conservative, nostalgic realist, and ardent ultra-Catholic. Monsieur Déléstang has decided to give the Chassepot a particular destiny. After spending fourteen days and nights in a deposit in the *vieux port* of Marseille, the rifle embarked in one of the company's ships: the *Saint-Antoine.*

The Atlantic crossing follows, without incident. The ship anchors in Limón Bay, Panama, United States of Colombia. The Chassepot is taken by boat to the railway depot (this has already been mentioned). On board freight car number 3 (this, on the other hand, has not), it covers the fifteen leagues between Colón and Panama City, where it is the object of a clandestine transaction. Night has just fallen. At the Waterfront Market, under an awning among bunches of Urubá bananas, a meeting is held between the Polish steward Józef Korzeniowski, the Corsican adventurer Dominic Cervoni, the Conservative General Juan Luis De la Pava, and the interpreter Leovigildo Toro. While General De la Pava hands over the sum agreed, through multiple intermediaries, with Déléstang & Fils, the Chassepot and the one thousand two hundred and ninety-two like it are taken to the port in mule-drawn carts and loaded onto the *Helena* steamship, whose Pacific route comes from California, via Nicaragua, and has as its final destination the port of Lima, Peru. Hours later, on board the *Helena*, General De la Pava gets repeatedly drunk and, to shouts of "Death to the Government! Death to President Aquileo Parra! Death to the damned Liberal Party!" shoots six shots into the air with the Smith & Wesson model 3 revolver he bought in Panama from a California miner (Bartholomew J. Jackson, 1834). On August 24, the steamer reaches port in the city of Buenaventura, on the Pacific coast of Colombia.

And so, covering the difficult trail from Buenaventura to Tuluá on muleback—the mules walk sometimes two or three days in a row without resting, and one of them collapses on the way up the Cordillera—the contraband arrives, under General De la Pava's supervision, at the front at Los Chancos. It is August 30, and it is almost midnight; General Joaquin María Córdoba, who will command the battle against the monster of Liberal atheism, sleeps peacefully in his tent but wakes when he hears the sound of mules and carts. He congratulates De la Pava; he makes his generals kneel and pray for the Déléstang family, pronouncing the surname variously as Delestón, Colestén, and Del Hostal. In a matter of minutes the four thousand and forty-seven Conservative soldiers are reciting the Sacred Heart of Jesus in which they trust and requesting eternal health for the crusaders of Marseille, their distant benefactors. The following morning, after years of inactivity on the noble stages of war, the Chassepot is placed in the hands of Ruperto Abello (1849), brother-in-law of the Buga parish priest, and goes back into combat.

At 6:47 a.m., its shot pierces the throat of Wenceslao Serrano, an artisan from Ibagué. At 8:13, it hits the right quadriceps of Silvestre E. Vargas, fisherman from La Dorada, making him fall; and at 8:15, after a failed reloading attempt, its bayonet is plunged into the thorax of the same Vargas, between the second and third ribs. It is 9:30 when its shot perforates the right lung of Miguel Carvajal Cotes, *chicha* producer; it is 9:54 when it blows apart the neck of Mateo Luis Noguera, a young journalist from Popayán who would have written great novels had he lived longer. The Chassepot kills Agustin Iturralde at 10:12, Ramón Mosquera at 10:29, Jesús María Santander at 10:56. And at 12:44, Vicente Noguera, older brother of Mateo Luis and first reader of his first poems—"Elegy for My Donkey" and "Immortal Jubilation"—who has followed Ruperto

Abello for three hours across the battlefield, disobeying the orders of General Julián Trujillo and exposing himself to a court-martial that will later absolve him, takes cover behind Barrabás, his own dead horse, and fires. He does not do so with the Spenser rifle that had been issued to him before the battle but with the 20-caliber Remington that his father used to take when he went hunting in the Cauca River Valley. The bullet hits Ruperto Abello's left ear, destroys the cartilage, breaks the cheekbone, and exits through the eye (green and celebrated in his family). Abello dies instantly; the Chassepot remains in the grass, among cow pies from a dairy herd.

Like Abello, two thousand one hundred and seven Conservative soldiers, many of them bearers of contraband Chassepots, die in Los Chancos. On the other side, one thousand three hundred and five Liberal soldiers die by the smuggled bullets of those rifles. Scouring the battlefield as part of the victorious army, young Fidel Emiliano Salgar, General Trujillo's ex-slave, picks up the Chassepot and takes it with him as the Liberals advance toward the State of Antioquia. The Battle of Los Chancos, one of the bloodiest in the 1876 civil war, has left a profound mark on Salgar's soul, as well as a profound hole in his left hand (produced by the rusty bayonet of Marceliano Jiménez, farm laborer). If Fidel Emiliano Salgar were a poet and French, he would undoubtedly have embarked on a sonnet called "L'ennui de la guerre." But Salgar was neither French nor a poet, and he has no way of sublimating the unbearable tension of the last few days or the persistent image of every one of the dead men he has seen. Armed with the Chassepot, Salgar begins to talk to himself; and that night, after using the same bayonet that killed Silvestre E. Vargas to kill the sentinel (Estanislao Acosta González, 1859), Salgar reveals—by the look in his eye, by his gestures—that he has gone mad.

The Chassepot's life ends shortly thereafter.

Correctly aimed, the rifle allows Salgar to terrorize several of his battalion comrades and enjoy doing so (it's like a small revenge). Many of them let him be, in spite of the danger an unstable and armed man represented to a military contingent, because the magnitude of his madness was not visible from outside. By the night of September 25, the battalion, Salgar, and the rifle have crossed the State of Antioquia and arrived at the banks of the Atrato River, as part of their reconquest of Conservative territory. Night catches them at the Hacienda Miraflores. Salgar, barefoot and shirtless, points the gun at General Anzoátegui, who had been sleeping in his tent, and they walk toward the river; Salgar manages to push off in a dugout he finds on the bank, all the time with the bayonet pressed against the General's ribs and his eyes loose and turbulent like those of a broken doll. But the dugout has gone barely ten meters into the current of the Atrato when the guards arrive at the riverbank and form an authentic firing squad. In the midst of his cloudy reasoning, Salgar raises the Chassepot, aims at the General's head, and his last shot pierces the skull before anyone has time to do anything. The rest of the soldiers, whose names no longer matter, open fire.

The bullets—of various calibers—hit Salgar in various parts of his body: they perforate both lungs, his cheek and tongue; they destroy one of his knees and reopen the almost closed wound in his left hand, burning nerves, scorching tendons, crossing through the carpel tunnel the way a boat crosses a canal. The Chassepot floats in the air for a second and falls into the rough waters of the Atrato; it sinks, and before touching bottom is swept a few meters ahead by the current. Following it, falling backward, the corpse of a man (sixty-nine kilograms in weight) who was a slave and will not now be free.

At the moment Fidel Emiliano Salgar lands on the sandy riverbed,

startling a ray and receiving a sting—not that the dead body feels anything, not that his tissues retract in reaction to the venom, not that
his muscles suffer fevers or his blood is contaminated—at that very
moment, the apprentice sailor Korzeniowski, on board the *Saint-
Antoine*, takes one last look at the coastline of the port of Saint-Pierre
in Martinique. Several days have gone by since, having completed the
rifles-to-overthrow-Liberal-governments mission, they left Colón and
the territorial waters of the United States of Colombia. And, since this
seems to be the chapter of things unknown, I better state what Korzeniowski doesn't know at that moment.

He doesn't know the names or ages of the one thousand three hundred and thirty-five victims of the Chassepots. He doesn't even know
there were one thousand three hundred and thirty-five victims of the
Chassepots. He doesn't know that the contraband will have been in vain,
that the Liberal and Masonic government will win the war against the
Conservative Catholics and it will take another war—or a resumption of
the same one—to alter that state of things. He doesn't know what Monsieur Déléstang will think, in Marseille, when he finds out about it, or
if he'll go on to interfere in other crusades. He doesn't know that one of
the gutter press newspapers, *La Justicia*, will invent many years later an
absurd version of his sojourn on the Colombian coast: in it, Korzeniowski takes charge of all the negotiations and sells the weapons to a certain Lorenzo Daza, delegate of the Liberal government who later "gives
them up for lost" and resells them "for double their price" to the Conservative revolutionaries. Korzeniowski, who doesn't even know who
Daza is, carries on with his gaze fixed on Martinique, and carries on
not knowing things. He doesn't know that the coastline of Saint-Pierre
will not ever be the same, at least not for him, for the city known as Old
Paris will be erased from the map in a quarter of a century, completely

obliterated like an undesirable historical fact (but this is not the time to speak of that disaster). He doesn't know that, in a matter of hours, when they sail between St. Thomas and Port-au-Prince, he will meet the violence of the East Wind and the West Wind, and doesn't know that much later he'll write about that violence. Between Port-au-Prince and Marseille he will turn nineteen, and won't know that at home awaits the most difficult chain of events of his youth, events that will culminate, for him, with a gunshot to the heart.

And while that birthday unfolds on board the *Saint-Antoine*, with songs and embraces from Cervoni, in another vessel somewhere else other things (or shall I say: correspondences) are happening. Allow me to introduce the steamer *Lafayette*, flagship of the French West Indies line that will play extremely important roles in our small tragedy. Aboard, Lieutenant Lucien Napoléon Bonaparte Wyse, illegitimate son of a famous mother (in the worst sense) and unknown father (in the only sense), this Lieutenant Wyse, dear readers, is preparing to leave on an expedition. His mission is to search through the Colombian Darien Jungle for the best place to open an inter-oceanic canal, which some— in Paris, in New York, in Bogotá itself—have begun to call That Fucking Canal. I'll say it once and for all: for reasons that will soon become apparent, for reasons impossible to reduce to the golden cage of a single pretty phrase, at that moment it wasn't just the Canal that began to be fucked up but my entire life.

Chronology is an untamed beast; the reader doesn't know what inhuman labors I've gone through to give my tale a more or less organized appearance (I don't rule out having failed in the attempt). My problems with the beast can be reduced to one alone. You'll see, with the passing of the years and the reflection on the subjects of this book, which I'm now writing, I have discovered what undoubtedly comes as no surprise to anyone: that stories in the world, all the stories that are known and told and remembered, all those little stories that for some reason matter to us and which gradually fit together without us noticing to compose the fearful fresco of Great History, they are juxtaposed, touching, intersecting: none of them exists on their own. How to wrest a linear tale from this? Impossible, I fear. Here is a humble revelation, the lesson I've learned through brushing up against world events: silence is invention, lies are constructed by what's not said, and since my intention is to tell faithfully, my cannibalistic tale must include everything, as many stories as can fit in the mouth, big ones and little ones. Well then, in the days before the departure of the *Lafayette* one of the latter occurred: the encounter between another two travelers. It was a few meters from the port of Colón and, therefore, from Lieutenant Wyse and his men. And in the next chapter, if my life has not ended by then, if there is still enough strength in my hand to hold my pen, I'll have to concentrate on it. (At my age, which is more or less the age of a dead novelist, Polish by birth and sailor before he became a writer, there's no point in making plans too far ahead.)

But first, responding to the peculiar order events have in my tale, I must concern myself with another matter, or rather with another man. Let's call him a facilitator; let's call him an intermediary. It's obvious, I think: if I'm going to devote so many pages to describing my encounter with Joseph Conrad, it's at least necessary that I explain a little who the person responsible for our meeting was, the host of my disgrace, the man who fostered the theft . . .

But it's still too early to speak of the theft.

Let us return, readers, to the year 1903. The location is a dock on the Thames: a passenger steamer has arrived from the Caribbean port of Barranquilla, in the convulsive Republic of Colombia. A passenger descends from the ship carrying all his worldly goods: a small trunk of clothes and personal items, more fitting to someone who plans to spend a couple of weeks away from home than to someone who'll never return to his homeland. Let's say that it is not the trunk of an émigré but of a traveler, and not just from its humble size but because its owner does not yet know that he has arrived to stay. . . . Of that first evening in London I remember details: the advertising flyer, received from a dark hand on the dock itself, on which were listed the services and virtues of Trenton's Hotel, Bridgewater Square, Barbican; the supplements that had to be paid, one for the use of electricity, another for cleaning my boots; the fruitful negotiation with the night porter, from whom I demanded a special rate, with breakfast included, in spite of the fact that my identity documents were neither North American nor colonial. The next morning, more memories: a pocket map I bought for tuppence, a folded map with covers the color of bile; bread with marmalade and two cups of cocoa that I had in the dining room of the hotel while searching through those white streets and yellow streets for the address I had written down in my journalist's notebook. A bus left me in Baker Street; I crossed Regent's Park instead of going around it, and through already bare trees and slushy paths I arrived at the street I was looking for. It was not difficult to find the number.

I still have the map I used that morning: its thin spine has been devoured by moths, its streaked pages resemble a crop of fungi for scientific use. But objects speak to me, dictate things to me; they call me to account when I lie, and in the opposite case they offer willingly to serve as proof. Well then, the first thing this old, unusable, out-of-date (London changes every year) map announces is the encounter with the aforementioned intermediary. But who was Santiago Pérez Triana,

the famous Colombian negotiator who in time would become pleni-
potentiary ambassador to the courts of Madrid and London? Who was
that man, one of so many who in Colombia inherit that undesirable and
dangerous monster: a Political Life? The answer, which will strike some
of you as strange, is: I don't care. The important thing is not who that
man was but rather what version I am prepared to give of his life, what
role I want him to play in this tale of mine. So right now I make use of
my narrator's prerogatives, I take the magic potion of omniscience and
enter, not for the first time, the head—and the biography—of another
person.

In those years, a Colombian arriving in London necessarily called
on Santiago Pérez Triana, at 45 Avenue Road. Pérez Triana, son of a former president and secret writer of children's stories, political target and
amateur tenor, had arrived in the city a few years before and presided
with his toad face and anecdotes in four languages over a table designed
for an audience: his dinners, his soirees in the Victorian drawing room,
were small tributes in his own honor, masterful speeches destined to
exhibit his talents as Athenian orator long before the addresses that distinguished him at the courts of The Hague. The evenings in that dining
room, or in the special room where coffee was taken, were always the
same: Pérez Triana took off his round-framed spectacles to light a cigar,
straightened his bow tie while the cups of his private audience were
filled to the brim, and began to speak. He spoke of his life in Heidelberg
or of the opera in Madrid, of his readings of Henry James, of his friendship with Rubén Dario and Miguel de Unamuno. He recited his own
poems: "Sepulchers Safeguard My Secrets" could burst out all of a sudden, or "I Have Heard the Crowds Moan." And his guests, Liberal politicians or erudite businessmen of the Bogotá bourgeoisie, applauded
like trained seals. Pérez Triana nodded with modesty, closed his eyes

already worn out like the slots in a piggy bank, calmed spirits with a gesture of his pudgy hand as if tossing a couple of sardines to the seals. And he would go on without wasting time to the next anecdote, to the next poem.

But at night, when everyone had gone, Pérez Triana would be enveloped by a distant and almost affectionate dread, a sort of tame but fearsome animal that still stayed with him even after all these years. It was a well-defined physical sensation: an intestinal discomfort similar to the moments preceding hunger. When he felt it coming on, the first thing the man would do was to make sure Gertrud, his wife, was asleep; he would immediately leave the dark bedroom and go down to his library, in his green dressing gown and leather slippers, and light all the lamps in the place. From his drawing room he could see the black stain that in the morning would be Regent's Park, but Pérez Triana didn't much like to look out at the street, except to confirm the rectangle of light that his window projected onto the dark pavement or the comforting presence of his own disheveled silhouette. He settled down at his desk, opened a wooden box with adjustable compartments, took out a few blank sheets of paper and a few Perfection-brand envelopes, and wrote long and always solemn letters in which he asked how things were in Colombia, who else had died in the most recent civil war, what was really happening in Panama. And the news came back to him in North American envelopes: from New York, from Boston, even from San Francisco. This was, as everyone knew, the only way to evade the censors. Pérez Triana knew as well as his correspondents did that a letter addressed to him would be opened and its contents read by governmental authorities and no one could do anything about it; if the authority considered it necessary, the letter would be lost before arriving at its destination, and could still provoke more or less unpleasant questioning for the sender.

So his accomplices in Bogotá soon grew accustomed to the routine of transcribing the news by hand; they also grew accustomed to receiving envelopes bearing U.S. stamps, inside of which appeared, as if playing hide-and-seek, the handwriting of their banished friend. And one of the questions most often repeated in the clandestine letters from London was this: Do you think that I can come back now? No, Santiago, his friends replied. You shouldn't come back yet.

Readers of the Jury: allow me to give you a very brief lesson in Colombian politics, to synthesize the pages turned up till now and prepare you for those to come. The most important event in the history of my country, as you'll perhaps have noticed, was not the birth of its Liberator, or its independence, or any of those fabrications for high school textbooks. Nor was it a catastrophe on an individual level like those that frequently mark the destinies of other lands either: no Henry wanted to marry some Boleyn, no Booth killed any Lincoln. No, the moment that would define the fate of Colombia for all history, as always happens in this land of philologists and grammarians and bloodthirsty dictators who translate *The Iliad*, was a moment made of words. More precisely, of names. A double baptism took place at some imprecise moment of the nineteenth century. The gathered parents of the two chubby-cheeked and already spoiled infants, those two little boys smelling since birth of vomit and liquid shit, agreed that the calmer of the two would be given the name Conservative. The other (who cried a little more) was called Liberal. Those children grew up and multiplied in constant rivalry; the rival generations have succeeded each other with the energy of rabbits and the obstinacy of cockroaches ... and in August of 1893, as part of that indisputable inheritance, former—Liberal—President Santiago Pérez Manosalva, a man who in other times had won the respect of General Ulysses S. Grant, was banished with a total lack of consideration by the—Conservative—regime of Miguel Antonio Caro. His son, Santiago Pérez Triana, inherited the condition of undesirable, more or less the way one inherits premature baldness or a hooked nose.

Perhaps a recap would not go amiss, as I'm not forgetting that some of my readers do not have the good fortune of being Colombian. It was all the fault of the subversive columns that the former—Liberal—President wrote in *El Relator*, real depth charges that would have breached and sunk in a matter of seconds any European government. *El Relator* was the pampered son of the family: a newspaper founded for the sole reason of dislodging the Conservatives from power and closed in a timely fashion, with decrees worthy of tyranny, by those who did not want to be dislodged. It was not the only one: former President Pérez—eyelids drooping, beard so thick his mouth was completely hidden—used to convoke clandestine meetings with other journalistic conspirators in his house on Carrera Sexta in Santa Fe de Bogotá. And thus, while on the other side of the street the Bordadita church filled with praying *godos*, the Pérez's drawing room filled with the editors of *El Contemporáneo, El Tábano,* and *El 93*, all newspapers closed down under charges of supporting the anarchist camp and preparing for civil war.

Well now: politics in Colombia, Readers of the Jury, is a strange class game. Behind the word *motivation* is the word *whim*; behind *decision* is *tantrum*. The matter that concerns us happened according to these simple rules, and it also happened as swiftly as mistakes usually happen. . . . At the beginning of August, Miguel Antonio Caro, Supreme Whimsical One of the Nation, has heard by chance that *El Relator* would be prepared to moderate its stance if it were allowed to go back into circulation. There is something in this news that tastes of victory to him: the Conservative Regeneration, which has set out censorship laws tougher than any ever seen in the democratic world, has defeated the written subversion of Liberal atheism. That's what Caro thinks; but *El Relator* shakes him out of his deception with the next day's edition, defying the censorship with one of the strongest invectives the institutions of the Conservative Regeneration have ever received. President Caro—inevitably—feels deceived. No one has promised him anything, but something terrible happened in his world, in his tiny little private world, made of Latin classics and a deep disdain for all who are not on his side: reality has not conformed to his fantasies. The President pounds and stamps on the wooden floors of the San Carlos Palace, hurls his rattle to the ground, pouts and throws tantrums, and refuses to eat his lunch . . . and nevertheless reality is still there: *El Relator* still exists and is still his enemy. Those with him then listen to him say that Santiago Pérez Manosalva, former President of Colombia, is a liar and a fake and a man who doesn't keep his word. They listen to him predict with the certainty of an oracle that that Liberal without a nation or a god will take the country to war and that banishment is the only way to prevent it. The definitive decree, the decree that fixes his expulsion, is dated 14 August.

The father complied, of course—the death penalty for exiles who didn't go into exile was common currency in Caro's Colombia—and left for Paris, natural homing instinct for the Latin American haute bourgeoisie. The son, after receiving the first threats, tried to leave the country by going down from Bogotá to the Magdalena River and embarking at the port of Honda on the first steamer prepared to take him to Barranquilla, and from there to European exile. "The truth is, I didn't feel I was in danger," he would tell me much later, when our relationship allowed this tone and these confidences. "I was leaving Colombia because, after the affront to my father, the atmosphere had become unbreathable; I was going to punish, in my own way, the country's ingratitude. But when I arrived at Honda, a foul village with a population of three and savage temperatures, I realized how mistaken I was." At night in London, Pérez Triana kept dreaming that the police who arrested him in Honda took him back to the Ciega—the most feared prison on the Magdalena—but in the dream the youngest policeman explained, smoothing the down on his upper lip, what hadn't been explained in reality: that the orders had come from the capital. But what orders? On what charges? In the dream it was as impossible to find out as it had been in reality. Pérez Triana had never spoken to anyone, not even to Gertrud, about the hours he spent in the Ciega, in the darkness of a cell, his eyes watering with the stench of human shit and soaked to the skin by the corrosive humidity of the tropics. He would have needed more than one hand to count the cases of yellow fever he had word of during his very short imprisonment. At some point, he thought, it would be his turn: each mosquito, each microbe was his enemy. He was then sure he'd been sentenced to death.

The prisoner had no way of knowing, but at dawn on his second day in the Ciega, while he grudgingly accepted the *arepa* without cheese that was all there was for breakfast, the Bogotá lawyer Francisco Sanin, who was vacationing at the time in Honda, received news of his imprisonment. By the time Sanin arrived at the Ciega, Pérez Triana had sweated so much that the starched collar of his shirt no longer pressed against his throat; he had the feeling, impossible to confirm, that his cheeks were sagging, but he passed a hand over his face and found only rough traces of stubble. Sanin weighed the situation, asked about the charges, and received evasive answers, and his complaints reached Bogotá and returned with neither replies nor solutions. Then it occurred to him that the only solution lay in a lie. At some stage, operating as a businessman in the United States, Pérez Triana had had to sign some letters of loyalty. Sanin wrote to the U.S. envoy, a certain MacKinney, citing those letters and telling him one of his citizens was in danger of dying in an insalubrious prison. It was a risky lie, but it worked: MacKinney believed every word with the candor of a small child and protested before the relevant judge, raising his voice and pounding the desk, and in a matter of hours Pérez Triana found himself on his way to Bogotá, looking back over his shoulder, confoundedly grateful for the power that Uncle Sam's husky voice has in these submissive latitudes. This time (he was thinking) there was no room for doubt, there was no anticipated nostalgia. He had to flee; every detail of his mistreated person pointed him toward the path to flight. If the Magdalena River route was forbidden him, he would search out less obvious ways. And so he fled through the Eastern Plains, he disguised himself as a priest and baptized incautious Indians along the way, he paddled down three rivers and saw animals he'd never seen and reached the Caribbean without having been recognized by anyone but also feeling that he no longer recognized himself. And then he told the whole story in a book.

Down the Orinoco in a Canoe was translated into English and published by Heinemann, with a prologue by the Scottish adventurer, dilettante writer, and socialist leader Robert Cunninghame Graham, whose perception of Bogotá as a kind of Chibcha Athens still strikes me as more ingenious than fitting. The book appeared in 1902; in November 1903, a few hours before I knocked on his door—one exile requesting help from another, a disciple in search of a master—Pérez Triana had received a letter from Sydney Pawling, his editor. "One last thing I should like to mention, Mr. Triana," it read. "As you will no doubt know, Mr. Conrad, whose magnificent *Typhoon* we published this past April, is immersed in a difficult project relating to current Latin American reality. Aware of his own limited knowledge of the subject, Mr. Conrad has sought out and received the aid of Mr. Cunninghame Graham to pursue the work; but he has also read your book, and has now requested I ask you, Mr. Triana, if you would be prepared to answer a few questions that Mr. Conrad would like to send you by way of us."

Joseph Conrad has read me, thinks Pérez Triana. *Joseph Conrad wants my help.*

Pérez Triana opens the drawer and takes out a blank sheet and another Perfection envelope. (He likes this invention, so simple and at once so ingenious: you had to pass your tongue along the flap as ever, but the glue was not there, it was on the envelope itself. His family physician, Dr. Thomas Wilmot, had told him of it after describing various tongue infections, and Pérez Triana had gone immediately to the stationer's in Charing Cross. He had to look after his health, of course; how many envelopes a day could a man like him end up licking?) He wrote: "My delay in replying to your letter, Mr. Pawling, is utterly inexcusable. Do relate to Mr. Conrad my absolute availability to answer as many questions as he cares to send me, no matter how lengthy." And then he put the paper in the envelope and licked the flap.

But he did not send the letter at once. A few hours later he would be pleased he hadn't. He threw that letter into the wastepaper basket, took out another piece of paper, and wrote again the same lines about tardiness and availability, but then added: "Pass on to Mr. Conrad, however, that certain recent events allow me now to have other ways of helping him. I do not presume to know better than the author what his needs might be, but the information he could receive from an exile of long standing, by way of a questionnaire sent by third parties, is invariably inferior to what he could be given in person by a direct witness to events. Well then, what I can offer is even better than a witness. I offer him a victim, Mr. Pawling. A victim."

What had happened between the two letters?

A man from his distant country had arrived to visit him. A man had told him a story.

That man, of course, was me.

That story is the one that you, dear Eloísa, are reading at this moment.

PART TWO

The words one knows so well have a nightmarish meaning in this country. Liberty, democracy, patriotism, government— all of them have a flavor of folly and murder.

Joseph Conrad, *Nostromo*

IV

The Mysterious
Laws of Refraction

I spent two whole days looking for my father, following his faint
but still visible trail, his slimy snail trail, through the streets of Colón.
But I was not successful. I didn't want to leave messages, notes, warnings, because I'm fond of surprises and I suspected—for no reason, of
course—that this fondness came from my paternal side. In the hospital
the mulatta nurses spoke of my father with (it seemed to me) too much
familiarity; they told me at once, between impertinent giggles, that he'd
been there that morning and had spent at least three hours chatting with
a tubercular young man, but they didn't know what his next destination
was; when I spoke to the tubercular young man, I found out several
things, but not my father's whereabouts. He'd been born in Bogotá and
was a lawyer by profession, that oh so frequent combination in my centralist and pettifogging country; two weeks after arriving in Colón he'd
woken up with a swelling under his jaw; by the time of my visit, the
infection had left the inflamed gland and invaded the lungs and blood;

he had, in the best of cases, a few months to live. "That fellow's a friend of yours?" he said, half opening his bile-colored eyes. "Well, tell him I'll be expecting him tomorrow. Tell him not to leave me abandoned here. In those three hours he looked after me better than all these damn doctors. Tell him, OK? Tell him that before I die I want to know what the hell happens to D'Artagnan." And as he pronounced the guttural r, with a zeal for correctness that struck me as at the very least curious in the case of a dying man, he brought his left hand up to his inflamed gland, covering it as if it hurt.

In the offices of the Railroad Company—which some natives called by its English name, giving me the strange sensation of living in two countries at once, or of crossing an invisible border over and over again—the North Americans confused me with a potential ticket buyer and conscientiously sent me to the ticket office, shaking the cuffs of their impeccable shirtsleeves in the direction of the street, and one of them even donning his felt hat to accompany me to the place. That whole exchange was in English; it was only after saying good-bye that I realized it, with rather greater surprise than modesty allows me to confess. In the place the impeccable cuff had indicated, a finely clothed arm moved to inform me that no, tickets were no longer sold there, then at another window a sweaty forehead told me that I should simply board the train and someone would come by to ask for my ticket. "But no, I'm looking for—" "Don't worry, nothing will happen. In the carriage they'll ask for it." And meanwhile, the heat was afflicting me like poison; as I crossed a threshold and entering any shade, a solitary drop of sweat trickled down my side, beneath my clothes; and in the street I marveled that a Chinese man could wear black while not a single pore on his face seemed open. I sought refuge in a liquor store full of gambling cart drivers in whose hands an innocent pair of dice managed to seem like high-stakes poker. And it was then, at the hottest hour of the day, with Front Street empty of pedestrians—only a lunatic or a recent arrival would dare to walk out in the sun at that moment—that I saw him. A restaurant door opened; a decadent place was revealed, a wall covered in mirrors; and through the door came a rash creature. Like in the old joke about twins who meet in the street and recognize each other instantly, I recognized my father.

You, readers of romantic novels; you, sensitive victims of our melo-dramatic culture, now await a standard reunion scene, with initial gestures of skepticism, lachrymose concessions to the physical evidence, sweaty embraces in the middle of the street, resounding promises to make up for lost time. Well then, allow me to say that I'm (not) sorry to disappoint you. There was no *re*union whatsoever, because there was no union to renew; there was no promise, because for my father and for me there'd been no time lost. Yes, there are some things that dissociate me from a certain English novelist, Polish by birth and sailor before he became a writer. My father did not teach me to read Shakespeare or Victor Hugo on our estate in Poland, nor did I immortalize the scene in my memoirs (surely exaggerating it along the way, it has to be said); he did not await me in bed when, the two of us living in cold Kraków, I returned from school to console him over the death of my mother in exile. . . . Please, understand: my father was my mother's story. A character, a version, and little more. Well then, there, in the middle of the scorching street, that father in his fifties spoke through the already graying beard that covered his face and defined his features. Or rather the absence of them: for the whiskers of his mustache covered his lips (and had turned yellow, or perhaps always had been), and those on his cheeks went so close to his eyes that my father could have looked at them himself with a little effort. And through that curtain of smoke, from that gray Birnam Wood advancing toward the deforested regions of his face, spoke my father's invisible mouth: "So I have a son." Hands clasped behind his back and his gaze fixed on the ground, on the waves of heat at the height of his shiny boots, he began to walk. I understood that I should follow him, and from behind, like a geisha following her lord, I heard him add: "Not a bad thing, at my age. Not bad at all."

And that's how it began: it was that simple. Thus I had a father, and he a son.

His house was on the north side of Manzanillo Island, in the makeshift and yet ostentatious city the founders of the railroad—which is to say, Aspinwall-Colón—had built for their employees. A ghetto surrounded by groves of trees, a luxurious hamlet on stilts, the city of the Panama Railroad Company was an oasis of salubriousness in the swamp of the island, and to enter it was to breathe a different air: the clean air of the Caribbean instead of the sickly vapors of the Chagres River. The white-walled, red-roofed house, paint peeling off the walls from the humidity and screen doors dirty with the accumulated bodies of mosquitoes, had belonged to a certain Watts, an engineer murdered five days after the inauguration of the railway, when, during a dry summer on his way back from buying two barrels of fresh water in Gatún, he was stabbed by mule thieves (or maybe water thieves); and my idealistic father, inheriting it, had felt that he inherited much more than walls and hammocks and mosquito nets. . . . But if someone—his recently discovered son, for example—had asked him what that legacy consisted of, he wouldn't have known how to answer; instead, he would have taken out of a Spanish trunk, covered in leather and closed with a lock strong enough to guard a dungeon in times of the Inquisition, the semi-complete collection of his articles published since his arrival in Colón-Aspinwall. That's what he did with me. In many more words and a few gestures, I asked him: Who are you? And he, without a single word and with the simple gesture of opening the chest and leaving it open, tried to answer the question. And the results, at least for me, were the first big surprise of the many that awaited me in the city of Colón. Do share, readers, my filial astonishment, such a literary thing. For there, lying in a hammock in San Jacinto and with a sherry cobbler in my free hand, I embarked on the task of reviewing my father's articles, that is, of finding out who this Miguel Altamirano was, into whose life I had just burst. And what did I discover? I discovered a symptom, or a complex, as one of these new Freudian disciples who accost us from everywhere would say. Let's see if I can explain it. I must be able to explain it.

I discovered that over the course of two decades my father had produced, from his mahogany desk—bare but for the skeleton of a hand on a marble pedestal—a scale model of the Isthmus. No, *model* is not the word, or perhaps it is the applicable word to the first years of his journalistic labors; but starting from some imprecise moment (futile, from a scientific point of view, to try to date it), what was represented in my father's articles was more than a distortion, a version—again the damned little word—of Panamanian reality. And that version, I began to realize as I read, only touched on objective reality at certain select points, the way a merchant ship only concerns itself with certain ports. In his writings, my father did not fear for a moment changing what was already known or what everyone remembered. With good reason, besides: in Panama, which after all was a state of Colombia, almost no one knew, and most of all, no one remembered. Now I can say it: that was my first contact with the notion, which would so often appear in my future life, that reality is a frail enemy to the power of the pen, that anyone can found a utopia simply by arming himself with good rhetoric.

In the beginning was the word: the contents of that biblical vacuity were revealed to me there, in the port of Colón, in front of my father's desk. Reality real like a creature of ink and paper: that discovery, for someone of my age, is of the sort that shakes worlds, transforms beliefs, makes atheists devout and vice versa.

Let's clear this up once and for all: it's not that my father wrote lies. Surprised and at the same time full of admiration, over the first few months of life with my father I began to notice the strange illness that a few years back had begun to guide his perception and, therefore, his pen. Panamanian reality entered his eyes as if from a stick for measuring water depth from the shore: it folded, it bent, folded at the beginning and bent afterward, or vice versa. The phenomenon is called "refraction," as more competent people have told me. Well then, my father's pen was the largest refractive lens of the Sovereign State of Panama; only the fact that Panama was in itself a place so prone to refraction can explain why nobody, I mean *nobody*, seemed to notice. At first I thought, as any respectful son would, that the fault was mine, that I had inherited the worst of distortions: my mother's cynicism. But I soon accepted the obvious.

In Miguel Altamirano's first articles, the railway's dead had been almost ten thousand; in one from 1863 the sum was less than half that, and toward 1870 he wrote about "the two thousand five hundred martyrs to our well-being." In 1856 my father was one of those who wrote with an indignant wealth of detail of an incident that happened near the stations, when a certain Jack Oliver refused to pay a certain José Luna the price of a slice of watermelon, and for several hours Panamanians of the neighborhood shot it out with Gringo train passengers, at a cost of fifteen dead and an indemnity the Colombian government had to pay in installments to the government of the victims. Examining my father's articles: in one from 1867, the fifteen dead had become nine; in 1872 he mentions nineteen wounded, seven of them seriously, but not a word about deaths; and in one of his most recently published texts—April 15 the year of my arrival—my father recalled "the tragedy of the nine victims" (and he even turns the watermelon into an orange, though I don't know what that could mean). Readers of the Jury, I now reach for a phrase that is the resource of lazy writers and say: examples abound. But I am interested in leaving a record of one in particular, the first of those to occur in my presence.

I have already mentioned Lieutenant Lucien Napoléon Bonaparte Wyse and his expedition to the Darien; but I have not mentioned the results. That November morning, my father presented himself at the anchorage of the port of Colón to see off the *Lafayette* and the eighteen explorers, and then he wrote for the *Star & Herald* (which the *Panama Star* was now called) a page-and-a-half-long panegyric, wishing good luck to the pioneers and courage to the conquerors in that first step toward the Inter-oceanic Canal. I was with him at that moment; I went with him. Six months later, my father returned to the port to welcome back the delegation of pioneers and conquerors, and again I was with him; and there, in the same port, he found, or we found, that two of the men had died of malaria in the jungle, and two others on the high sea, and that the rain had made several of the routes impassable, so the terrains the expedition wanted to investigate remained convincingly virginal. The conquerors returned to Colón dehydrated, ill, and depressed, and most of all victims of a resounding failure; but two days later Miguel Altamirano's version appeared in the newspaper:

THE WYSE EXPEDITION IS AN UNQUALIFIED SUCCESS
THE LONG ROAD TO THE CANAL BEGINS

The French Lieutenant had not managed to establish the best route for a task of such magnitude, but my father wrote: "All doubts have been dispelled." The French Lieutenant had not managed to establish whether a canal with culverts and locks would be better than one at sea level, but my father wrote: "For the science of engineering, the Darien Jungle has ceased to hold secrets." And no one contradicted him. The laws of refraction are a complicated business.

But it's the same all over and the same thing was happening on the other side of the Atlantic. So now we travel to Marseille. The reason? I would like to show, simply to be fair, that others also have the enviable capacity to distort truths (and more: they manage to do so with greater success, with better guarantees of impunity). Now I return to Korzeniow-ski, and I do so rather overwhelmed by shame and excusing myself in advance for the direction this tale is about to take. Who could have told me that one day my pen would be occupied with such shocking matters? But there is no way to avoid it. Sensitive readers, people of delicate constitutions, demure ladies and innocent children: I beg or suggest that you close your eyes, cover your ears (in other words, skip to the next chapter), because here I shall refer, more than to young Korzeniowski himself, to the most private of his parts.

We are in the month of March in 1877, and in the city of Marseille, Korzeniowski's anus is suffering. No, let us be frank or, at least, more scientifically precise: he has an abscess. It is, in all probability, the most well-documented anal abscess in the history of anal abscesses, for it appears, at least, in two of the young sailor's letters, two of those from a friend, one of his uncle's, and in the first officer's report. Before such proliferation, I have often asked myself the inevitable question: Are there allusions to the anal abscess in the literary oeuvre of Joseph Conrad? Dear readers, I confess: if they are there, I have not found them.

Of course, I don't share the opinion of a certain critic (George Galla-her, *Illustrated London News*, November 1921, page 199), according to whom that abscess is the "true heart of darkness," nor do I believe that in real life it was Korzeniowski who, in an attack of private discomfort, cried out, "The horror! The horror!" Be that as it may, no abscess, anal or any other kind, has had such intense consequences from a metaphysi-cal point of view as that which oppresses Korzeniowski that spring. For due to its pain he is obliged to remain on land while his ship, the *Saint-Antoine*, sails again to the Caribbean.

During these days of enforced terra firma, a disconsolate and mor-tally bored Korzeniowski devotes himself to theoretical studies of tech-nical materials to qualify as a ship's mate. But this training is theoretical in more than one sense, for what happens in practice is quite differ-ent: Korzeniowski spends his time walking around the *vieux port* and frequenting people with questionable reputations. Summer begins and Korzeniowski tries to complement his education: in his very poor room at 18 rue Sainte, between two applications of Madame Fagot's ointment, he receives English lessons from one Henry Grand, who lives at number 22 of the same street; in the Café Bodoul, between two drinks or two cigars, he receives lessons in politics from the Nostalgic Realists. The anal abscess does not prevent him from noticing that the followers of Monsieur Déléstang are right: King Alfonso XII, who is the same age as our Polish sailor, is no more than a puppet of Republican atheists, and the only legitimate owner of the crown of Spain is Don Carlos, the poor, pursued Catholic who had to hide on the other side of the French border. This, of course, is only one way of seeing things; the other is that Korzeniowski doesn't give a fig about the Carlists, the monarchy, the Republic, and Spain in general; but the anal abscess that has left him on land has also deprived him of the salary he had anticipated. . . .

Korzeniowski suddenly finds himself short of funds. How will he buy his good brandy, the good Havana cigars he's grown accustomed to on recent voyages? European politics then provides an opportunity he cannot waste: smuggling rifles for the Colombian Conservatives had gone so well, had worked so easily, that now Korzeniowski accepts the invitation of a certain Captain Duteuil. He puts a thousand francs on the table to get weapons to the Carlists; after a few days, the investment produces a return of four hundred. "Viva Don Carlos!" shouts Korzeniowski through the streets of Marseille, producing a sort of involuntary echo from a certain bellicose Conservative and Colombian general. Death to the Republic! Death to Alfonso XII! Korzeniowski, enthusiastic about his talent for business, invests for a second time in the Carlist crusade. But the contraband for political-ends market is capricious and variable, and this time the young investor loses it all. While another dose of ointment is applied, this time prepared by a friend of Madame Fagot's, Korzeniowski thinks: It is all the fault of the abscess. Viva Madame Fagot's friend! Death to anal abscesses!

It is then that he meets Paula de Somogyi, Hungarian actress, lover of the aspirant Don Carlos, activist for his restitution to the throne and *belle dame sans merci*. Paula is beautiful and closer in age to the contrabandist than to the pretender; and what happens in romantic novels happens to Korzeniowski, when the disoriented young man and Don Carlos's brazen lover become involved. They have clandestine and frequent encounters in portside hotels. To keep from being recognized, Paula covers her head with a hood, in the best Milady de Winter style; Korzeniowski enters and leaves through the window, and becomes an habitué of the rooftops of Marseille. . . . But the paradise of clandestine love cannot endure (it's one of the laws of romanticism). Enter John Young Mason Key Blunt, an American adventurer who had lived in

Panama during the gold rush and made himself rich, in those days before the railway, taking prospectors from one side of the Isthmus to the other. Blunt—who would have imagined?—had taken a liking to the Hungarian. He pursues her, he hounds her in scenes worthy of a cabaret (she with her back against a wall, he wrapping his arms around her while speaking fish-scented obscenities too close to her face). But Paula is a virtuous woman, and her religion only allows her to have one lover; so she tells Korzeniowski all about it, holding the back of her hand against her forehead and leaning back her head. The young man knows that his honor and that of the woman he has fallen in love with leave him no alternative. He challenges Blunt to a duel to the death. In the tranquillity of the Marseille siesta, shots are suddenly heard. Korzeniowski lifts a hand to his chest: "I'm dying," he says. And then, as is obvious, he does not die.

Oh, dear Conrad, what an impetuous lad you were.... (You don't mind if I address you informally, do you, dear Conrad? We know each other so well, after all, and we're so close. . . .) Later you would leave written evidence of these activities, of your own voyage as a Mediterranean gunrunner on the *Tremolino*, of the encounter with the coast guard—someone had denounced the smugglers—and of the death of César, the informant, at the hands of his own uncle, none other than Dominic Cervoni, the Ulysses of Corsica. But *written evidence* is undoubtedly a condescending and generous phrase, dear Conrad, because the truth is this: despite the passing of the years, which turn everything true, I do not manage to believe a single word of what you say. I don't believe you were a witness to the moment Cervoni murdered his own nephew; I don't believe the nephew sank to the bottom of the Mediterranean with the weight of the ten thousand francs he'd stolen. Let's admit, dear Conrad, that you have been deft in the art of rewriting your own life; your little white lies—and another few running closer to beige—have passed into your official biography unquestioned. How often did you speak of your duel, dear Conrad? How many times did you tell that romantic and also sterilized story to your wife and sons? Jessie believed it till the end of her days, and so did Borys and John Conrad, convinced that their father was a musketeer for modern times: noble like Athos, kind like Porthos, and religious like Aramis. But the truth is different and, most of all, much more prosaic. It's true, Readers of the Jury, that on Conrad's chest was the scar of a bullet wound; but the similarities between Conradian reality and real reality end there. As in so many other cases, real reality has been left buried under the verbiage of the novelist's profuse imagination. Readers of the Jury: I am here, again, to give the contradictory version, to dispel the verbiage, to bring discord into the tranquil house of received truths.

The young Korzeniowski. I can see him now, and I'd like my readers to see him, too. Photos of the time show a baby-faced lad, smooth hair, long, straight brows, almond-colored eyes: a young man who regards his aristocratic origins at once with pride and affected disdain; he was five-foot-eight but at this time appears shorter due simply to timidity. Look at him, readers: Korzeniowski is first and foremost a boy who has lost his bearings . . . and that's not all. He has lost his faith in people; he's lost all his money, wagering it on the habit-forming horse of contraband. Captain Duteuil had betrayed him: he'd taken his money and fled to Buenos Aires. Do you see him, readers? Korzeniowski, disoriented, wanders round the port of Marseille with an anal abscess and not a single coin in his pockets. . . . The world, thinks Korzeniowski, has suddenly turned into a difficult place, and all through the fault of money. He had quarreled with Monsieur Déléstang; he would never again step on a ship of his fleet. All paths seem closed to him. Korzeniowski thinks—it is to be thought that he thinks—of his uncle Tadeusz, the man whose money has kept him afloat since he left Poland. Uncle Tadeusz writes regularly; for Korzeniowski his letters should be a source of joy (contact with the homeland and so on), but in truth they torment him. Each letter is a judgment; after each reading, Korzeniowski is found guilty and condemned. "In two years you have by your transgressions used up your maintenance for the whole third year," his uncle writes. "If the allowance that I have allotted you does not suffice, earn some money—and you will have it. If, however, you cannot earn it, then content yourself with what you get from the labor of others—until you are able to supplant it with your own earnings, and gratify yourself." Uncle Tadeusz makes him feel useless, childish, irresponsible. Uncle Tadeusz has suddenly come to represent all that is detestable about Poland, every constraint, every restriction that had forced Korzeniowski to escape. "Hoping that it is the first and last time you cause me so much trouble, you have my embrace and my blessing." First time, thinks Korzeniowski, last time. First. Last.

At the age of twenty, Korzeniowski has learned what it means to get into debt up to his neck. While waiting for the profits from the smuggled guns, he'd lived on the money of others; with other people's money he'd bought the basic necessities for a trip that never came off. And that's when he turns, for the last time—first, last—to his friend Richard Fecht. He takes a loan of eight hundred francs and leaves for Villa Franca. His intention: to join up with a North American squadron that was anchored there. What follows happens very quickly, and will continue happening very quickly in Korzeniowski's mind, and also in Conrad's, for the rest of his life. On the U.S. ships there are no available places: Korzeniowski, Polish citizen with no military papers, no stable employment, no certificates of good conduct, without a single piece of testimony to his skills on deck, is turned away. The Korzeniowskis are rash, passionate, impulsive: Apollo, his father, had been imprisoned for conspiring against the Russian Empire, for organizing several mutinies, and he had staked his life on a patriotic ideal; but the desperate young sailor does not think of him when he manages to get a lift to Monte Carlo, where he will stake his life for—shall we say?—less altruistic motives. Korzeniowski closes his eyes. When he opens them again, he finds himself standing before a roulette wheel. Welcome to Roulettenbourg, he thinks ironically. He doesn't know where he's heard that name before, sardonic code of hardened gamblers. But he doesn't exert himself in pursuit of the memory. His concentration is elsewhere: the ball has begun to spin.

Korzeniowski takes his money, all his money. Then he pushes the chips across the smooth surface of the table; the chips settle contentedly on a black-colored diamond. *"Les jeux sont faits,"* shouts a voice. And as the roulette spins and on it the black ball, black like the diamond under the chips, Korzeniowski is surprised to recall words not his own and whose providence is unknown.

No, he does not recall them: the words have invaded him, they have taken him by storm. They are Russian words, the language of the empire that killed his father. Where do they come from? Who is speaking, and to whom? "If one begins cautiously," says the new and mysterious voice rising in his head, ". . . and can I, can I be such a baby! Can I fail to understand that I am a lost man?" The roulette spins, the colors disappear, but in Korzeniowski's head the voice persists and keeps talking: "But—can I not rise again! Yes! I have only for once to be prudent and patient and—that is all! I have only for once to show willpower and in one hour I can transform my destiny! The great thing is willpower. Only remember what happened to me seven months ago at Roulettenbourg just before my final failure." There it is, thinks Korzeniowski: that strange word. He doesn't know what Roulettenbourg is or where it is; he doesn't know who, from deep in his head, mentions this ignoble place. Is it something I've heard, something I've read, something I've dreamed? Who's there? wonders Korzeniowski. And the voice: "Oh! it was a remarkable instance of determination; I had lost everything, then, everything . . ." Who is it, who's speaking? asks Korzeniowski. And the voice: "I was going out of the casino, I looked, there was still one gulden in my waistcoat pocket. Then I shall have something for dinner, I thought. But after I had gone a hundred paces I changed my mind and went back." The roulette is coming to a stop. Who are you? asks Korzeniowski. And the voice: "There really is something peculiar in the feeling when, alone in a strange land, far from your home and from friends, not knowing whether you will have anything to eat that day, you stake your last gulden, your very last! I won, and twenty minutes later I went out of the casino, having a hundred and seventy guldens in my pocket. That's a fact! That's what the last gulden can sometimes do! And what if I had lost heart then? What if I had not dared to risk it?" But who are you? asks Korzeniowski. And the voice: "Tomorrow, tomorrow it will all be over!"

The roulette has stopped.

"Rouge!" shouts a man's bow tie.

"Rouge," repeats Korzeniowski.

Rouge. Red. Rodz.

He has lost everything.

Back in Marseille, he knows very well what he should do. He invites his friend Fecht to his apartment on rue Sainte for tea. There is no tea in the house, nor money to buy any, but that doesn't matter. *Rouge. Red. Rodz*, he thinks. *Tomorrow it will all be over.* He goes out for a stroll around the port, he approaches an English sailing ship and stretches out his arm, as if to touch it, as if the sailing ship were a newborn donkey. There in front of the sailing ship and the Mediterranean, Korzeniowski suffers a violent attack of sadness. His sadness is that of skepticism, disorientation, the complete loss of a place in the world. He had arrived in Marseille drawn by adventure, and by the desire to break with a life that didn't include adventure, but now he feels lost. An exhaustion that is not physical undermines him from within. Now he realizes that over the last seven days he has not slept seven whole hours. He raises his head and looks at the cloudy sky extending behind the sailing ship's three masts; there, in the middle of the subtle racket of the port, the universe presents itself as a series of incomprehensible images. A few minutes after five, Korzeniowski is back in his room. Madame Fagot asks if he might not have the money he owes her. "One more day, please," Korzeniowski says, "one more day." And he thinks: *Tomorrow it will all be over.*

The first thing he does upon entering his room is to open the only window. A solitary, dense gust of sea air rushes in and the smell almost makes him cry. He opens his trunk of personal belongings and from the bottom extracts a book of names and addresses—all the people he has known in his short life—and places it delicately, like a sleeping child, on the bedspread, so it would catch any visitor's eye. In the trunk he has also found a revolver: it is a Chamelot-Delvigne with six metal cartridges, but Korzeniowski opens the drum and removes five of them. At that moment he hears voices: it's Fecht, who has arrived for tea unaware there is no tea to be had; Fecht, courteous as ever, greets Madame Fagot and asks after her daughters. Korzeniowski hears footsteps climbing the stairs and sits down on the bed. He leans against the wall, lifting up his shirt at the same time, and as he puts the cold barrel of the revolver against his chest, in the place where he imagines his heart must be, he feels his nipples harden and the hairs on the back of his neck stand on end like a furious cat's. *Tomorrow it will all be over*, he thinks, and at that moment a light comes on in his head: it's a line from a novel, yes, the last line of a Russian novel, and the mysterious words that he'd been hearing in the casino are the last words of that novel. He thinks of the title, *Igrok*, and it strikes him as too elementary, almost insipid. He wonders if Dostoevsky is still alive. Strange, he thinks, that the image of an author he finds unpleasant should be the last thing that passes through his head.

Konrad Korzeniowski smiles as he considers this idea, and then he fires.

The Chamelot-Delvigne's bullet goes through Korzeniowski's body without touching a single vital organ, zigzagging improbably to avoid arteries, tracing ninety-degree angles if necessary to miss lungs and thus postpone the death of the desperate young man. The bedspread and pillow are soaked in blood, blood splashes the walls and headboard. Minutes later, the friend Fecht will find first the wounded man and then the address book, and will write the famous telegram to Uncle Tadeusz that will later become a synthesis of the young man's situation: KONRAD BLESSÉ ENVOYEZ ARGENT. Uncle Tadeusz will travel from Kiev to Marseille on express trains, and upon arrival will pay the debts that must be paid—discovering as he does so that the creditors are several—as well as the medical bills. Korzeniowski will recover gradually, and after a few years, once he has made a more or less profitable profession out of lying, he will begin to lie about the origin of the scar on his chest as well. He will never confess the true circumstances of the injury; he will never find himself obliged to do so. . . . Let's get to the point: once Uncle Tadeusz was dead, once Richard Fecht was dead, the failed suicide of Joseph Conrad disappeared from world events. And I myself was deceived . . . for at the beginning of 1878 I was the victim of a sharp chest pain, which at that moment, before the unpredictable law of my correspondences with Joseph Conrad was revealed to me, was diagnosed as the main symptom of a light form of pneumonia. Many years later— when I at last discovered the invisible ties that bind me to my kindred spirit, and was able to interpret correctly the most important events of my life—I prided myself at first that the monstrous pain, which attacked me accompanied by a dry (to begin with) and (eventually) productive cough, overwhelming me with breathing difficulties and loss of sleep, should have been the noble echo of a duel, a sort of participation in the chivalrous history of humanity. Finding out the truth, I confess, was a slight disappointment. Suicide is not noble. As if that weren't enough: suicide is not very Catholic. And Korzeniowski/Conrad, Catholic and noble, knew it. If not, Readers of the Jury, he would not have taken the trouble to hide it.

The supposed pneumonia kept me laid up in bed for ten weeks. I suffered the shivers not thinking and not knowing that another man, in another part of the world, was suffering them, too, at that precise instant; and when I sweated whole rivers, was it not more sensible to attribute it to the supposed pneumonia instead of thinking of the metaphysical resonances of someone else's distant sweating? The days of the supposed pneumonia are associated in my memory with the Altamirano guest house; my father confined me to his house—he sequestered me, kept me in quarantine—for he knew what so many people said in so many different words but which could be synthesized in these: in Panama, the unhealthy, feverish, contagious Panama of that time, going into the hospital meant never coming out. "Ill on arrival, dead on departure" was the refrain that summed the matter up (and that went round Colón in every language, from Spanish to English to Caribbean Creole). So the white-walled, red-roofed house, bathed by sea air, with treatments from Miguel Altamirano, amateur physician, became my private little sanatorium. My Magic Mountain, in other words. And I, Juan Castorp or Hans Altamirano, received in the sanatorium the various lessons my father lavished on me.

So time passed, as they say in novels.

And so (stubbornly) it continued to pass.

There, in the place of my isolation, my father would arrive to tell me of the magnificent things that were happening all over the world. One pertinent clarification: my father the optimist referred to almost anything related to the by then ubiquitous subject of the Inter-oceanic Canal as *magnificent things*; by *all over the world* he meant Colón, Panama City, and the piece of terra more or less firma that stretched between them, that strip where the railway ran and that, for reasons the reader can already imagine, would soon become something like the Apple of Western Discord. Nothing else existed then. Nothing else was worth talking about, or maybe it was that nothing was happening in any other part of the world. For example (it's just an example), my father didn't tell me that on one of those days a U.S. warship had arrived in Limón Bay, armed to the teeth and determined to cross the Isthmus. He didn't tell me that Colonel Ricardo Herrera, commander of the Colón Sappers battalion, had to declare that he "would not consent to their crossing Colombian territory as they intended," and even went so far as to threaten the Gringos with "the armed defense of the sovereignty of Colombia." He didn't tell me that the commander of the North American troops finally gave up his attempt and crossed the Isthmus by train, like everyone else. It was a banal incident, of course; years later, as will be seen, that unusual attack of Sovereign Pride would take on importance (a metaphorical importance, shall we say?), but my father could not know it, and so he condemned me to ignorance as well.

On the other hand, I was one of the first people to know, through my father's news and with a wealth of detail, that Lieutenant Lucien Napoléon Bonaparte Wyse had traveled to Bogotá on an urgent mission, covering the four hundred kilometers in ten days by the Buenaventura route, and that he'd arrived smelling of shit and in terrible need of a razor. And thus I also discovered that two days later, clean-shaven and cologne-scented, he'd had an interview in Bogotá with Don Eustorgio Salgar, Secretary of Foreign Relations, and had obtained from the government of the United States of Colombia the exclusive privilege, valid for ninety-nine years, to construct the Fucking Canal. Thus I found out that Wyse, with the concession in his pocket, had traveled to New York to buy from the Gringos the results of their isthmian expeditions; thus I found out that the Gringos had roundly refused to sell them and, what's more, had refused to show a single map or reveal a single measurement, share a single piece of geological data or even listen to the proposals of the French. "Negotiations are advancing," wrote my refracting father in the *Star & Herald*. "They advance like a locomotive, and nothing can stop them."

Now, when I remember those distant days, I see them as the last period of tranquillity my life would know. (This melodramatic declaration contains less melodrama than it seems at first: for someone born in the tropical isolation in which I was born, in that Remote Kingdom of Humidity that is the city of Honda, any halfway worldly experience is an example of rare intensity; in the hands of someone less timid, that pastoral, riverbank childhood could be material for many cheap lines of verse, things like *The turbulent waters of my plains childhood* or *The turbulent childhood of these plains waters* or even *The young and plainly turbulent water*.) But what I want to say is this: those first years of my life in Colón, beside my newfound father—who seemed no less improvised and makeshift than the house on stilts he lived in—were moments of relative peace, although at the time I didn't realize it. My crystal ball did not allow me to see what was coming. How could I have foreseen what was going to happen, anticipate the Cascade of Great Events waiting for us around the corner, concentrated as I was on that novelty that excluded everything else: the acquisition of a father? I will now write something very rash, and I hope it will be tolerated: in those days, talking with Miguel Altamirano and sharing his activities and enjoying his attentions, I felt that I had found my place in the world. (I didn't feel it with much conviction; I didn't go so far as to delight in such temerity. In the end, as often happens, it turned out that I was wrong.)

In exchange for his care, Miguel Altamirano demanded nothing but my unconditional attention, the presence of the blank face of the listener. My father was a talker in search of an audience; he sought an ideal listener possessed of a no less ideal insomnia, and everything seemed to indicate that he'd found him in his son. For months, long after my chest had overcome the supposed pneumonia, my father kept talking to me as he had done while I was ill. I don't know why, but my illness and my seclusion in the Magic Mountain had provoked curious pedagogical enthusiasms, and those enthusiasms carried on afterward. My father gave me his hammock, as he would a convalescent, and brought a chair over to the wooden porch steps; and there, both of us immersed in the dense, damp heat of the Panamanian night, as soon as the mosquitoes' habits allowed, under the occasional flutter of a hungry bat, the monologue began. "Like most of his countrymen, he was carried away by the sound of fine words, especially if uttered by himself," wrote a certain novelist, who never even met my father, much later in a certain Damn Book. But the description is apt: my father, enamored of his own voice and his own ideas, used me the way a tennis player uses a practice wall.

So a strange routine settled over my new life. During the day, I walked the baking streets of Colón, accompanying my father on his labors as Chronicler of the Isthmus like a witness to a witness, visiting and revisiting the offices of the Railroad Company with such assiduity that they became for me a second home (like a grandmother's house, for example, a place we are always welcome and where there is always a plate for us on the table), and during the no less baking nights I attended the Altamirano Lectures on "The Inter-oceanic Canal and the Future of Humanity." During the day, we visited the white wooden offices of the *Star & Herald*, and my father would receive commissions or suggestions or missions that we would go straight out to fulfill; during the night, my father explained to me why a canal built at sea level was better, cheaper, and less problematic than one built with locks, and how anyone who said the opposite was simply an enemy of progress. During the day, my figure soaked in sweat accompanied the figure of my father to visit an engine driver and listen to him talk about how the Railroad Company had changed his life, in spite of having been attacked more times than he could remember in his years of work and having, to prove it, scars of a dozen knife wounds still visible in his torso ("Touch them, sir, go ahead and touch them, doesn't bother me"); during the night, I found out with a wealth of detail that Panama was a better territory than Nicaragua for opening the Canal, in spite of the Gringos' expeditions producing the opposite findings ("Out of pure spite toward Colombia," according to my father). During the day . . . During the night . . . During the day . . . et cetera.

I had no reason to know it, but at that time meetings were taking place at 184 boulevard Saint-Germain, in Paris, between representatives of more than twenty countries, including the United States of Colombia. For two weeks they had devoted themselves to doing the same thing

my father and I did in the Colón nights: discuss the plausibility (and
the difficulties and the implications) of constructing a sea-level canal
across the Isthmus of Panama. Among the distinguished orators was
Lieutenant Lucien Napoléon Bonaparte Wyse, who was still stopping
in the middle of the street, like a mangy dog, to scratch bites from isthmian mosquitoes, or waking up screaming in horror after being visited,
during a sweaty dream, by one of the dead engineers from the Darien
Jungle. In spite of having failed on his expedition, in spite of lacking
engineering knowledge, Lieutenant Wyse—recently shaved and with
the concession signed by Eustorgio Salgar safely tucked into the pocket
of his jacket—ventured that Panama was the only place on Earth able
to host the colossal undertaking of an inter-oceanic canal. He also ventured that constructing a canal at sea level was the only method able
to bring the project to a successful conclusion. To a question about the
monstrous volume of the Chagres River, the history of its floods that
seemed taken from Genesis, and the inventory of shipwrecks that lay on
its bed as if it weren't a river but a mini Bermuda Triangle, he replied: "A
French engineer does not know the word problem." His opinion, backed
up by the heroic figure of Ferdinand de Lesseps, maker of Suez, convinced the delegates. Seventy-eight of them, of which seventy-four were
personal friends of de Lesseps, voted unreservedly in favor of Wyse's
project.

There followed several tributes, banquets all over Paris, but one
interests me in particular. In the Café Riche, representing the illustrious
Colombian community, a certain Alberto Urdaneta organized a lavish
banquet: two musical ensembles, silver dinner service, a liveried servant for each diner, and even a couple of interpreters who circulated
throughout the salon to facilitate communication among the guests.
His intention was to commemorate both Colombian independence and

de Lesseps's victory over the delegates of the boulevard Saint-Germain Congress. The banquet was a sort of quintessence of Colombianness and of Colombia, that country where everybody—I mean, *everybody*—is a poet, and anybody who isn't is an orator. And so it was: there was poetry, and there were also speeches. On the back of the gilded lithographed menu were portraits of Bolívar and Santander. Behind Bolívar, three verses which themselves resembled gilded lithographs and that were, viewed from whichever angle, as close as you can get to political masturbation, so much so that I think them superfluous here. Behind Santander, on the other hand, was this gem of adolescent versification, a quartet that could have come out of the composition book of a refined señorita from one of the finest private schools in Bogotá.

> *Courageous, unwavering skipper*
> *Proud monarchs you cut down to size*
> *Now your foot wears a magistrate's slipper*
> *And your hand is unflinching and wise.*

The speech was the responsibility (in a manner of speaking) of a certain Quijano Wallis. The orator said: "Thus as the sons of Arabia who, wherever they may find themselves on this earth, overcoming the distance in spirit, bow toward their holy city, so, too, we send our thoughts across the Atlantic, where they are warmed in the tropical sun, and fall to our knees on our beloved beaches to greet and bless Colombia on her day of rejoicing. Our fathers made us independent from the Mother Country; Monsieur de Lesseps will make universal commerce independent of the obstacle of the Isthmus and perhaps free Colombia forever from civil discord."

His thought, I suppose, crossed the Atlantic, warmed itself, and knelt

and greeted and blessed and all those things. . . . And at the end of that
year, in the hottest and driest season, the ones who did cross the Atlantic (without kneeling, to be sure) were the French. The *Star & Herald*
commissioned my father to write—in prose, if at all possible—about
Ferdinand de Lesseps and his team of Gallic heroes. After all, the representatives of the government, the bankers and journalists, the analysts of
our incipient economy and historians of our incipient republic, all were
for once in perfect agreement: for Colón, that was the Most Important
Visit since the long-ago day when Cristóbal Colón himself accidentally
discovered our convulsive lands.

From the moment de Lesseps disembarked from the *Lafayette*, speaking perfect Spanish with everyone, looking with his curious, sleepy feline
gaze, throwing left and right a smile the likes of which Panamanians had
never seen in their lives, flaunting a full head of white hair that made him
look like a half-finished Santa Claus, my father didn't let him out of his
sight for an instant. In the evening he walked a few steps from his prey
down the main street of Colón, passing beneath tissue-paper lanterns
that seemed about to burst into flames, in front of the railway station and
later in front of the dock where Korzeniowski and Cervoni had unloaded
the contraband weapons, in front of the hotel where his son had stayed
his first night in Colón, before he knew he had a son, and in front of the
premises where the most famous piece of watermelon in the world was
sold and where diners and other onlookers died under gunfire. The next
morning he spied on him from a prudent distance and saw him go out
with three velvet-clad children beneath the unbearable sun, and saw the
children running happily among the carrion on the streets and the smell
of rotting fruit, and running up to startle a flock of black buzzards snack-
ing on a newborn donkey a few steps from the sea. He saw him catch an
Indian woman off guard on the Pacific Mail pier (when the band hired

by the Mayor exploded into metallic sounds to celebrate his arrival) and try to dance with her to music that was not danceable but rather martial, and when the woman yanked herself away from him and crouched down at the edge of the sea to wash her hands with a look of disgust, de Lesseps kept smiling, and what's more, began to chuckle and shout out his love for the tropics and the bright, the radiant (*radieux*) future awaiting them.

De Lesseps climbed aboard the train to Panama City and my father climbed up after him, and when the train arrived at the Chagres River, he saw him shout to the man in charge and order him to stop the locomotive because he, Ferdinand de Lesseps, had to take home a glass of the enemy's water, and the entire delegation—the Gringos, the Colombians, the French—raised glasses and toasted the victory of the Canal and the defeat of the Chagres River, and while the glasses clinked in the air one of de Lesseps's envoys jogged through the hamlet of Gatún, along muddy paths and across pastures that came up to his knees, and arrived at an improvised dock where a canoe rested, and crouched down beside the canoe as the Indian woman had crouched down by the pier and collected in a recently emptied champagne glass a greenish liquid that came out full of slimy algae and dead flies. The only time my father spoke to de Lesseps was when the train passed Mount Hope, where employees had buried their dead during the construction of the railway, and he decided to speak to him in a burst of enthusiasm about the Chinamen in barrels of ice he'd had sent to Bogotá—"Where?" asked de Lesseps. "Bogotá," repeated my father—and that, if they hadn't been of use to the student doctors in the university of the capital, they would surely have ended up here, under this earth, under the orchids and mushrooms. Then he shook hands with de Lesseps and said, "Pleasure to meet you," or "Pleasure to make your acquaintance" (pleasure, in any case, was present in his phrase), and swiftly returned to the edge of the group, trying not to disturb, and from the edge observing de Lesseps during the rest of the journey of that fortunate train, that historic train, through the leafy darkness of the jungle.

He followed him closely when de Lesseps visited the old church of Santo Domingo, whose arch defied the laws of gravity and of architecture, and took note of every admiring comment the admiring tourist came out with. He followed him while de Lesseps shook the hands of the Mayor and military officials in the Panama City station (neither the Mayor nor the officers would wash their hands for the rest of the day). He followed him while he walked through the recently swept and cleaned streets, under French flags sewn ad hoc by the wives of the most distinguished politicians (just as years later another flag would be sewn, the first one of a country that perhaps began to exist the very afternoon when de Lesseps visited the city, but let's not get ahead of ourselves or jump to conclusions), and he accompanied him to the Grand Hotel, a colonial cloister recently opened with every luxury along one of the longest flanks of the cathedral plaza, whose paving stones—those of the plaza, of course, not the hotel—were normally occupied by carriages pulled by old horses, the noise of their hooves on the stones, and this time by baby-faced soldiers dressed in white and as silent as nervous children about to take their first communion. In the Grand Hotel, before my father's fascinated gaze, the welcome banquet was held with French food and a pianist brought from Bogotá—"From where?" asked de Lesseps. "From Bogotá," he was told—to play a barcarole or some gentle polonaise while the local leaders of the Liberal Party told de Lesseps what Victor Hugo had said, that the constitution of the United States of Colombia was made for a country of angels, not human beings, or something along those lines. For those Colombian politicians, who barely sixty years before were inhabitants of a colony, the mere attention of that prophet, author of *The Last Day of a Condemned Man* and of *Les Misérables*, the defense counsel of humanity, was the greatest praise in the world, and they wanted de Lesseps to know it: because the attention of de Lesseps was also the greatest praise in the world. De Lesseps asked a banal question, his eyes widened slightly at an anecdote, and the colonized suddenly felt that their entire existence would take on new meaning. If Ferdinand de Lesseps had wished, they would have danced a *mapalé* or a *cumbia* right there for him, or better yet a cancan, so he wouldn't go away thinking we were all Indians here. For there, in the Isthmus of Panama, the colonial spirit floated in the air, like tuberculosis. Or maybe, it occurred to me at some point, Colombia had never stopped being a colony, and time and politics simply swapped one colonizer for another. For the colony, like beauty, is in the eye of the beholder.

When the banquet was over, my father, who had already reserved a room with a view of the interior patio and its fountain where brightly colored fish swam, followed de Lesseps until he saw him retire at last, and was getting ready to retire as well when the door to the billiard room opened and a young man with a waxed mustache and chalk stains on his fingers came out into the corridor and began to speak to him as if he'd known him his whole life. He was part of the *Lafayette* delegation, had arrived with Monsieur de Lesseps, and would be part of the press office of the Compagnie back in Paris. People had spoken to him very highly of my father's journalistic work, he said, and even Monsieur de Lesseps had a very good impression from meeting him. He had read some of his articles about the Railroad, his columns in the *Star & Herald*, and now he would like to propose a permanent connection to the Magnificent Canal Venture. "A pen like yours would be a great help to us in the struggle against Skepticism, which is, as you know so well, the worst enemy of Progress." And before the night was over, my father found himself playing a three-cushion frame with a group of Frenchmen (and, by the way, losing by several caroms and tearing the imported baize), and he would forever associate the resplendent green of that baize and the clinking of the immaculate ivory balls with the moment when he said yes, that he accepted and felt it an honor to do so, that starting tomorrow he would be the Panama correspondent of the *Bulletin du Canal Interocéanique*. The *Bulletin*, to its friends.

And the next morning, before going to stand by the hotel entrance to wait for de Lesseps's departure, before accompanying him to the hotel dining room where three elite engineers were waiting to talk about the Canal and its problems and its possibilities, before going out with him and getting in the same dugout as him to navigate two or three bends of the enemy Chagres beneath a pulverizing sun, before all that, my father told me what I hadn't seen with my own eyes. He did so with the evident (and very problematic) feeling of having begun to form part of history, of having begun to imitate the Angel, and perhaps, in a certain sense, he wasn't wrong. Of course I didn't speak to my father of the Refractive Effect of his journalism or of the possible impact that effect might have had on the decision of those Frenchmen thirsty for contracted propaganda; I asked him, instead, what opinion he'd formed of that Old Diplomatic Fox, a man who to me was the bearer of a smile much more dangerous than any furrowed brow, author of handshakes more lethal than a stabbing, and at my impudent question and comments my father turned serious, very serious, more serious than I'd ever seen him, and said, with something halfway between frustration and pride: "He's the man I would have liked to be."

V

Sarah Bernhardt
and the French Curse

"Let there be a canal," said de Lesseps, and the Canal . . . began to come into being. But this did not happen before his sleepy feline eyes: the Great Man returned to Paris—and his return in perfect health was tangible proof that the murderous Panamanian climate was nothing but a myth—and from the offices on rue Caumartin acted as general in chief of an army of engineers managed from the distance, an army sent to these savage tropics to defeat the guerrillas of the Climate, to achieve the subjugation of treacherous Hydrology. And my father would be the narrator of that clash, yes sir, the Thucydides of that war. For Miguel Altamirano, something obvious emerged in those days, vivid and prophetic like a solar eclipse: his manifest destiny, which only now, at sixty-some years of age, was being revealed to him, was to leave written testimony to the supreme victory of Man over the Forces of Nature. Because that's what the Inter-oceanic Canal was: the battlefield where Nature, legendary enemy of Progress, would at last sign an unconditional surrender.

In January 1881, while Korzeniowski was sailing Australian seas, the good old *Lafayette* entered those of Panama, bringing a shipment that my father described in his article as a Noah's Ark for modern times. Down the gangplank came not pairs of all the animals in creation but something much more definitive: fifty engineers and their families. And for a couple of hours there were more École Polytechnique graduates in the port of Colón than porters to take them to the hotel. On February 1, one of those engineers, a certain Armand Reclus, wrote to the rue Caumartin offices: TRAVAIL COMMENCÉ. The two glorious words of the telegram reproduced like rabbits in every newspaper in the *hexagone* of France; that night my father stayed on Front Street in Colón, going from the General Grant to the nearest Jamaican shack, and from there to the groups of inoffensive drunks (and others who were a little less so) to the loading docks, until dawn reminded him of his respectable age. He arrived at the house on stilts with the first light, drunk on brandy but also on *guarapo*, because he'd shared toasts and drinks with anyone willing to humor him. "Three cheers for de Lesseps and three cheers for the Canal!" he shouted.

And all of Colón seemed to respond: "Hurrah!"

Eloísa, dear: if my tale had taken place in these cinematographic times (ah, the cinematographer: a creature my father would have liked), the camera would focus right now on a window of Jefferson House, which was, let's be frank, the only hotel in all of Colón worthy of the engineers from the *Lafayette*. The camera approaches the window, hovers briefly over the slide rules, protractors, and compasses, moves to focus on the fast-asleep face of a five-year-old child and the trickle of saliva that darkens the red velvet of the cushion, and after passing through a closed door—nothing is forbidden the magic of cameras—captures the last movements of a couple at the height of ecstasy. That they're not local is obvious from their respective levels of perspiration. I will refer to the woman at length a few lines further on, but for now it is important to note that her eyes are closed, that she's covering her husband's mouth to keep him from waking the child with the inevitable (and imminent) noises of his orgasm, and that her small breasts have always been a cause of disputes between her and her bodices. As for the man: between his thorax and that of his wife is an angle of thirty degrees; his pelvis moves with the precision and the invincible regularity of a piston; and his ability to conserve these variables—the angle and the frequency of movement—is due, in large part, to his ingenious use of a lever of the third kind. In which, as everyone knows, the Power is between the Weight and the Fulcrum. Yes, my intelligent readers, you have guessed: the man was an engineer.

His name was Gustave Madinier. He had graduated with honors first from the Polytechnique and later from the École des Ponts et Chaussées; during his brilliant career, he had found himself obliged on more than one occasion to repeat that he was no relation to the other Madinier, the one who fought with Napoleon at Vincennes and later developed a mathematical theory of fire. No, our Madinier, our dear Gustave, who at this very moment is ejaculating into his wife while reciting to himself, "Give me a lever and a fulcrum on which to place it and I shall move the earth," was responsible for twenty-nine bridges that cover the French Republic, or rather her rivers and lakes, from Perpignan to Calais. He was the author of two books: *Les fleuves et leur franchissement* and *Pour une nouvelle théorie des câbles*; his works had caught the attention of the Suez team, and his participation was decisive in the construction of the new city of Ismaelia. Coming to Panama as part of the Compagnie du Canal had been, for him, as natural as having children after marriage.

And now that we're on that subject: Gustave Madinier had married Charlotte de la Môle in early 1876, that magic year for my father and for me, and five months later Julien was born, weighing 3,200 grams and generating an equal number of malicious comments. Charlotte de la Môle, the woman whose small breasts were a challenge for any bodice, had been a challenge for her husband, too: she was stubborn, willful, and unbearably attractive. (Gustave liked the way her breasts contracted to her ribs when she was cold, because it gave him the feeling he was fornicating with a very young girl. But these were guilty pleasures; Gustave was not proud of them, and only once, while drunk, had he confessed them to his wife.) The fact of the matter was that the collective voyage to Panama had been Charlotte's idea, and she hadn't needed more than a couple of couplings to convince the engineer. And there, in the room in the Jefferson House, while her husband falls into a satisfied sleep and begins to snore, Charlotte feels that she made the right decision, for she knows that behind every great engineer stands a very determined woman. Yes, their first images of Colón—its putrefying odors, the unbearable assiduousness of its insects, the chaos of its streets—had provoked a brief disenchantment; but soon the woman fixed her gaze on the clear sky, and the dry heat of February opened her pores and entered her blood, and she liked that. Charlotte did not know that the heat was not always dry, the sky not always clear. Someone, some charitable soul, should have told her. No one did.

It was during those days that Sarah Bernhardt arrived. Readers' eyes widen, skeptical comments are uttered, but it's true: Sarah Bernhardt was there. The actress's visit was another symptom of the navelization of Panama, the sudden displacement of the Isthmus to the very center of the world. . . . La Bernhardt arrived, for a change, in that dispenser of French figures that was the *Lafayette*, and stayed in Colón only long enough to catch the train to Panama City (and earn her brief inclusion in this book). In a tiny and sweltering theater, set up in haste in one of the lateral salons of the Grand Hotel, before an audience made up entirely, with one exception, of French people, Sarah Bernhardt appeared on a stage with two chairs and, with the help of a young amateur actor she'd brought with her from Paris, recited, from memory and without a slip, all the speeches of Racine's *Phèdre*. A week later she'd taken the train again, but in the opposite direction, and returned to Europe without having spoken to a single Panamanian . . . but securing, nevertheless, a place in my tale. For that night, the night of *Phèdre*, two people applauded more than the rest. One was Charlotte Madinier, for whom the presence of Sarah Bernhardt had been like a balsam against the unbearable tedium of life in the Isthmus. The other was the man in charge of registering every beneficial or worthwhile experience that occurred as a consequence (directly or indirectly) of the construction of the Canal: Miguel Altamirano.

I'll tell it plainly: Charlotte Madinier and Miguel Altamirano met that night, exchanged names and pleasantries and even classical alexandrines, but it was quite some time before they would see each other again. Something, in any case, quite normal: she was a married woman, and all her time was taken up in being respectably bored; he, for his part, was never still, because at that time there was never an instant when there wasn't something happening in Panama worthy of review in the *Bulletin*. Charlotte met my father, forgot him straightaway, and carried on with her own routine, and from the vantage point of that routine watched the dry February air grow denser as the weeks passed, and one night in May she awoke in a fright, because she thought the city was being bombed. She looked out the window: it was raining. Her husband looked out with her, and in a glance calculated that in the forty-five minutes the downpour lasted more water had fallen than fell on France in a whole year. Charlotte saw the flooded streets, the banana peels and palm leaves that passed floating in the current, and every once in a while caught sight of more intimidating objects: a dead rat, for example, or a human turd. Identical downpours occurred eleven more times over the course of the month, and Charlotte, who watched from her seclusion as Colón turned into a swamp over which flew insects of all sizes, began to wonder if the trip hadn't been a mistake.

And then one day in July, her son woke up with chills. Julien was shaking violently, as if his bed had a life of its own, and the chattering of his teeth was perfectly audible in spite of the downpour lashing the terrace. Gustave was at the Canal construction site, evaluating the damage caused by the rains; Charlotte, dressed in the still-damp clothes she'd had laundered the previous day, carried the child in her arms and arrived at the hospital in a dilapidated buggy. The chills had ceased, but as she laid Julien down in the bed he'd been assigned, Charlotte put the back of her hand against his forehead more out of instinct than anything else, and in the same instant realized the boy was burning up with fever and that his eyes had rolled back in his head. Julien moved his mouth like a grazing cow; he stuck out his dry tongue and there was no saliva in his mouth. But Charlotte could not find enough water to quench his thirst (which, in the middle of a downpour, was nothing if not ironic). Gustave arrived mid-afternoon, having run all over the city asking in French if anyone had seen his wife, and had finally decided, in order to exhaust all possibilities, to go to the hospital. Sitting in hard wooden chairs with backs that fell off if you leaned on them, Gustave and Charlotte spent the night, sleeping upright when exhaustion overcame them, taking turns in a sort of private superstition to take Julien's temperature. At dawn, Charlotte was awakened by silence. It had stopped raining and her husband was doubled over asleep, his head between his knees, his arms hanging down to the floor. She reached out her hand and felt a wave of relief at finding the fever had gone down. And then she tried, without success, to wake Julien up.

And once again I write this phrase I've written so often: enter Miguel Altamirano.

My father insisted on being the one to accompany the Madiniers through those diabolical proceedings: take the child out of the hospital, put him in a coffin, put the coffin in the ground. "It was Sarah Bernhardt's ghost's fault," my father would tell me much later, trying to explain the reasons (which remained unexplained) he'd dived headfirst into the suffering of a couple he barely knew. The Madiniers felt a gratitude I should call eternal: in the midst of their loss and the disorientation of loss, my father had served them as interpreter, undertaker, lawyer, and messenger. There were days when the presence of mourning overwhelmed him; he would think at those moments that his task was complete, that he was intruding; but Charlotte asked him not to go, not to leave them, to keep helping them with the simple help of his company, and Gustave put a hand on his shoulder with the gesture of a brother-in-arms: "You're all we have," he said . . . and then Sarah Bernhardt went past, dropped a line from *Phèdre* and continued on her way. And my father was unable to leave: the Madiniers were like puppies, and they depended on him to confront that inhospitable and incomprehensible isthmian world in which Julien no longer was.

Maybe it was around then that people in Colón began to speak of the French Curse. Between May and September, as well as the Madiniers' son, twenty-two Canal workers, nine engineers, and three engineers' wives fell victim to the killer fevers of the Isthmus. It carried on raining—the sky turned black at two in the afternoon, and the downpour began almost immediately, not falling in drops but solid and dense, like a heavy wool poncho coming down through the air—but the work carried on, in spite of the earth excavated one day being found back in the trench the next morning due to the weight of the rain. The Chagres River rose so much in one weekend that the railway had to stop running, because the line was under thirty centimeters of water and weeds; and with the railway paralyzed, the Canal was paralyzed, too. The engineers met in the mediocre restaurant of the Jefferson House Hotel or in the 4th of July, a saloon with tables wide enough for them to spread out their topographical maps and architectonic plans—and perhaps play a quick hand of poker on top of the maps and plans—and there they spent hours arguing about where they'd carry on the works when it finally cleared up. It would frequently happen that the engineers would say adieu at the end of an afternoon, arranging to meet the next morning at the excavations, only to discover the next morning that one of them had been admitted to the hospital with an attack of chills, or was at the hospital watching over his wife's fever, or was with his wife at the hospital attending to their child and regretting ever having come to Panama. Few survived.

And here I enter conflictive terrain: in spite of all that, in spite of his relationship with the Madiniers, my father (or rather his strange Refractive Pen) wrote that "the rare cases of yellow fever that have presented among the heroic artisans of the Canal" had been "imported from other places." And since no one stopped him, he carried on writing: "No one denies that tropical plagues have been present among the non-local population; but one or two deaths, especially among the workers who came from Martinique or Haiti, should not be cause for unjustified alarm." His chronicles/reports/articles were read only in France. And there, in France, the relatives of the Canal read them and were reassured, and the shareholders kept buying shares because all was going well in Panama. . . . I have often thought that my father would have made himself rich if he'd patented that invention: the Journalism of Refraction, so much abused since then. But I am unjust in thinking that. After all, in this lay his extraordinary gift: in not being aware of the gap—no, the immense crater—between the truth and his version of it.

Yellow fever carried on killing tirelessly, and killing French recent arrivals most of all. For the Bishop of Panama, that was sufficient proof: the plague was choosing, the plague had intelligence. The Bishop described a long hand that arrived at night in the houses of the dissolute—the impious, adulterers, drinkers—and took away their children as if Colón were the Egypt of the Old Testament. "Men of upright morals have nothing to fear," he said, and for my father his words had the taste of old battles against Presbyter Echavarría: it was as though time were repeating itself. But then Don Jaime Sosa, the Bishop's cousin and administrator of the old cathedral of Porto Bello, a relic of colonial times, said one day that he was feeling bad, then that he was thirsty, and three days later he was buried, in spite of having been bathed by the Bishop himself in a solution of whiskey, mustard, and holy water.

During those months funerals became part of the daily routine, like meals, for the fever dead were buried in a matter of hours to prevent their decomposing fluids from carrying the fever on the wind. The French began walking around with their hands over their mouths, or tying an improvised mask of fine cloth over their mouths and noses like the outlaws of legend; and one afternoon, masked to his cheekbones, a few meters from his masked wife, Gustave Madinier—defeated by the climate, the mourning, the fear of the incomprehensible and treacherous fever—sent my father a farewell note. "It is time to return home," he wrote. "My wife and I need a change of air. You know, sir, you will always be in our hearts."

Well now: I would have understood. You, hypocritical readers, my fellows, my brothers, would have understood, even if only out of simple human sympathy. But not my father, whose head was beginning to circulate on different rails, pulled by independent locomotives . . . I invade his head and this is what I find: a multitude of dead engineers, a number of other deserters, and an abandoned half-built canal. If hell is personal, a distinct space for each biography (made out of our worst fears, the ones that are not interchangeable), that was my father's: the image of the works abandoned, of the cranes and steam-powered excavators rotting under moss and rust, the excavated earth returning from the deposits in the freight cars to their damp origins on the jungle floor. The Great Trench of the Inter-oceanic Canal forsaken by its constructors: this, Readers of the Jury, was Miguel Altamirano's worst nightmare. And Miguel Altamirano was not about to let such a hell establish itself in reality. So there, beside the ghost of Sarah Bernhardt who tossed him Racine's alexandrines at the least provocation, my father steadied his hand to write these lines: "Honor, Monsieur Madinier, the memory of your only son. Bring the works to completion and little Julien will forever have this Canal as his monument." By the way, when Gustave Madinier read these lines, it was not in a private note, but on the front page of the *Star & Herald*, beneath a headline that was little less than blackmail: OPEN LETTER TO GUSTAVE MADINIER.

And one December afternoon, as the sun of the dry season—which had returned with that strange December talent of making us forget past rains, making us believe that in reality Panama is like this—shone over the streets of Colón and over the whole zone of the Great Trench of the Canal, in Jefferson House an engineer and his wife unpack trunks. The clothes go back in the wardrobes and the implements back on the desk, and the portraits of the dead child go back onto the dresser.

And there they stayed, at least until some unpredictable force knocked them off.

After all, these were convulsive times.

Allow me to say it again: these were convulsive times. No, dear readers, I'm not referring to that spoiled idea of politicians who have nothing else to say. I'm not referring to the elections that the Conservatives stole in the Colombian State of Santander, getting rid of Liberal votes and fabricating Conservative ones where there weren't any; nor am I referring to the Liberal reaction already beginning to think of armed revolutions, of convening revolutionary juntas and raising revolutionary funds. No, Eloísa dear: I'm not referring to the fear of another civil war between Conservatives and Liberals, the constant fear that accompanied Colombians like a faithful dog, and that would not take long, not very long at all, to materialize again. . . . I'm not referring to the declarations in a secret session of a certain radical leader, who assured the Senate of the Republic that he had news that "the United States had resolved to take possession of the Isthmus of Panama," much less to the reply of an unsuspecting Conservative for whom "the alarmist voices" should not frighten the nation, for "the Panamanian is happy as a citizen of this Republic, and would never swap his honorable poverty for the soulless comforts of those gold diggers." No, I'm not referring to any of that. When I say these were convulsive times, I'm referring to less metaphorical and much more literal convulsions. Let us put it clearly: Panama was a place where things shook.

In the space of one year, the inhabitants of the Isthmus took fright at each explosion of the imported dynamite, and very soon grew accustomed to each explosion of imported dynamite: Panama was a place where things shook. There were months when Panamanians were dropping to their knees and beginning to pray every time the steam-powered dredgers opened the earth, and then the dredgers began to form part of the auditory landscape and Panamanians stopped kneeling, for Panama was a place where things shook. . . . In the yellow-fever wards, the beds reverberated on the wooden floors, lifted by the force of the shivering, and nobody, nobody was surprised: Panama, Readers of the Jury, was a place where things shook.

Well then: on September 7, 1882, came the great shake.

It was 3:29 in the morning when the movements started. I hasten to say they did not last more than a minute; but in that short minute I managed to think first of dynamite, then that this was no time to be setting charges in the Canal zone, then of the French machines, and I ruled them out for the same reason. At that moment a ceramic flowerpot, which had belonged to Mr. Watts, the previous resident of the house on stilts, and which had slept peacefully on top of the cupboard until then, walked four hand spans and threw itself off the edge. The whole cupboard fell immediately after that (crash of crockery smashing, shards of glass scattered dangerously across the floor). My father and I barely had time to grab the bony hand of the dead Chinaman and a drawer from the filing cabinet and get out of the house before the earthquake broke the stilts and the house came down, clumsy and heavy and hulking like a shot buffalo. And at the same time, not far from the residential neighborhood of the Panama Railroad Company, the Madiniers went outside, both in pajamas and both frightened, before the portraits of Julien were smashed against the floor of Jefferson House, and before, luckily, Jefferson House—or at least its façade—crashed to the street, raising a dust cloud that made several of the witnesses sneeze.

The earthquake of 1882, which for many was a new episode of the French Curse, brought down the Colón church as if it were made of cards, ripped up the railway sleepers for 150 meters, and ran down Front Street tearing it as if with a dull knife. Its first consequence: my father got down to work. The bed of the Great Trench collapsed and the walls of the excavation collapsed, ruining a good deal of the work already done, and an encampment near Miraflores disappeared—instruments, personnel, and a steam-powered digger—into the earth that opened as the dynamite had not been able to open it. And in the midst of that disconsolate panorama, my father wrote: "No one is worried, no one is wary, work proceeds without the slightest delay."

In his writings that followed, did he mention the Colón City Hall, of which not one stone remained on top of another? Did he mention the roofs of the Grand Hotel that buried the general headquarters of the Company, several maps, a contractor recently arrived from the United States, and one or two engineers? No, my father did not see any of that. The reason: at that moment he had acquired, definitively now, the famous Colombian illness of SB (Selective Blindness), also known as PB (Partial Blindness) and even as RIP (Retinopathy due to Interests of a Political nature). For him—and, in consequence, for the readers of the *Bulletin*, actual and potential shareholders—the Canal works would be finished in half the time predicted and would cost half the anticipated money; the machines that were working were double the existing number but had cost half as much; the cubic meters of earth excavated per month, which was never more than 200,000, was transformed in the *Bulletin* reports to a good million with all its zeros in place. De Lesseps was happy. The shareholders—actual ones, potential ones—too. Three cheers for France, and three cheers for the Canal, damn it.

Meanwhile, in the Isthmus, the War for Progress was being fought on three fronts: the construction of the Canal, the repair of the railway, and the reconstruction of Colón and Panama City, and Thucydides reported the news in detail (with the details his RIP allowed him to see). Now that the house on stilts had fallen down, I witnessed for the first time the practical effects of my father's Blindness: not four days passed before he was allocated one of the picturesque habitations of Christophe Colomb, the hamlet built for the white technicians of the Canal Company. It was a prefabricated construction, set down beside the sea with its own hammock and brightly colored blinds like a doll's house, and we would live in it at no charge whatsoever. It was regal treatment, and my father felt at the back of his neck the unsubtle blow of the Flattery of the Powerful, that which in other places is known under different aliases: sweetener or bribe, enticement or kickback.

The satisfaction, besides, was double: four houses along the way, almost simultaneously, another couple displaced by the earthquake moved in, Gustave and Charlotte Madinier. Everyone was agreed that getting out of that horrible hotel full of dark memories would bring about notable benefits, tabula rasa and all that. In the evenings, after dinner, my father walked the fifty meters that separated us from the Madiniers' little house, or they walked over to ours, and we sat on the veranda with brandy and cigars to watch the yellow moon dissolve in the waters of Limón Bay and be glad that Monsieur Madinier had decided to stay. Dear readers, I don't know how to explain it, but something had happened after the earthquake. A transformation of our lives, maybe, or maybe the beginning of a new life.

They say in Panama that the nights in Colón favor intimacies. The causes are, I suppose, scientifically indemonstrable. There is something in the melancholy moan of a certain owl that seems always to be saying

"*Ya acabó*—All done"; there is something in the darkness of the nights that makes you feel you could reach up a hand and grab a piece of the Great Bear; and most of all (to leave off the schmaltz) there is something very tangible in the immediacy of danger, whose incarnations are not limited to a bored jaguar who decides to make an excursion out of the jungle, or the occasional scorpion who sneaks into your shoe, or the violence of Colón-Gomorrah, where since the arrival of the French there were more machetes and revolvers than picks and shovels. Danger in Colón is a daily and protean creature, and one becomes accustomed to its smell and soon forgets its presence. Fear unites; in Panama, we were afraid although we did not know it. And that's why, it occurs to me now, that a night facing Limón Bay, as long as the sky was clear and the rainy season was over, was able to produce intimate friendships. That's how it was for us: under my secretarial gaze, my father and the Madiniers spent one hundred and forty-five evenings of friendship and confessions. Gustave confessed that the Canal works were an almost inhuman challenge, but confronting that challenge was an honor and a privilege. Charlotte confessed that the image of Julien, her dead son, no longer tormented her but rather kept her company in moments of solitude, like a guardian angel. The Madiniers confessed (in unison and slightly out of tune) that never, since their marriage, had they felt so close.

"We owe it to you, Monsieur Altamirano," said the engineer.

"Sir," said my diplomatic father, "Colombia owes you so much more."

"It's the earthquake you owe," I said.

"None of that," said Charlotte. "We owe it to Sarah Bernhardt."

And laughter. And toasts. And alexandrine verses.

At the end of April, my father asked the engineer to take him to see the machines. They left at dawn, after a spoonful of whiskey with quinine to avert what Panamanians called a temperature and the French *paludisme*, and they took a dugout down the Chagres to go over to the excavations at Gatún. The machines were my father's latest love: a steam-powered digger could absorb his attention for long minutes; a North American dredger, like the ones that had arrived at the beginning of that year, could arouse sighs from him like the ones my mother had surely aroused on the *Isabel* (but that was another time). One of those dredgers, parked a kilometer from Gatún like a gigantic beer barrel, was the dugout's first port of call. The rowers approached the shore and stuck their oars into the riverbed so my father could contemplate, still and hypnotized in spite of the harassment of the mosquitoes, the magic of the hulking great thing. Panama was a place where things shook: the chains of the monster sounded like a medieval prisoner's shackles, the iron buckets jolted as they lifted the extracted earth, and then came the spitting of pressurized water that launched the earth away from the work site with a hissing that gave him goose bumps. My father took attentive notes on all of that, and began to think of comparisons taken from some book on dinosaurs or from *Gulliver's Travels*, when he turned around to thank Madinier but found him with his head between his knees. The engineer said the whiskey had not agreed with him. They decided to go back.

That evening they gathered (we gathered) on the veranda, and the ritual of cigars and brandy was repeated. Madinier said he felt much better; he didn't know what had happened, he said, he was going to have to take better care of his stomach from then on. He had a couple of drinks, and Charlotte thought it was because of the alcohol when she saw him stand up in the middle of the conversation to go and lie down in the hammock. My father and Charlotte were not talking about Sarah Bernhardt or about Racine's *Phèdre* or about the improvised theater in the

Grand Hotel, because now they were friends, now they felt like friends, and they didn't need those codes. They were talking, not without nostalgia, of their pasts in other places; until now they hadn't realized that my father was also a stranger in Panama, that he had also gone through the processes of the recent arrival—the efforts to learn, the anxiousness to adapt—and having that in common stimulated them. Charlotte told how she'd met Gustave. They had attended a more or less private sort of celebration in the Jardin des Plantes; they were celebrating the departure of a team of engineers to Suez. There they had met, said Charlotte, and soon they were lost on purpose in Buffon's labyrinth, just so they could talk without anyone interrupting them. Charlotte was repeating what Gustave had explained to her that evening—that in order to get out of a labyrinth, if the walls are all connected, you need only keep the same hand on one of the walls, and sooner or later you would find the exit or return to the entrance—when she stopped mid-sentence and her flat chest was as still as the surface of a lake. My father and I turned instinctively to look at what she was looking at, and this is what we saw: the hammock, swollen under the weight of the engineer Gustave Madinier, molded to the curve of his buttocks and the angle of his elbows, had begun to tremble, and the beams from which it hung creaked desperately. I'm not sure if I've mentioned it yet: Panama, dear readers, was a place where things shook.

In a matter of minutes the chills stopped and the fever and thirst began. But there was something new: with the little lucidity he had left, Madinier began to say that his head ached, and the pain was so savage that at one point he asked my father to shoot him, for pity's sake, to shoot him. Charlotte refused to let us take him to the hospital, in spite of my father's insistence, and what we did was lift up the aching body and carry it to my bed, which was the closest to the veranda. And there, on my linen sheets recently purchased at half price from a West Indian shopkeeper, Gustave Madinier spent the night. His wife stayed with him as she had stayed with Julien, and undoubtedly the memory of Julien plagued her during the night. When dawn broke, and Gustave told her that his head was feeling better, that there was no longer such terrible pain in his legs and back, just a vague restlessness, Charlotte didn't even notice the yellowish tone that had invaded his skin and eyes, but let herself be swept up with relief. She admitted she should sleep a little; the exhaustion kept her slumbering well into the evening. It was already dark when I chanced to see the moment when her husband began to vomit a black and viscous substance that could not be blood, no, sir, I swear it could not be blood.

Gustave Madinier's death was sadly famous in the neighborhood of Christophe Colomb. The neighbors obliged my father to burn the linen sheets, along with every glass/cup/piece of cutlery that might have entered into contact with the contaminated lips of the poor engineer; the same obligation held, obviously, for Charlotte. Of course, the stubborn and willfull woman put up some resistance at first: she was not going to part with those memories, she wasn't going to burn the last mementos of her husband without putting up a fight. The French Consul in Colón had to come and force her, by way of an insolent decree adorned with all the stamps in the world, to carry out that purifying bonfire in front of everyone. (The Consul would die of yellow fever, with spasms and black vomit, three weeks later; but that small piece of poetic justice is not relevant now.) My father and I were the labor force for that inquisitional ceremony; and in the middle of the main street of Christophe Colomb a pile gradually grew of blankets and ties, of boar-bristle hairbrushes and straight razors, treatises on Resistance Theory and family photo albums, untrimmed editions of *Les fleuves et leur franchissement* and of *Pour une nouvelle théorie des câbles*, crystal goblets and porcelain plates, and even a loaf of rye bread with dirty bite marks. It all burned with a mixture of smells, with black smoke, and once the flames died down a scorched, dark mass remained. I saw my father hug Charlotte Madinier and then get a pail, walk to the edge of the bay, and return with enough water to extinguish the last fading embers. When he came back, when he emptied the pail over the recognizable cover of an album of picture cards that had been blue velvet, Charlotte was no longer there.

She lived four doors down from us, but we lost sight of her. Every day, after the burning, my father and I passed by her veranda and rapped on the wooden frame of the screen door. But there was never an answer. It was futile to try to peek indiscreetly: Charlotte had covered the windows with dark clothing (Parisian capes, long taffeta skirts). It must have been about five or six months after the engineer's death when we saw her go out, very early, and leave the door open. My father followed her; I followed my father. Charlotte walked toward the port carrying in her right hand—for the left was covered up to the wrist in a badly wrapped bandage—a small case like the ones doctors use. She didn't hear or didn't want to hear my father's words, his greetings, his reiterated condolences; when she arrived at Front Street, she headed, like a horse heading home, to the Maggs & Oates pawnshop. She handed over the case and received in exchange a sum that seemed previously agreed upon (on some of the notes was a drawing of a railway, on others a map, on still others an old ex-President); and all this she did with her face turned toward Limón Bay and her eyes fixed on the *Bordeaux*, a steamer that had anchored in the bay thirty days earlier and now floated there deserted, for the entire crew had died of fever. *"Je m'en vais,"* repeated Charlotte with her eyes very wide. My father followed her all the way back home and all she said was: "*Je m'en vais.*" My father climbed the porch steps behind her and managed to receive a solid whiff of human filth, and all she said was: "*Je m'en vais.*"

Charlotte Madinier had decided to leave, yes, but she couldn't or didn't want to do so immediately. During the day, she was seen walking alone around Colón, after visiting her husband's grave in the cemetery and even passing by the hospital like a shadow and staying for hours in front of the bed of any fever victim, watching him with such intensity that she would end up disturbing him and asking the nurses why the chart said gastritis when the truth was obviously quite different. There were people who saw her asking the railway passengers for alms; some saw her defy all laws of decency by stopping to chat with a French prostitute from the Maison Dorée, famous all over the Caribbean. I don't know who first called her the Widow of the Canal, but the nickname stuck with the persistence of an epidemic, and even my father began to use it after a while. (I suspect that for him it didn't have the scornful and slightly heartless tone it had for the rest; my father spoke of the Widow of the Canal with respect, as if in truth the engineer's tomb contained a code of the fate of the Isthmus.) The Widow of the Canal, as tends to happen in the Talkative Tropics, began to turn into a legend. She was seen in Gatún, kneeling in the mud to speak to a child, and in the Culebra Pass, discussing the latest advances of the works with the laborers. It was said she didn't have the money for the passage, and that's why she hadn't left; and from then on she was often seen in the Callejón de Botellas charging Canal workers for a quick fuck, and giving others, not so quick and free as well, to the recently arrived workers from Liberia. But the Widow of the Canal, deaf to and distant from rumors, kept wandering the streets of Colón, saying "*Je m'en vais*" to anyone who would listen and in every tone of voice possible, but never going. Until the day when . . .

But no.

Not yet.

It's still too soon.

Later I'll get to the curious destiny of the Widow of the Canal. Now it's more important to deal with other rumors that took place far from there, and which the Widow of the Canal did not hear either. For now the demanding lady Politics peremptorily requires my attention and I, at least for the duration of this book, am her deferential servant. In the rest of the country, politicians were making speeches about the "imminent danger to social order" and "the threatened peace." But in Panama no one heard their words. The politicians kept talking with suspicious determination of "interior commotion," of the "revolutions" that were being hatched in the country and of their "somber accompaniment of misfortunes." But in Colón, and more so in that ghetto of Colón formed by the employees of the Canal Company, we were all deaf to and distant from those speeches. The politicians spoke of the country's destiny using alarmist words: "Regeneration or Catastrophe," but their words got snagged in the Darien Jungle or drowned in one of our oceans. Finally, the fatal rumor, the rumor of rumors, arrived in Panama; and so we inhabitants of the Isthmus found out that, in that remote land to which the Isthmus belonged, an election had been held, a party had won in confusing circumstances, another party was rather unhappy. What bad losers the Liberals were! exclaimed the (Conservative) Panamanian priests in the salons of Colón. The facts were simple: some votes had gone missing, some people had difficulties getting to the polling stations, and some who were going to vote Liberal changed their minds at the last minute, thanks to the opportune and divine intervention of that bastion of democracy, the Priesthood. What blame could be ascribed to the Conservative government for such electoral vicissitudes? And that's what the topic was in the salons of Colón when they received the detailed report of what was going on outside: the armed uprising of the dissenters.

The country, incredibly, was at war.

The first victories belonged to the rebels. The Liberal General Gaitán Obeso took Honda and therefore control of the boats that navigated the Magdalena and entered Barranquilla. His successes were immediate. The Caribbean coast was close to falling into the red hands of the revolution; then, for the first time in history, the writers of that long comedy that is Colombian democracy decided to give a small role, just a couple of easy lines, to the State of Panama. Panama would be the defender of that coast; the martyrs destined to rescue the country from the hands of the Masonic devil would sail from Panama. And one fine day, a contingent of veteran soldiers gathered at the port of Colón under the command of the Governor of Panama, General Ramón Santodomingo, and set sail swiftly for Cartagena, ready to make history. From the port, Miguel Altamirano and his son saw them leave. They weren't the only ones, of course: onlookers of all nationalities crowded around the port, talking in all languages, asking in all languages what was going on there and why. Among the onlookers there was one who knew well what was going on, and who had decided to make use of it, to take advantage of the absence of soldiers. . . . And at the end of March, the mulatto lawyer Pedro Prestán, in command of thirteen barefoot West Indians, dressed in rags and armed with machetes, declared himself General of the Revolution and Civil and Military Chief of Panama.

The war, Eloísa dear, had finally arrived in our neutral province, in this place that until then had been known as the Caribbean Switzerland. After half a century of wooing the Isthmus, of knocking on her isthmian doors, war had managed to force them open. And its consequences . . . yes, here come the disastrous consequences, but first an instant of pithy and cut-price philosophy. Colombia—as we know—is a schizophrenic country, and Colón-Aspinwall had inherited the schizophrenia. In truth, Aspinwall-Colón had a mysterious capacity to double, to multiply, to divide, to be one and another at the same time, cohabitating without too much effort. Allow me to take a brief leap into the future of my narration, and along the way to ruin all the effects of suspense and narrative strategy, to tell how this episode ends: the Colón fire. I was in the new house of the French city, lying in the hammock (which had become like a second skin to me), holding in my hand an open copy of Jorge Isaacs's novel *María*, which had just come off the boat from Bogotá, when the sky behind the book turned yellow, not like feverish eyes but like the mustard that works for some as an antidote.

I ran outside. A long time before getting to Front Street, the air stopped moving and I felt the first slap of heat that wasn't tropical. At the entrance to the Callejón de Botellas, where legend had seen the Widow of the Canal conversing with the Liberians, I caught the scent of burned flesh, and soon saw emerge out of the shadows the figure of a mule lying on its side, the back legs already charred, the long tongue spread over fragments of green glass. It wasn't me, but rather my body, that approached the flames like an alligator hypnotized by a burning torch. People ran past me, pushing the hot air, like expulsions from the bellows of a balloon, into my face: the smell of flesh shook me again. But this time it didn't come from any mule but from the body of *mesié* Robay, a Haitian beggar of unknown age, family, and place of residence, who had arrived in Colón before all of us and had specialized in stealing meat from the Chinese butchers. I remember I bent down to vomit, and as my face got close to the paving stones they felt so hot that I didn't dare touch them. Then a strong and constant wind began to blow from the north, and the fire traveled on the wind. . . . In a matter of hours, during the evening and night of March 31, 1885, Colón, the city that had survived the floods and the earthquake, was turned into charred planks of wood.

The reader will imagine our great surprise when, in that country of impunities, in that world capital of irresponsibility that is Colombia, the one who'd started the fire was put on trial a short time later. My father and I, I remember, turned pale with shock when we learned how events had transpired; but paler still shortly afterward, sitting at the table on the veranda at home, when we realized our evaluations of what had happened were radically different, for our versions of events were different. In other words, conflicting stories were circulating about the Colón fire.

What are you saying, Mr. Narrator? the audience protests. Facts don't have versions, the truth is but one. To which I can only answer by telling what was told that midday, in the recently burned tropical heat, in my Panamanian house. My version and that of my father coincided at the beginning of the story: we both knew, as did every *Colónial* who was keeping up with events in the city, the origin of the Colón fire. Pedro Prestán, that mulatto and Liberal lawyer, has risen in arms against the distant Conservative government, only to realize almost immediately that he doesn't have enough weapons; when he finds out that a shipment of two hundred rifles is coming from the United States on board a private boat, Prestán buys it at a good price; but the shipment is intercepted by an opportunistic and not at all neutral North American frigate that had received very clear instructions from Washington to defend the Conservative government. Prestán, in reprisal, has three North Americans arrested, including the Consul. Meanwhile, Conservative troops disembark in Colón and oblige the rebels to retreat; meanwhile, American marines disembark in the city and also oblige the rebels to retreat. The rebels, in retreat, realize that defeat is near. . . . And here occurs the schizophrenic attack of Panama politics. Here my version of subsequent events separates from that of my father. The inconsistent Angel of History gives us two different gospels, and the chroniclers will carry on banging their heads against a brick wall till the end of their days, because it is simply impossible to know which deserves the credence of posterity. And thus it is that there, at the Altamiranos' table, Pedro Prestán splits in two.

Seeing himself defeated, Prestán One, charismatic leader and anti-imperialist national hero, flees by sea toward Cartagena to join the Liberal troops fighting there, and the Conservative soldiers, on the orders of their own government and in connivance with the Wicked Marines, torch Colón and put the blame on the charismatic leader. Prestán Two, who after all is little more than a resentful murderer, decides to satisfy his deep-seated pyromania, because nothing seems more attractive to him than attacking the interests of the whites and burning down the city he's lived in for the last few years. . . . Before escaping, Prestán One manages to hear the cannon blasts the frigate *Galena* unleashes on Colón and which, in a matter of hours, will have started the conflagration. Before escaping, Prestán Two gives orders to his West Indian machete men to wipe the city off the map, for Colón prefers death to occupation. The months pass for Prestán One, and they also pass for Prestán Two. And in August of that same year, 1885, Prestán One is arrested in Cartagena, taken to Colón, court-martialed, and found guilty of the fire on irrefutable evidence, having been given full procedural guarantees and the right to a learned, competent lawyer free of racial or class prejudices.

Prestán Two, on the other hand, was not so lucky. The court-martial that tried him did not hear witnesses for the defense; it did not investigate the version that was going round the city—and had earned the credibility of the French Consul, no less—according to which the man responsible for the fire was a certain George Burt, former general manager of the Railroad Company and agent provocateur; it didn't manage to produce any other witnesses than one North American, one Frenchman, a German and an Italian, none of whom spoke a word of Spanish, whereupon their declarations were never translated or made public; and it did not establish why, if Pedro Prestán's motive was hatred of the North Americans and the French, the only properties in Colón that were not damaged by the fire were the Railroad Company and the Canal Company.

On August 18, 1885, Prestán One was sentenced to death.

What a coincidence: so was Prestán Two.

Readers of the Jury: I was there. Politics, that Gorgon that turns to stone those who look it in the eye, passed very close by me this time, refusing to be ignored: The morning of the eighteenth, the authorities of the Conservative government, victorious in the Umpteenth Civil War, drove Pedro Prestán to the railway lines, guarded at regular intervals (and without anyone finding it odd) by U.S. Marines armed with cannons. From the second floor of a fire-damaged building I saw four laborers, mulatto like the condemned man, erect a wooden archway in a couple of hours; then a freight platform appeared, rolling along the rails without making any noise. Pedro Prestán mounted the platform, or rather was shoved onto it, and behind him climbed a man who was not wearing a hood but who would undoubtedly act as hangman. There, under the arch of cheap wood, Prestán looked like a lost child: his clothes were suddenly too big for him; his bowler hat seemed about to fall off his head. The hangman put down a canvas bag that he'd been carrying and took a rope out of it so well greased that from the distance it looked like a snake (absurdly I thought they were going to kill Prestán with its venomous bite). The hangman threw the rope over the crossbeam and put the other end, delicately, around the condemned man's neck, as if afraid of scratching his skin. He tightened the slip knot; he climbed down off the platform. And then, along the rails of the Panama Railroad, the platform slid away with a whistle, and the body of Prestán was left hanging in midair. The noise of his neck breaking blended in with that of the tug of the rope, the jolt of the wood. It was cheap wood, and Panama, in any case, was a place where things shook.

The execution of Pedro Prestán, in those days when the Constitution for Angels with its explicit prohibition of the death penalty was still in force, was a real shock for many. (There were later another seventy-five shocks, when seventy-five citizens of Colón, arrested by the Conservative troops, were lined up with their backs to the charred remains of the walls and shot without the courtesy of a trial.) Of course my father, in his article for the *Bulletin*, took out his Refraction stick and rearranged reality as he so well knew how. And so, the French shareholder, so concerned about the political convulsions of that remote country and the damage they could cause his investments, found out about the "regrettable fire" that, after an "unforeseeable, inadvertent accident," burned down "a few unimportant shanties" and several "cardboard shacks that had been on the verge of falling down anyway." After the fire, "sixteen Panamanians were admitted to the hospital with breathing troubles," wrote my father (the breathing trouble consisted of the fact that they were not breathing, because the sixteen Panamanians were dead). In my father's article, the Canal workers were "true war heroes" who had defended the "Eighth Wonder" tooth and nail, and whose enemy was "fearsome nature" (no mention was made of fearsome democracies). Thus it was: through the workings and grace of Refraction, the war of 1885 never existed for the French investors, nor was Pedro Prestán hanged above the railway lines the French used to transport materials. The defeated rebel General Rafael Aizpuru, after listening to the clamor of several notable Panamanians, had offered to declare the independence of Panama if the United States would recognize him as its leader: Miguel Altamirano did not report that.

Like the installations of the two companies, the hamlet of Christophe Colomb was unscathed, as if a firebreak had separated it from the city in flames, and my father and I, who were already starting to feel like nomads on a domestic scale, didn't have to move again. Shortly after the fire, while the employees of the railway/gallows were busy rebuilding the city, I told my father that we'd had good luck, and he answered with a cryptic expression on his face that must have been melancholy. "It wasn't luck," he said. "What we had were Gringo ships." Under the paternal vigilance of the USS *Galena* and the USS *Shenandoah*, under the irrefutable authority of the USS *Swatara* and the USS *Tennessee*, works on the Great Trench tried to carry on. But things were no longer as they had been. Something had changed that month of August when the Colombian war arrived in the Isthmus, that ill-fated month when Pedro Prestán was executed. I will say it quickly and without anesthesia: I felt that something had begun to sink. The shareholders, the readers of the *Bulletin*, had begun to listen to those grotesque rumors: that their brothers, their cousins, their sons, were dying by the dozens in Panama. Could it be true, they wondered, if the *Bulletin* says the opposite? Workers and engineers arrived from the Isthmus at Marseille or Le Havre, and the first thing they did upon disembarking was to come out with contemptible slander, saying that work was not advancing as had been foreseen, or that costs were rising at a scandalous rate. . . . Incredibly, those baseless falsehoods began to leak into the credulous minds of the French. And meanwhile, my country was beginning to shed its name and constitution like a snake sheds its skin, and sink headfirst into the darkest years of its history.

VI

In the Belly
of the Elephant

My country would sink metaphorically, of course, just as the sinking of the Canal Company (of which more later) would be metaphorical. But there were other much more literal sinkings in those days; the qualities of each, of course, depended on the object sinking. On the other side of the Atlantic, for example, the sailing ship *Annie Frost* sank, which wouldn't have had any significance if you, dear Korzeniowski, had not shamelessly invented for yourself a role in the shipwreck. Yes, I know: you needed money, and Uncle Tadeusz was the nearest bank and the one that requested the fewest guarantees; so you wrote an urgent telegram: SHIPWRECKED STOP ALL LOST STOP NEED HELP . . . And since the correspondences that overwhelm me have not ceased, even though I've left the space of a few pages to put them on the record, allow me to note one of them now. For while Korzeniowski was pretending to have been on board a sinking ship, another sinking of perhaps more modest proportions was taking place but with much more immediate consequences.

One early morning in the dry season, Charlotte Madinier rented a dugout—undoubtedly similar to the one that had once carried her husband and my father—and, without anyone seeing, paddled herself along the Chagres River. She was wearing a coat that had belonged to her husband and that she'd saved from the famous postmortem burn; she had the pockets stuffed full with a collection of rocks her husband had accumulated over the early days of the explorations. I sneak into her head and I find, in the midst of fears and nostalgia and disorderly thoughts, the words *Je m'en vais* repeated like a mantra and piling up on top of one another; in her pockets I find chunks of basalt and slabs of limestone. Then Charlotte puts her hands in her pockets, with the left she clutches a large piece of granite and with the right a ball of blue clay the size of an apple. She drops into the water, backward, as if lying down, and the Panamanian ground, the oldest geological formation of the American continent, drags her to the bottom in a matter of seconds.

Let's imagine: as she sinks, Charlotte loses her shoes, so when she gets to the riverbed, the bare skin of her feet touches the sand. . . . Imagine: the pressure of the water in her ears and on her closed eyes, or maybe they're not closed but wide open, and maybe they see trout swim by and water snakes, weeds, sticks, or branches broken off trees by the humidity. Imagine the weight that rushes against Charlotte's airless chest, against her small breasts and shrunken nipples, oppressed by the cold water. Imagine that all the pores of her skin close like stubborn little mouths, tired of swallowing water and aware that very soon they'll be able to resist no longer, that death by drowning is right around the corner. Let's imagine what Charlotte is imagining: the life she managed to have—a husband, a son who learned to talk before he died, a few sexual, social, or economic satisfactions—and most of all the life she won't have, that which is never easy to imagine, because imagination (let's be honest) doesn't really get us that far. Charlotte starts to wonder what it feels like to drown, which of her senses will disappear first, if there's pain in this death and where this pain will be located. She already lacks air: the weight against her chest has increased; her cheeks have contracted: the air that had been in them has been consumed by the involuntary voracity—no, by the gluttony—of her lungs. Charlotte feels that her brain is turning off.

And then something goes through her head.

Or: something goes on *in* her head.

What is it? It is a memory, an idea, an emotion. It is something (unique) to which I, despite my prerogatives as narrator of this tale, do not have access. With a shrug of her narrow shoulders, of her elegant arms, Charlotte shakes off her husband's coat. Lumps of lignite, slabs of schist fall to the bottom. Immediately, with the swiftness of a freed buoy, Charlotte's body lifts off the riverbed of the Chagres.

Her body begins to emerge.

Her ears hurt. Saliva returns to her throat.

I anticipate all my curious readers' doubts and questions: no, Charlotte would never speak of what she thought (or imagined, or felt, or simply saw) a few seconds before what would have been a terrible death in the depths of the Chagres River. I, who am so given to speculation, in this case have been unable to speculate, and as the years have gone by this incapacity has become more firmly ingrained. . . . Any hypothesis on what happened pales in the face of that reality: Charlotte decided to go on living, and when she came out on the cloudy green surface of the Chagres, she was already a new woman (and had probably already decided she'd take the secret with her to her grave). This process of radical renovation cannot be emphasized too much, the reinvention with a capital *R* of herself that the Widow of the Canal undertook after her head—puffing and panting, her mouth gulping for air with the desperation of a landed salmon—appeared again in the superficial world of the Isthmus, that world she had come to despise and which she now forgave. I'm not afraid to record the physical manifestations of that transformation: the color of her eyes became lighter, her voice took on a graver tone, and her chestnut-colored hair grew down to her waist, as if the water of the Chagres River had formed a perpetual cascade down her back. Charlotte Madinier, who, as she sank into the Chagres River with her pockets bulging with Panamanian geology, had been a beautiful but wasted woman, when revived—because that's what it was, a resurrection, that occurred that day—seemed to return to the disturbing beauty of a not too distant adolescence. It was an almost mythic event. Charlotte Madinier as a Siren of the Chagres River. Charlotte Madinier as a Panamanian Faust. Readers of the Jury, did you want to witness another Metamorphosis? This one is unpredictable and also without precedents; this is the most powerful I've ever seen, because it eventually involved me. For the new woman did not just rise from the bottom of the Chagres, which was a portent in itself, but carried out a deed even more portentous: she entered my life.

And she was transformed, of course she was. There is no doubt: at the end of the convulsive decade of the 1880s, Metamorphosis was in the spirit of the times. On the other side of the world, in Calcutta, Korzeniowski was suffering a series of subtle identity shifts and was beginning—just like that—to sign his contracts as Conrad; the Widow of the Canal did not change her name, for we had a tacit agreement according to which she would keep her married name and I would understand her reasons without her having to explain them to me, but she would change her attire. She opened the doors of her house in

Christophe Colomb, took the skirts and capes down from the windows, and I accompanied her to the Liberian neighborhood and helped her exchange her heavy, stubbornly dark Parisian clothes for green and blue and yellow cotton shifts, which gave her pale skin the tone of unripe fruit. Another bonfire in the middle of the street: but this time the bonfire was one of exorcism and not purification, the attempt to cast out the demons of past lives. There, in the port of Colón, during the final days of 1885, Charlotte began a reincarnation in which I participated. The initiation ceremony (the details of which, out of chivalry, I must keep to myself) took place one Saturday night, and was fed by certain shared solitudes, by nostalgias that remained unshared and by the guaranteed fuel of French brandy. In my private dictionary, which might not correspond with those of all my readers, *reincarnation* means "returning to the carnal." I returned every Saturday; every Saturday Charlotte Madinier's generous flesh awaited me ravenously, with the desperate abandon of one with nothing to lose. But never, not in those days of initiation or later, did I manage to find out what happened at the bottom of the Chagres River.

I spent the night of New Year's Eve in Charlotte's house, not in my father's, and the first sentence I heard in 1886 was a plea inside of which lurked an order: "Don't ever leave again." I obeyed (willingly, I should add); at the age of thirty-one I found myself, suddenly and unexpectedly, cohabiting with a widow who barely spoke a couple of words of Spanish, colonizing her youthful body like an explorer who doesn't know he's not the first and feeling myself to be brazenly, convincingly, dangerously happy. Our place of residence and Charlotte's nationality, those two items of census data, constituted a sort of moral safe conduct, carte blanche to move through the rigid system of the Panamanian bourgeoisie to which, much to our dismay, we still belonged. Dear readers: I'm not talking, however, about impunity. On one occasion, the Jesuit priest, Father Federico Ladrón de Guevara, called Charlotte a "woman of sullied reputation" and stressed that France was historically a "lair of Liberals and nurturer of anti-Christian revolutions." I remember it well because it was then, as if trying to respond to those accusations, that Charlotte summoned me one night to the veranda. The first April downpour had just fallen, and the air was still thick with the earth's dampness, with the smell of dead worms and stagnant ditch water, with clouds of mosquitoes like floating nets. The most redundant phrase tends to be the one that announces humanity's defining moments: "I have something to tell you," says the person who—obviously—has something to say. Charlotte was faithful to this tradition of superfluity. "I have something to tell you," she said. I thought she was going to confess once and for all what had happened at the bottom of the Chagres River, that stubborn incorruptible mystery; but she, lying in the hammock and wearing an orange shift and a red scarf wrapped around her head, turned her back to me but held my hand and, as the heavens opened and unleashed another downpour, told me she was pregnant.

Our private history is sometimes capable of the most remarkable symmetries. In Charlotte's belly, a new Altamirano announced its presence with the will to continue the isthmian branch of the lineage; at the same time my father, Altamirano Senior, began to back away, to leave the world like a mortally wounded boar. Like a hibernating bear. Like whichever animal you'd prefer to use for the simile.

He began to distance himself from me. Charlotte, the new Charlotte, retained (in spite of her reincarnation) enormous contempt for my father. Do I need to spell it out? Something inside her blamed Miguel

Altamirano for the deaths of her son and her husband. He, for his part, did not manage to grasp it. The idea that there was a direct link between his Selective Blindness and the deaths of the Madiniers would have struck him as absurd and indemonstrable. If someone had told him that the two Madiniers had been murdered, and that the weapon (in one of the murders, at least) was a certain open letter that appeared on a certain day in a certain newspaper, my father, I swear, would not have understood the reference. Miguel Altamirano shed a couple of tears for the extinction, at the hands of Panama, of a whole family; but they were innocent tears, since they weren't guilty, and also innocent, since they were not wise. Miguel Altamirano elevated predictable defense mechanisms—denial and rejection—to the level of an art form. And the process extended to other parts of his life. For the news from the European press had begun to reach us, and to my indignant father, enraged and frustrated, the only way to preserve his sanity was to pretend that certain things were not certain.

Now, for the space of a few pages, my tale transforms into a very personalized collection of press cuttings, something you, Readers of the Jury, will appreciate, I think, in particular. Imagine the gray pages of these newspapers, the cramped columns, the tiny and sometimes incomplete letters... What excessive power those dead characters have! How much can they affect a man's life! The twenty-six letters of the alphabet had traditionally been on my father's side; now, suddenly, a few seditious and subversive words were agitating the political panorama of the Republic of Journalism.

Round about the same time that Pedro Prestán's neck snapped, *The Economist* of London warned the entire world, but in particular the shareholders, that the Canal Company had become a suicidal venture. At the same time as Liberal and rebel forces were capitulating in Los Guamos, and bringing the civil war to an end, a long report in *The Economist* said that de Lesseps had deliberately duped the French, and finished by saying: "The Canal will never be finished, among other reasons because finishing it was never the intention of the speculators." France, Ferdinand de Lesseps's beloved *hexagone*, began little by little to turn its hexagonal back on the Canal Company. My father received this news in the streets of Colón (in the Company offices, at the port where some newspapers came in) openmouthed and slavering like a tired bull, each article another *banderilla*. But I don't believe—I can't believe—that he was prepared for the final sword thrust, the pitiless stab in the neck that fate had in store. I understood that the world had stopped being my father's, or that my father had stopped belonging to this world, when in the space of a few days two decisive things happened: in Bogotá they reformed the Constitution; in *The Economist* they published the famous denunciation of the press. In Bogotá, President Rafael Núñez, a strange turncoat who'd gone from the most radical Liberalism to the staunch-est Conservatism, put the name of God, "the source of all authority," back into the Constitution. In London, *The Economist* made this absurd accusation: "If the Canal does not advance, and if the French had not noticed the monstrous swindle they have been the victims of before, it is because Monsieur de Lesseps and the Canal Company have invested more money in buying journalists than excavators, spent more on bribes than on engineers."

Dear readers of the gutter press, dear lovers of cheap scandal, dear spectators fascinated by the misfortunes of others: the denunciation in *The Economist* was like a bag of shit that someone threw as hard as they could against a fan. The room—let's think, for example, of the offices on rue Caumartin—was soiled from floor to ceiling. Heads rolled at every newspaper: publishers, editors, reporters, whom the pertinent investigations revealed all to have been on the Canal's payroll. And the shit, whose volatile properties are very little recognized, crossed the ocean and reached Colón, also splattering the walls of the *Correo del Istmo* (three reporters on salary) and those of *El Panameño* (two reporters and two editors), and most of all ending up on the face of one poor innocent man who suffered from Refraction Syndrome. The *Star & Herald* was the newspaper in charge of translating *The Economist*'s denunciation and did so with unusual alacrity. My father experienced the event as a betrayal in every sense of the word. And one day, while in Bogotá, Núñez, the metamorphosed President, declared that education in Colombia would either be Catholic or would not be, in Colón Miguel Altamirano feels like he's been the victim of an accident, a stray bullet from a skirmish in the street, a lightning bolt that splits a tree and drops it on the head of a passerby. It is incomprehensible to him that the *Star & Herald* could accuse all those journalists who'd written about the Canal (who'd only described what they'd seen) of venality, and in a mere thirty lines go from that accusation to a more direct one of fraud (against those whose only interest had been to collaborate in the cause of Progress). It's incomprehensible.

FRANCE BEGINS TO EMERGE FROM UNDER DE LESSEPS'S SPELL read the headline in *Le Figaro*. And that was the general feeling: de Lesseps was a cheap conjurer, a circus magician and, at best, a high-quality hypnotist. But whatever the designation conferred, beneath it—sleeping a long siesta like a hibernating bear—persisted the idea that the terms of construction of the Canal, from cost to duration, by way of engineering, had been a monstrous lie. "It would not have been possible," said the journalist, "had it not been for the solicitous collaboration of the print media and its unscrupulous writers." But my father defended himself: "In an endeavor of this magnitude," he wrote in the *Bulletin*, "contretemps are part of day-to-day life. The virtue of our workers does not lie in an absence of obstacles, but in the heroism with which they've overcome them and will continue to overcome them." My idealistic father, who at times seemed to recover the vigor he'd had at twenty, wrote: "The Canal is a work of the Human Spirit; it needs humanity's support in order to reach a successful conclusion." My comparativist father looked to other great human undertakings—the argument of the Suez Canal now seemed stale—and wrote: "Did the Brooklyn Bridge not cost eight times as much as expected? Did the Thames Tunnel not cost triple its original budget? The Canal's story is humanity's story, and humanity cannot dwell on debates about centimes." My optimistic father, the same man who years before had left the comforts of his native city to put his shoulder to the wheel where it was most needed, kept writing: "Give us time and give us francs." Around then one of our daily downpours fell on the Isthmus, no worse or any friendlier than those that fell every year; but this time the excavated earth absorbed the rainwater, got swept by the current, and returned to its place, wet and stubborn and impossible like a gigantic clay balcony ripped off the side of a hilltop cottage. In one afternoon of intense Panamanian rain, three months of work were lost. "Give us time," wrote my idealist-optimist father, "give us francs."

The last item in my press anthology (in my files, clippings fight for me to quote them, elbow each other out of the way, stick fingers in each other's eyes) appeared in *La Nación*, the newspaper of the ruling party. For all practical purposes—known and future ones—that text was a threat. Yes, of course we all knew of the badly disguised hostility the central government harbored against the French in general and de Lesseps in particular; we knew the government, after months and more months of meticulously bleeding the Public Treasury dry, had asked the Canal Company for a loan, and the Company had refused to lend them any money. Telegrams came and went, telegrams so dry the ink absorbed into the paper once they were read, and this was known. It was also known that the fact had generated resentment, and in the Presidential Palace this phrase was heard: "We should have given this to the Gringos, who really are our friends." But we could not predict the profound satisfaction that seemed to emanate from that page.

CANAL COMPANY ON THE BRINK OF BANKRUPTCY read the headline. The body of the article explained that many Panamanian families had mortgaged properties, sold family jewels, and plundered savings accounts to invest everything in Canal stocks. And the last sentence was this one: "In the case of collapse, it will be obvious who is responsible for the absolute ruin of hundreds of our fellow countrymen." And then it transcribed an extensive list of writers and journalists who had "lied, deceived, and defrauded" the public with their reports.

The list was alphabetical.

There was just one name under the letter *A*.

For Miguel Altamirano, it was the beginning of the end.

Now my memory and my pen, irremediable addicts to the vicissitudes of politics (fascinated by the stone horrors left in the Gorgon's wake), must address without distractions those terrible years that begin with the strange lines from a national anthem and end with a thousand one hundred and twenty-eight days of a war. But an almost supernatural event paralyzed the political evolution of the country, or paralyzes it in my memory. On September 23, 1886, after six and a half months of pregnancy, Eloísa Altamirano was born, a baby girl so small that my two hands could cover her completely, so scrawny that her legs still showed the curve of her bones and the only thing visible of her genitals was the tiny point of her clitoris. Eloísa was born so weak that her mouth was unable to wrestle with her mother's nipples, and she had to be fed with spoonfuls of twice-boiled milk for the first six weeks. Readers of the Jury, common readers of breeding age, fathers and mothers everywhere: the arrival of Eloísa paralyzed the entire world, or rather annulled it, erased it pitilessly the way color is erased from the world of a blind man. . . . Out there, the Canal Company made desperate attempts to stay afloat, issuing new bonds and even organizing peripatetic lotteries to recapitalize the business, but none of that mattered to me: my task consisted in boiling Eloísa's spoon, holding her cheeks with two fingers to make sure the milk didn't spill, massaging her throat with the tip of my index finger to help her swallow; I am indifferent to the knowledge that Conrad was writing his first story, "The Black Mate," at the time. Shortly before he turned twenty-nine, Conrad passed his captaincy exam in London, and was transformed for us into Captain Joseph K.; but that seems banal to me compared with the moment when Eloísa first put a bumpy nipple in her mouth and, after weeks and weeks of slow learning and gradual strengthening of her jaw, sucked so strongly that she cut it with her gums and made it bleed.

And nevertheless, there is an event that escapes my comprehension: in spite of Eloísa's birth, in spite of the great care that determined her slow and laborious survival, the annulled world kept spinning, the country kept moving with insolent independence, in the Isthmus of Panama life went on with complete indifference to what was happening to its most loyal subjects. How to talk about politics thinking at the same time of those years, evoking moments that in my memory belong exclusively to my daughter? How to get down to work recuperating events of a national character, when the only thing that interested me at the time was seeing Eloísa gain one more gram and then another? Every day, Charlotte and I took her, all wrapped up in freshly boiled linens, to Tang's butcher shop and unwrapped her to place her like a fillet steak or a piece of liver in the big bowl of his scales. On the other side of the high wooden counter Tang put the weights on, those solid rust-colored discs, and for us parents there was no greater pleasure than seeing the Chinese butcher look through his shiny lacquered box for a bigger weight, because the previous one hadn't been heavy enough. . . . I bring this memory into my tale and immediately wonder: How do I search out, in the midst of my warm personal memories, the aridity of public memories?

Self-sacrificing man that I am, I'll try, dear readers, I'll try.

Because in my country things were about to happen of the sort that historians always end up recording in their books, asking with sonorous question marks how on earth we could have come to this and then answering I know, I have the answer. Which, of course, isn't all that clever, for even the most muddle-headed person would have sensed something odd in the air during those years. There were prophecies everywhere: one had only to interpret them. I don't know what my father might have thought, but I should have recognized the imminent tragedy the day when my nation of poets was no longer able to write poetry. When the Republic of Colombia lost its ear, mistook literary taste, and rejected the most basic lyric rules, I should have sounded the alarm, shouted man overboard, stop the ship. I should have stolen a lifeboat and descended immediately, though I might have run the risk of not finding terra firma, the day I first heard the verses of the National Anthem.

Ah, those verses . . . Where did I hear them first? It's more important to ask myself now: Where did those words come from, words that nobody understood and which would have struck any literary critic as worse than terrible literature, more like the product of an unstable mind? Readers, let us go over the traces of the crime (against poetry, against decency). The year is 1887: one José Domingo Torres, a civil servant whose foremost talent was setting up nativity scenes at Christmas time, decides to become a theater director, and also decides that for the next national holiday a Patriotic Poem Produced by Presidential Plume shall be sung. And this for those blessed not to know it: the President of our Republic, Don Rafael Núñez, was in the habit of whiling away his free time composing adolescent verse. He was following a deeply entrenched Colombian tradition: when he wasn't signing new accords with the Vatican to satisfy the elevated morals of his second wife—and to persuade Colombian society to forgive him for the sin of having married a second time, abroad and in a civil ceremony—President Núñez put on his pajamas, with a nightcap and everything, threw a poncho on top of that against the cold of Bogotá, ordered a cup of chocolate with cheese, and sat down to vomit lines of verse. And one November afternoon, the Bogotá Varieties Theater witnesses a group of profoundly disconcerted young people, through no fault of their own, intoning these ineffable stanzas:

> *From the fields of Boyacá*
> *An unconquered hero*
> *Is crowned with each new shoot*
> *The genius of glory.*

> *The virile breath*
> *Of bare-chested soldiers*
> *Serves as their shield*
> *And wins the victory.*

Meanwhile, in Paris, Ferdinand de Lesseps devotes all his time to that protracted task: accepting. He accepted that the Canal would not

be ready in time but would require several more years. He accepted that
the billions of francs put up by the French would be insufficient: they
needed six hundred million more. He accepted that the idea of a sea-level
canal was a technical impossibility and an error of judgment; he accepted
that the Panama Canal would be constructed by means of a system of
locks. . . . He accepted and accepted and kept accepting: this proud man
made more concessions in two weeks than he'd made in his entire life.
However—and this is quite a large however—it wasn't enough. What
nobody (where *nobody* means "de Lesseps") had imagined had happened:
the French were fed up. The day the bonds that would save the Canal
Company went on sale, an anonymous note arrived at all the European
newspapers saying that Ferdinand de Lesseps had died. It wasn't true, of
course; but the damage was done. The sale of bonds failed. The lottery
had failed. When they announced the dissolution of the Canal Company
and named a liquidator to take charge of its machines, my father was in
the offices of the *Star & Herald*, begging them to take him back, offering
to write the first five articles for free if they would give him space in their
pages again. Witnesses assure me they saw him cry. And meanwhile, all
over Colombia the people were singing:

A lock of the virgin's hair
Torn out in agony
Of her deceased love
Around the cypress branch entwined.

Beneath a cold tombstone
Her hope she mourns
While a glorious halo of pride
Her pale countenance enshrined.

Work on the Panama Canal, the Great Trench, was officially interrupted or stopped in May of 1889. The French began to leave; in the port
of Colón the trunks and hemp sacks and wooden crates piled up daily,
and the porters couldn't cope with all the work of getting the moment's
luggage onto the moment's steamer. The *Lafayette* seemed to have tri-
pled its weekly runs during that exodus (because that's what it was, an
exodus, what happened in the Isthmus, the French like a persecuted
race fleeing in search of friendlier lands). The French city of Christophe
Colomb was gradually deserted, as if the plague had invaded and exterminated its residents; it was a ghost town coming into being, but it happened before our eyes, and in itself the spectacle would have fascinated
anyone. The recently emptied houses all took on the same smell of freshly
washed cupboards; Charlotte and I liked to take Eloísa by the hand and
go for walks through the abandoned houses and look through the drawers for a revealing diary full of secrets (something we never did find) or
some old garment that Eloísa could use to play dress-up (something we
found quite often). On the walls of the houses were marks from nails,
rectangles of a whiter white where a portrait of the grandfather who
fought with Napoleon had been. The French sold everything that wasn't
indispensable, not to reduce the dimensions of their belongings, but
because, from the moment they knew they could leave, Panama became
a wretched place they needed to forget as soon as possible and whose
objects were capable of carrying curses with them. One of those belongings, sold at public auction a little while later, was a still life the owners
had bought, out of charity, from a Canal worker. The man was a poor
unhinged Frenchman who claimed to be a banker and also a painter, but
who was really no more than a vandal. He claimed to be related to Flora
Tristan, which would have interested my mother; he'd disembarked in
Panama City, on his way from Peru, and was arrested there for urinating

in public. He left in a matter of weeks, frightened off by the mosquitoes and the labor conditions. The world later learned more about his life, and perhaps his name will not be unknown to my readers. He was called Paul Gauguin.

> *Thus the country was formed*
> *Thermopylae springing forth,*
> *The Cyclops constellation*
> *From the night sky shining down.*
> *While the trembling flower*
> *Seeks a safe shelter,*
> *From the menacing gale*
> *Beneath the laurel crown.*

The uninhabited houses of Christophe Colomb began to fall to pieces (I'm not saying it was partly the fault of the anthem, but you never know). After every rainy season, a whole wall would give way in some sector of the city, the wood so rotten it wouldn't break but bent like rubber, the beams eaten through to the center by termites. Our strolls through the houses had to end: one afternoon in June, in the middle of a downpour, a Cuna Indian slipped into the former house of the engineer Vilar while waiting for the weather to clear; reaching under a wardrobe out of curiosity, he received two bites from a rather small coral snake and died before he got back to Colón. No one could explain why snakes were so interested in the empty houses of Christophe Colomb, but as the years passed the city began to fill with these visitors, bushmasters and fer-de-lances, perhaps just looking for food. My father, who after the publication of the famous Canal payroll in the *Star & Herald* had become a sort of undesirable, a pariah of isthmian journalism, wrote during those days a short article about two Indians who met in the house of the engineer Debray to test which of them knew the best antidotes. They covered the neighborhood of Christophe Colomb from one end to the other, going into every house and sticking their hands under every wardrobe and every basket and every loose floorboard, getting bitten by as many snakes as they could find to then prove their skill with verbena, with *guaco*, and even with *ipecacuanha*. My father recounted how toward the end of the night one of the Indians had crawled under one of the houses, and felt a bite but had not managed to identify the snake. The other let him die: that was his way of winning the contest. And the winner celebrated his victory in the Colón jailhouse, sentenced by a Panamanian judge for culpable homicide.

Readers of the Jury: this passage, despite appearances, is not an ingenious touch of local color on the part of the narrator, anxious as he is to please audiences in England and even in continental Europe. No, the anecdote of the Indians and the snakes plays an active role in my narration, for that antidote competition marks my father's disgrace like a boundary stone. Miguel Altamirano wrote a simple chronicle about the Panamanian Indians and the valuable medical information that had come down to them through their traditions; but he did not manage to get it published. And thus, with all the irony implied by what I am about to write, this apolitical and banal tale, this inoffensive anecdote that had nothing to do with the Church, with History, or with the Inter-oceanic Canal, was his ruin. He sent it to Bogotá, where the taste for exoticism and adventure was greater, but seven daily papers (four Conservative, three Liberal) turned it down. He sent it to a newspaper in Mexico and another in Cuba but didn't even get a reply. And my seventy-year-old father began shutting himself up inside himself (wounded boar, hibernating bear), convinced that everyone was his enemy, that the whole world had turned its back on him as part of a conspiracy led by Pope Leo XIII and the Archbishop of Bogotá, José Telésforo Paul, against the forces of Progress. When I went to visit him, I was met by a resentful, sour-faced, embittered figure: the shadow of a silver beard dominated his face, his restless hands trembling and keeping busy with idle pastimes. Miguel Altamirano, the man who in other times had been able, with a column or a pamphlet, to generate enough hatred that a presbyter would call for his death, now spent his hours inoffensively interchanging the lines of that patriotic song as if he could take revenge on someone like that. The verses he composed might be irreverent:

> *A lock of the virgin's hair*
> *Torn out in agony*
> *The virile breath*
> *Serving as shield.*

But there were also verses of intense political criticism:

> *From the fields of Boyacá*
> *The genius of glory*
> *Seeks a safe shelter*
> *Beneath the laurel crown.*

And there were also some that were simply absurd:

> *Thermopylae springing forth*
> *And win the victory.*
> *The Cyclops constellation*
> *Her pale countenance surrounds.*

Playing with paper, playing with words, spending the day as a child spends it, laughing at things no one else understands (because no one else was there to hear the explanations or, of course, the laughter), my father entered his own decline, his personal sinking. "Clearly," he'd say when I went to see him, "the little poem lends itself to anything." And he'd show me his latest discoveries. Yes, we'd laugh together; but his laughter was tinged with the new ingredient of bitterness, by the melancholy that had killed so many visitors to the Isthmus; and by the time I took my leave of him, when I decided it was time to go home where the miracle of domestic happiness awaited me—my concubine Charlotte, my bastard Eloísa—by that time I was fully aware that in my absence and without my help and in spite of the switched-around lines of the National Anthem, that night my father would sink back down again. His routine had become an alternation of sinking and resurgence. Had I wanted to see it, I would have realized that sooner or later one of those sinkings would be the last. And no, I didn't want to see it. Drugged by my own mysterious well-being, fruit of the mysterious events of the Chagres River and generated by the mysterious joys of fatherhood, I grew blind to the appeals for help Miguel Altamirano sent my way, the flares he let off from his ship, and I was surprised to find that the power of refraction could be hereditary, that I too was capable of certain blindnesses. . . . For me, Colón turned into the place where I allowed myself to fall in love and to cultivate the idea of a family; I didn't notice—I didn't want to notice—that for my father Colón did not exist, nor did Panama exist, nor was life possible, if the Canal did not exist.

And so we arrive at one of the fundamental crossroads of my life. For if there, in a rented house in Christophe Colomb, a man manipulates lines written by another on a piece of paper, thousands of kilometers away, in a rented house in Bessborough Gardens, London, another prepares to write the first pages of his first novel. In Christophe Colomb a life made of explorations through jungles and rivers is dying away; for the man in Bessborough Gardens the explorations—in another jungle, down another river—are just about to begin.

The Angel of History, expert puppeteer, begins to move the strings above our unsuspecting heads: unbeknownst to us, Joseph Conrad and José Altamirano begin to edge closer. My duty, as Historian of Parallel Lines, is to trace an itinerary. And I now devote myself to that task. We are in September of 1889, Conrad has just finished breakfast, and something happens to him at that moment: his hand grasps the bell and rings it, so someone will come and clear the table and take the tray away. He lights his pipe and looks out the window. It's a veiled and misty day, with the odd flash of fiery sunlight here and there on the houses opposite. "I was not at all certain that I wanted to write, or that I meant to write, or that I had anything to write about." And then he picks up a pen and . . . writes. He writes two hundred words about a man called Almayer. His life as a novelist has just begun; but his life as a sailor, which has not yet ended, is in trouble. It has been several months since Captain Joseph K. returned from his last voyage, and he has still not managed to obtain a captaincy anywhere. There is a project: travel to Africa to captain a steamer for the Société Anonyme Belge pour le Commerce du Haut-Congo. But the project is stalled . . . as is also, apparently for good, the project of the Inter-oceanic Canal. Has it failed? wonders Miguel Altamirano in Colón. All the stage lights now focus on that fateful space of time: the twelve months of 1890.

JANUARY. Taking advantage of the dry season, Miguel Altamirano hires a lighter and sails up the Chagres to Gatún. It is his first outing in sixty days, if you don't count the occasional foray down Front Street (no longer bedecked with flags or banners in every language, having ceased to be a boulevard in the center of the world in the space of a couple of months and gone back to being a lost wagon track of the colonized tropics) or his daily stroll to the statue of Christopher Columbus and back. He gets the same impression every time: the city is a ghost town, it is populated by the ghosts of its dead, the living hang around like ghosts. Abandoned by the French, German, Russian, and Italian engineers, by the Jamaican and Liberian laborers, by the North American adventurers who'd fallen from grace and looked for work on the Canal, by the Chinese and the sons of the Chinese and the sons of those sons who fear neither melancholia nor malaria, the city that until recently was the center of the world has now turned into an empty hide, like that of a dead cow devoured by vultures. The Cubans and Venezuelans have gone home: there's nothing for them to do here. Panama has died, thinks Miguel Altamirano. Viva Panama. His intention is to go to see the machines, which he visited seven years ago with the engineer Madinier, but he changes his mind at the last minute. Something has overcome him—fear, sadness, an overwhelming sense of failure—something he can't quite pinpoint.

FEBRUARY. On the advice of his uncle Tadeusz, Conrad writes to another of his maternal uncles: Aleksander Poradowski, hero of the revolution against the Tsar's empire, who was sentenced to death after the insurrection of 1863 and managed to flee Poland thanks, paradoxically, to the help of a Russian accomplice. Aleksander lives in Brussels; his wife, Marguerite, is a cultured and attractive woman who talks intelligently about books, who also writes terrible novels, and who, most of all, has all the contacts in the world with the Société du Haut-Congo.

Conrad announces that he intends to travel soon to Poland to visit Tadeusz, and that he will have to travel by way of Brussels; his uncle tells him he'll be welcome but warns that he is in poor health and might not be able to perform all his duties as host. Conrad writes: "I leave London tomorrow, Friday, at nine a.m. and should arrive in Brussels at five-thirty in the afternoon." But when he arrives he finds himself faced with another piece of fate's foul play: Aleksander dies two days later. Disappointed, Captain Joseph K. travels on to Poland. He does not even attend the funeral.

MARCH. On the seventh, Miguel Altamirano arrives very early at the train station. His intention is to go to Panama City, and at eight o'clock on the dot he has boarded the train as he had done so often over the last thirty years, settling down in one of the coaches at the back without telling anyone and opening a book for the journey. Out the window he sees a black man sitting on a barrel; he sees a mule cart cross the railway lines and stop over the rails long enough for the mules to shit. Miguel Altamirano distracts himself watching, on one side of the train, the sea and the distant ships in Limón Bay and, on the other side, the crowds stamping their heels on the paving stones waiting for the train to start moving. But then Miguel Altamirano receives the first slap of his new position in Panama: the ticket collector comes through asking to see all tickets, and when he arrives at Altamirano's place, instead of tipping his hat and greeting him as usual, holds out a rude hand. Altamirano looks at the fingertips grimy from handling the paper of the tickets and says, "I don't have one." He doesn't say that for thirty years he has traveled courtesy of the Railroad Company. He just says, "I don't have one." The ticket collector shouts at him to get off; Miguel Altamirano, gathering the last grams of dignity he has left, stands up and says he'll get off when he feels like it. A moment or two later the ticket collector reappears, this time accompanied by two *cargadores*, and between the three of them they lift the passenger up and shove him off the train. Altamirano falls on the paving stones. He hears murmurs that turn into laughter. He looks at his trousers: they are torn at the knee, and through the rip he sees the skin scraped by the blow and a stain of blood and dirt that will soon be infected.

APRIL. After two months in Poland, two months devoted to visiting for the first time in fifteen years the place where he was born and the places he lived until his voluntary exile, Captain Joseph K. returns to Brussels. He knows that his aunt Marguerite has recommended him to the authorities of the Société du Haut-Congo. But when he arrives he is surprised by a stroke of luck: a Danish captain named Freiesleben, in charge of one of the company's steamboats, has died suddenly and his position is available. Captain Joseph K. is not intimidated by the idea of replacing a dead man. On paper, the trip to Africa will last three years. Conrad hurries back to London, arranges his things, returns to Brussels, takes the train to the port of Bordeaux, and embarks on the *Ville de Maceio* en route to Boma, port of entry to the Belgian Congo. From the first port of call in Tenerife, he writes: "The screw turns and carries me off to the unknown. Happily, there is another me who prowls through Europe, who is with you at this moment. Who will get to Poland ahead of you. Another me who moves about with great ease; who can even be in two places at once." From Freetown, he writes: "Fever and dysentery! There are others who are sent home in a hurry at the end of a year, so that they shouldn't die in the Congo. God forbid!" From the port of call in Libreville, he writes: "For a long time I no longer have been interested in the goal to which my road leads. I go along it with my head lowered, cursing the stones. Now I am interested in another traveler: this makes me forget the petty miseries of my own path. While awaiting the inevitable fever, I am very well."

MAY. Miguel Altamirano travels to Panama City to visit the head offices of the *Star & Herald*. He is prepared to humiliate himself if necessary in order to be allowed to return to the pages of the newspaper. But the necessity does not arise: a novice editor, a baby-faced young man who turns out to be a son of the Herrera family, receives him and asks him if he'd like to review a book that is causing a sensation in Paris. Miguel Altamirano accepts, obviously, his curiosity piqued: the *Star & Herald* does not devote much space to reviews of foreign books. The young man hands him a five hundred and seventy-two–page volume, recently published by Dentu: *La dernière bataille*, it is called, and bears this subtitle: *New Psychological and Social Study*. The author is a certain Edouard Drumont, founder and promoter of the National Anti-Semite League of France and author of *La France juive* and also of *La France juive devant l'opinion*. Miguel Altamirano has never heard of him; on the train back to Colón, he begins to read the book, a leather-bound volume with a red spine and the name of a bookshop on the frontispiece. Before the train has gone as far as Miraflores, his hands have already begun to tremble, and the other passengers in the carriage see him lift his eyes off the page and look out the window with an incredulous expression (or is it indignant, or perhaps irate?). He understands why they've assigned him this book. *La dernière bataille* is a history of the construction of the Inter-oceanic Canal, where *history* should be understood as *diatribe*. De Lesseps is called a "delinquent" and "poor devil," "great fraud" and "compulsive liar." "The Isthmus has become a vast cemetery," it says, and also: "The blame for the disaster belongs to the Jewish financiers, plague of our society, and to their monstrous accomplices: corrupt journalists the world over." Miguel Altamirano senses that he is being derided; he feels like the target where the arrow has landed, and sees in that commission a conspiracy on a grand scale to ridicule him, at best, or deliberately drive him mad, at worst. (All of a sudden, all the fingers in the train lift up and point at him.) When they get to Culebra, where the train stops briefly, he throws the book out the window, he sees it fly through the foliage of the trees—imagines or perhaps hears the small crashing of the leaves—and land with a liquid sound in a small mud puddle. Then he looks up almost by accident, and his gaze, heavy with exhaustion, falls onto the abandoned French machines, the dredgers and excavators. It is as if he were seeing them for the first time.

JUNE. Captain Joseph K. disembarks, finally, in Boma. Almost immediately he sets off for Kinshasa, in the interior, to assume the captaincy of the steamboat he's been assigned: the *Florida*. In Matadi he meets Roger Casement, an Irishman in the service of the Société du Haut-Congo, in charge of recruiting labor, but whose most important work so far has been that of exploring the Congolese landscape with an eye to the construction of a railway between Matadi and Stanley Pool. The railway will be a real advance of progress: it will facilitate free trade and improve the living conditions of Africans. Conrad prepares to cover the same ground that the future railway will cross. He writes to his aunt Marguerite: "I leave tomorrow, on foot. Not an ass here but your very humble servant." Prosper Harou, the Société's guide, approaches him and says: "Pack for several days, Monsieur Conrad. We're going on an expedition." Captain Joseph K. obeys, and two days later is entering the Congo jungle in a caravan of thirty-one men, and for thirty-six days walks behind them in the inclement humidity of the African heat, and watches the black, half-naked men open a trail with their machetes while this white man in a loose shirt notes in his travel diary—and in English— everything he sees: the depth of the Congo River when they try to wade across it but also the trill of the birds, one resembling a flute, another the baying of a hound; the general gray-yellowish tone the dry grass gives to the landscape but also the great height of the oil palms. The journey is unbearable: the murderous heat, the humidity, the clouds of flies and mosquitoes the size of grapes, the lack of drinking water, and the constant threat of tropical diseases make that penetration of the jungle into a true descent into hell. Thus concludes the month of June for Captain Joseph K. On July 3 he writes: "Saw at a camp place the dead body of a Bakongo." On July 4 he writes: "Saw another dead body lying by the path in an attitude of meditative repose." On July 24 he writes: "A white man died here." On July 29 he writes: "On the road today passed a skeleton tied to a post. Also white man's grave."

JULY. The most scandalous details of the financial disaster of the Canal have begun to come to light. My father discovers through the print media that de Lesseps, his old idol, his model for life, has retired from Parisian life. The police have searched the rue Caumartin offices and soon will do the same to the private houses of those involved: no one doubts that the search will reveal frauds and lies and embezzlements at the highest level of French politics. On the fourteenth, the Republic's national holiday, documents and declarations are published in Paris and reproduced in New York and in Bogotá, in Washington and in Panama City. Among other revelations, the following emerge. More than thirty deputies of the French Parliament received bribes to take decisions in favor of the Canal. More than three million francs were invested in "buying good press." Under the heading "Publicity" the Canal Company accepted a transfer of ten million francs divided into hundreds of checks made out to the bearer. When the destination of those checks was investigated, it was found that several of them had ended up in the editorial departments of Panamanian newspapers. On the twenty-first, at an informal lunch given by the representatives of the central government (a governor, a colonel, and a bishop), my father denies ever having seen one of those checks. An uncomfortable silence descends over the table.

AUGUST. Captain Joseph K. arrives in Kinshasa to take command of the *Florida*. But the *Florida* has sunk; and Conrad then embarks on the *Roi des Belges*, in the capacity of supernumerary, for a reconnaissance journey up the Congo River. During the trip what hasn't happened yet happens: he gets ill. He suffers three attacks of fever, two of dysentery and one of nostalgia. Then he discovers that his mission, when he arrives in Stanley Falls, will be to relieve the agent of the interior station, who is gravely ill with dysentery. His name is Georges Antoine Klein; he is twenty-seven years old; he is a conventional young man, full of hopes and plans for the future, and eager to return to Europe. Conrad and Klein speak very little at the interior station. On September 6, with Klein on board and very ill, the *Roi des Belges* begins its journey downriver. The Captain of the boat has also fallen ill, and for the first part of the trip Captain Joseph K. takes charge. Then, under his captaincy and to some degree under his responsibility, Klein dies. His death will accompany Joseph K. for the rest of his life.

SEPTEMBER. In the Christophe Colomb house, which has undergone an extraordinary rebirth since I began living in it, we are celebrating

Eloísa's birthday. Miguel Altamirano has been to Chez Michel, the pastry shop of one of the few bold Frenchmen who decided to stay in the ghost town of Colón, and has brought his granddaughter a cake in the shape of the number 4, with three layers of cream inside and a shell of caramelized sugar on the outside. After dinner, we all go out on the veranda. A few days earlier Charlotte had hung over the railings a jaguar hide with white edges, yellow flanks, brown spots, and a brown stripe along its backbone. My father is leaning on the railing and begins to stroke the spotted pelt, his gaze lost in the tops of the palm trees. Charlotte is behind him, showing a servant from Cartagena how to serve coffee in a set of four cups from Limoges. I have stretched out in the hammock. Eloísa, in my arms, has fallen asleep, and her half-open mouth emits a tiny clean-scented little snoring that I enjoy as it reaches my face. And at that moment, without turning around and without stopping his stroking of the little jaguar, my father speaks, and what he says could be directed at me but also at Charlotte: "I killed him, you know. I killed the engineer." Charlotte bursts into tears.

OCTOBER. Back in Kinshasa, Conrad writes: "Everything here is repellent to me. Men and things, but above all men." One of those men is Camille Delcommune, manager of the station and Conrad's immediate superior. The aversion Delcommune feels for this English sailor—for Conrad, by this time, is already an English sailor—is comparable only to that which the sailor feels toward Delcommune. In those conditions, Captain Joseph K. realizes that his future in Africa is rather dim and not too promising. There are no possibilities of promotion, much less of an increase in salary. However, he has signed a contract for three years, and that reality is inescapable. What to do? Conrad, ashamed but defeated, decides to provoke a quarrel in order to resign and return to London.

But he does not have to resort to this extreme: a crisis of dysentery—quite real, besides—presents a better pretext.

NOVEMBER. On the twentieth my father asks me to come with him to see the machines. "But you've seen them so many times," I tell him, and he replies, "No, I don't want to see the ones here. Let's go to Culebra, where the big ones are." I don't dare tell him the railway fare has become, overnight, too expensive for him to afford, now that he's unemployed, and always has been for me. What he says, however, is true: at the moment when they stopped for good, the Canal works were divided into five sectors, from Colón to Panama City. The Culebra sector, the one that caused the engineers the most problems, consists of two kilometers of unpredictable and disobedient geography, and that was where the best dredgers were assembled as well as the most powerful excavators the Canal Company had acquired during the final years. And that's what my father wanted to see on that November 20: the abandoned remains of the biggest failure in human history. At that moment I didn't yet know that my father had attempted that nostalgic pilgrimage before. In spite of the profound sadness I notice in his voice, in spite of the tiredness that weighs down every movement of his body, I think the matter of going to see rusty hulks is just a disappointed man's whim, and I brush him off the way you might shoo away a fly. "You go on your own," I tell him. "And then you can tell me how you got on."

DECEMBER. On the fourth, after a grueling six-week journey—the long duration the result of his terrible state of health—Conrad has returned to Matadi. He had to be carried in a hammock on the shoulders of younger, stronger men, and the humiliation adds to the exhaustion. On his way back to London, Captain Joseph K. stops again in Brussels.

But Brussels has changed in those months: it is no longer the white-walled, lethally boring city Conrad had known before; now it is the center of a slave-holding, exploitative, murderous empire; now it is a place that turns men into ghosts, a real industry of degradation. Conrad has seen the degradation of the colony, and in his head those Congolese images begin to mix, as if he were drunk, with the death of his mother in exile, the failure of his insurrectionist father, the imperialist despotism of Tsarist Russia, the betrayal of Poland by the European powers. Just as the Europeans had divided up the Polish cake, thinks Conrad, now they will divide up the Congo, and then no doubt the rest of the world. As if replying to those images that torment him, those fears that he has undoubtedly inherited from his father, his health deteriorates: Captain Joseph K. goes from rheumatism in his left arm to cardiac palpitations, from Congolese dysentery to Panamanian malaria. His uncle Tadeusz writes: "I've found your writing so changed—which I attribute to the fever and dysentery—that since then there is no happiness in my thoughts."

The day of his pilgrimage to Culebra, several American passengers saw my father take the eight o'clock train on his own, and heard him making comments to nobody each time one of the work stations passed by the windows, from Gatún to Emperador. As they passed near Matachín they heard him explain that the name of the place came from the Chinamen who'd died and were buried around there, and as they passed Bohío Soldado they heard him translate both words into English—*Hut, Soldier*—without offering the slightest explanation. At midday, while the train filled with the smells of the meals the passengers had improvised for the journey, they saw him alight in Culebra, slip down the railway embankment, and disappear into the jungle. A Cuna

Indian who was collecting plants with his son caught sight of him then, and his way of walking struck him as so odd—the careless way he kicked a piece of rotten wood that could have been the refuge of a poisonous snake, the worn-out way he bent down to look for a stone to throw at the monkeys—that he followed him to where the Frenchmen's machines were. Miguel Altamirano arrived at the excavation, the gigantic gray and muddy trench that looked like a meteor's point of impact, and contemplated it from the edge the way a general studies a battlefield. Then, as if someone had defied the Isthmus's rules, it began to rain.

Instead of sheltering under the closest tree, whose impenetrable foliage would have provided a perfect umbrella, Miguel Altamirano began to walk in the rain, along the edge of the trench, until arriving at an enormous creature covered in creepers that towered ten meters above the ground. It was a steam-powered excavator. The downpours of the last eighteen months had covered it in a patina of rust, as thick and hard as coral, but that was only visible after pulling away the three hand-breadths of tropical vegetation that covered it all over, the vines and leaves with which the jungle was pulling it down into the earth. Miguel Altamirano approached the shovel and caressed it as if it were an old elephant's trunk. He walked around the machine slowly, stopping beside each leg, pulling the leaves away with his hands and touching each of the buckets that his arms could reach: the old elephant was ill, and my father circled it in search of symptoms. He soon found the elephant's belly, a little shed that served as the monstrous tank of the excavator's engine room, and there he took shelter. He did not come out again. When, after a fruitless two-day search of Colón and the surrounding area, I managed to discover his whereabouts, I found him lying on the damp floor of the excavator. Fate decreed it would rain that day as well, so I lay down beside my dead father and closed my eyes to feel what he would have felt during his last moments: the murderous clatter of the rain on the hollow metal of the buckets, the smell of the hibiscus, the shirt soaked through with the cold of the wet rust, and the exhaustion, the pitiless exhaustion.

PART THREE

The birth of another South American Republic.
One more or less, what does it matter?

Joseph Conrad, *Nostromo*

VII

A Thousand One Hundred and Twenty-eight Days, or The Brief Life of a Certain Anatolio Calderón

The saddest thing about my father's death, it sometimes occurs to me (I still think of it often), was the fact that he wasn't survived by anyone prepared to observe a decent mourning. In our house in Christophe Colomb there was no black clothing or any desire to wear any, and Charlotte and I had a tacit agreement to spare Eloísa contact with that death. I don't think it was a protective impulse but rather the notion that Miguel Altamirano hadn't been very present in our lives during those last years and it was futile to give the little girl a grandfather after that grandfather had died. So my father began to sink into oblivion as soon as his funeral was over, and I did absolutely nothing to prevent it.

By stipulation of the Bishop of Panama, my Masonic father was denied an ecclesiastical burial. He was buried in unconsecrated ground, beneath a gravelly headstone, among the Chinese and the atheists, unbaptized Africans, and all sorts of excommunicated people. He was buried, scandalizing those who knew, with a certain hand amputated a long time before from a certain Asian cadaver. The Colón gravedigger, a man who had already seen it all in this life, received the death certificate from the judicial authorities and handed it to me the way a bellhop gives you a message in a hotel. It was written on Canal Company stationery, which seemed anachronistic and somewhat disdainful; but the gravedigger explained that the stationery was already printed and paid for, and he preferred to keep using it than to let hundreds of perfectly usable sheets of paper rot away in an attic. So my father's particulars appeared above dotted lines, beside the words *Noms, Prénoms, Nationalité*. Beside *Profession ou emploi*, someone had written: *Journalist*. Beside *Cause du décès*, it read: *Natural causes*. I thought of going to the authorities to make it a matter of public record that Miguel Altamirano had died of disillusionment, though I was prepared to accept melancholy, but Charlotte persuaded me that I would be wasting my time.

When nine months of mourning had passed, Charlotte and I realized we hadn't visited Miguel Altamirano's grave even once. The first anniversary of his death arrived without our noticing, and we mentioned it with faces contorted by guilty expressions, hands full of remorse fluttering in the air. The second anniversary went by unnoticed by either of us, and it took the arrival of the news of the trials in Paris for my father's memory to make a brief, momentary appearance in the organized well-being of our household. Let's see how I can explain this: by way of some sort of cosmic result of my father's death, the house in Christophe Colomb and its three residents had become detached from the land of Panama and was now located outside the territories of Political Life. In Paris, Ferdinand de Lesseps and his son Charles were mercilessly interrogated by the hungry pack of swindled shareholders, thousands of families who had mortgaged their houses and sold their jewels to rescue the Canal in which they'd invested all their money; but that news reached me through a thick wall of glass, or from the virtual reality of a silent film: I see the actors' faces, I see their lips moving, but I can't understand what they're saying, or perhaps I don't care. . . . The French President, Sadi Carnot, shaken by the financial scandal of the Company and its various economic debacles, had found himself obliged to form a new government, and the ripples of the waves of such an event must have reached the beaches of Colón; but the Altamirano-Madinier household, apolitical and to some apathetic, remained on the margins. My two women and I lived in a parallel reality where uppercase letters did not exist: there were no Great Events, there were no Wars or Nations or Historic Moments. Our most important events, the humble peaks of our life, were very different during that time. Two examples: Eloísa learns to count to twenty in three languages; Charlotte, one night, is able to talk of Julien without collapsing.

Meanwhile, time passed (as they say in novels) and Political Life was up to its usual tricks in Bogotá. The President Poet, Author of the Glorious Anthem, had stretched out his finger and designated his successor: Don Miguel Antonio Caro, illustrious exemplar of the South American Athens who drafted Homeric translations with one hand and draconian laws with the other. Don Miguel Antonio's favorite pastimes were opening Greek classics and closing Liberal newspapers . . . and banishing, banishing, banishing. "We are not short of disoriented individualities," he said in one of his first speeches. "But the vehement perorations of the revolutionary school have no echo in the country." His own finger pointed dozens of disoriented individualities, hundreds of revolutionaries, down the road to forced exile. But in the apolitical, apathetic, and historical house in Christophe Colomb, Caro's name was never heard, despite the fact that many he banished were Panamanian Liberals. The unbearable pressure of the censorship measures was not complained of, despite the fact that several newspapers in the Isthmus suffered under them. One of those days was the hundredth anniversary of the famous day when the famous Robespierre made his famous remark: "History is fiction." But we, who lived in the fiction that there was no history, paid scant attention to that anniversary so important to others. . . . Charlotte and I took it upon ourselves to complete Eloísa's education, which basically took the form of reading together (and sometimes in costume) from all the fables we could find, from Rafael Pombo to good old La Fontaine. On the floorboards of our house, I was the grasshopper and Eloísa was the ant, and between the two of us we forced Charlotte to put on a bow tie and play the Outgoing Tadpole. At the same time, I made myself, dear Eloísa, this solemn promise: never again would I allow Politics to have free access to my life. Before the onslaught of Politics that had destroyed my father's life and so often disrupted my country, I would defend as best I could my new family's integrity. On any of the issues that would define the immediate future of my country, the Arosemenas or the Arangos or the Menocals (or the Jamaican with his blunderbuss, the Gringo with his railroad, or the lost *bogotáno* from the tailor's shop) asked me: "And what do you think?" And I would answer with an oft-repeated, mechanical phrase: "I'm not interested in politics."

"Will you vote Liberal?"

"I'm not interested in politics."

"Will you vote Conservative?"

"I'm not interested in politics."

"Who are you? Where are you from? Who do you love? Who do you hate?"

"I'm not interested in politics."

Readers of the Jury: how naïve I was. Did I truly think I would manage to avoid the influences of that ubiquitous and omnipotent monster? I wondered how to live in peace, how to perpetuate the happiness I'd been granted, without noticing that in my country these are political questions. Reality soon disabused me, for in those days a group of conspirators met in Bogotá, prepared to capture President Caro, depose him as if he were an old monarch, and set off the Liberal revolution. . . . But they did so with such enthusiasm that they were discovered and detained by the police before they had time to say a word. The government continued its repressive measures; uprisings, in answer to these measures, continued in various parts of the country. I kept Charlotte and Eloísa shut up at home in Christophe Colomb; I stocked up on provisions and drinking water and boarded up all the doors and windows with planks stolen from the ownerless houses. And that's what I was doing when I got the news that another war had broken out.

I hasten to say: it was a tiny war, a sort of prototype of a war or an amateur war. Government forces took less than sixty days to subdue the revolutionaries; the echo of the Battle of Bocas del Toro, the only clash of any importance the Isthmus saw, ricocheted off our boarded-up windows. The memory of Pedro Prestán and his broken-necked hanging body was fresh in Panamanian minds; when the echo reached us from Bocas of those Liberal gunshots so timid they turned back in midair, many of us began to think of more executions, of more bodies hanged over the railway lines.

But none of that happened.

However . . . in this story there's always a *however*, and here it is. The war barely touched the isthmian coasts, but it touched them; the war stayed with us for just a few hours, but there it was. And most important: that amateur war opened the appetites of Colombians; it was like the carrot before the horse, and from that moment on I knew something more serious was waiting for us round the corner. . . . Feeling in the air the appetite for warmongering, I wondered if staying holed up in my apolitical house would be enough, and immediately answered that it would, that it couldn't be otherwise. Watching the sleeping Eloísa—whose legs lengthened desperately under my scrutiny, whose bones mysteriously changed coordinates—and watching Charlotte's naked body when she went out into the yard under the palm tree to shower with that watering can that looked like it had just been brought from l'Orangerie, I thought: Yes, yes, yes, we're safe, no one can touch us, we have stationed ourselves outside of history and we are invulnerable in our apolitical house. But it is time for a confession: at the same time I thought of our invulnerability, I felt in my stomach an intestinal upset that resembled hunger pangs. The emptiness began to recur at night when we turned out the lamps. It came to me in dreams or when I thought of my father's death. It took me a week to identify the sensation and admit, with some surprise, that I was afraid.

Did I speak of my fear to Charlotte? Did I tell Eloísa? Of course not: fear, like phantoms, does more damage when invoked. For years I kept it by my side like a forbidden pet, feeding it in spite of myself (or was it the fear itself, tropical parasite, that fed off me like a pitiless orchid?) but without admitting its presence. In London, Captain Joseph K. also faced small personal and unprecedented terrors. "My uncle died on the 11th of this month," he wrote to Marguerite Poradowska, "and it seems everything has died in me, as though he carried off my soul with him." The months that followed were an attempt to recover his lost soul; it was around that time that Conrad met Jessie George, an English typist who had two very obvious qualities for the Polish writer: she was a typist and she was English. A few months later, Conrad proposed to her with this invincible argument: "After all, my dear, I'll not live long." Yes,

Conrad had seen it, he'd seen the chasm that opened at his feet, he'd felt that strange form of hunger and had run for shelter like a dog in a thunderstorm. That's what I should have done: run, cleared off, packed up my things and my family, taken them by the hand and evacuated without a backward glance. After writing *Heart of Darkness*, Conrad had been plunged into new depths of depression and bad health; but I didn't know it, I didn't realize other abysses were opening at my feet. On Good Friday in 1899, Conrad wrote: "My fortitude is shaken by the view of the monster. It does not move; its eyes are baleful; it is as still as death itself—and it will devour me." If I had been able to pick up the prophetic-telepathic waves those words were sending, maybe I would have tried to decipher them, figure out what the monster was (but now I can imagine, and so can the reader) and what to do to keep it from devouring us. But I didn't know how to interpret the thousand portents that filled the air during those years, I didn't know how to read the warnings in the text of events, and the warnings that Conrad, my kindred spirit, sent telepathically from so far away, did not reach me.

"Man is an evil animal," he wrote to Cunninghame Graham around that time. "His perversity must be organized." And then: "Crime is a necessary condition of organized existence. Society is essentially criminal—or it wouldn't exist." Józef Konrad Korzeniowski, why didn't your words reach me? Dear Conrad, why didn't you give me a chance to protect myself from the evil men and their organized perversity? "I am like a man who has lost his gods," you said at the time. And I didn't know how, dear Joseph K.: I didn't know how to see in your words the loss of mine.

On October 17, 1899, shortly after my daughter Eloísa menstruated for the first time, the department of Santander saw the longest and bloodiest civil war in the history of Colombia.

• • •

The Angel of History's modus operandi was basically the same as usual. The Angel is a brilliant serial killer: once he has found a good way to get men to kill each other he never gives it up, he clings to it with the faith and obstinacy of a St. Bernard. . . . For the war of 1899, the Angel spent about four months humiliating the Liberals. First he used the Conservative President Don Miguel Antonio Caro. Until his arrival in power, the national army had been composed of some six thousand troops; Caro increased the manpower to the legal maximum, ten thousand men, and in the space of two years quadrupled military expenditure. "The government has a duty to assure the peace," he said, while he filled his little ant's cave with nine thousand five hundred and fifty machetes with scabbards, five thousand and ninety Winchester 44 carbines, three thousand eight hundred and forty-one Gras 60 rifles, with well-polished bayonets. He was an ambidextrous and able man: with one hand he translated a bit of Montesquieu—for example: "Peace and moderation are the spirit of a republic"—and with the other signed recruitment decrees. In the streets of Bogotá he mobilized farm workers and hungry peasants in exchange for two *reales* a day, while their wives sat against the wall and waited for the money to go and buy potatoes for lunch; priests walked around the city promising adolescent boys eternal blessings in exchange for their service to the nation.

Soon the Angel, already bored by this Conservative President, decided to change him for another; to better affront the Liberals, he put Don Manuel Antonio Sanclemente in charge, an old man of eighty-four, who shortly after being sworn in received an order not open to appeal from his personal doctor to leave the city. "It gets so cold here, this playing-President lark could cost you a hefty price," he told him. "Go on down to the tropical lowlands and leave this business to the young folk." And the President obeyed: he moved to Anapoima, a little village with a tropical climate where his octogenarian lungs caused him fewer problems and his octogenarian blood pressure went down. Of course the country was then left without a government, but that little detail wasn't going to intimidate the Conservatives. . . . In a matter of days, the Minister of State in Bogotá invented a rubber stamp with a facsimile of the President's signature, and distributed copies to all interested parties, so that Sanclemente's presence in the capital was no longer necessary: every senator signed his own proposed laws, every minister validated any decrees he felt like validating, for it took only a blow from the magic stamp to bring them to life. And thus, amid the Angel's resounding guffaws, the new government evolved, to the indignation and dishonor of the Liberals. Then, one October morning, patience went astray in the department of Santander, and a general with many wars behind him fired the first shots of the revolution.

From the beginning we realized this war was different. In Panama the memory of the war of '85 was still vivid, and Panamanians were determined to take their destiny into their own hands this time. So Panama, the Isthmus detached from Colombian reality, the Caribbean Switzerland, joined in the hostilities as soon as it could. Several towns of the isthmian interior rose up in arms two days after the first shots; before a week was out, the Indian Victoriano Lorenzo had armed a force of three hundred men and started his own guerrilla war in the mountains of Cocle. When the news reached Colón, I was having lunch in the same mirrored restaurant from which I'd seen my father emerge a quarter of a century earlier. I was with Charlotte and Eloísa, who was gradually turning into an adolescent of dark and perturbing beauty, and the three of us heard a Jamaican waiter say, "Well, what difference is one more war going to make? The world's coming to an end anyway."

It was a commonly held conviction among Panamanians that on December 31 the Final Judgment would begin, that the world wasn't designed to see the twentieth century. (Every comet, every shooting star seen from Colón, seemed to confirm these prophecies.) And for several months the prophecies gained strength: the last days of the century witnessed battles bloodier than any seen since independence. The coordinates of the country were flooded with blood, and that blood was all Liberal: in every military clash, the revolution was destroyed by the numerical superiority of the government armies. In Bucaramanga, General Rafael Uribe Uribe, at the head of a mixed army of fed-up peasants and rebellious university students, was received with shots fired from the tower of the church of San Laureano. "Long live the Immaculate Conception!" shouted the snipers after each young Liberal death. In Pasto, Father Ezequiel Moreno fired up the Conservative soldiers: "Be like the Maccabees! Defend the rights of Jesus Christ! Kill the Masonic beasts without mercy!" Scenes were also staged on the Muddy Magdalene: in front of the port of Gamarra, Liberal ships were sunk by government cannons, and four hundred and ninety-nine revolutionary soldiers burned to death amid the flaming wood of the hulls, and those who didn't burn to death drowned in the river, and those who made it to the shore before they drowned were shot without any sort of trial and their bodies left to rot beside the morning's catfish. And gathered in the telegraph office, the people of Colón awaited the definitive telegram: PROPHECY TRUE STOP COMETS AND ECLIPSES WERE RIGHT STOP ENTIRE WORLD NEARS END. In the Republic of Colombia, the new century was greeted without any celebrations whatsoever. But the telegram never arrived.

Others arrived, however. (As you'll soon realize, my dear readers, a good part of the war of '99 was waged in Morse code.) DISASTER FOR REVOLUTIONARIES IN TUNJA. REVOLUTIONARY DISASTER IN CÚCUTA.

REVOLUTIONARY DISASTER IN TUMACO . . . In the midst of this disastrous telegraphic landscape, no one believed the news of the Liberal victory in Peralonso. No one believed that a Liberal army of three thousand poorly armed men—one thousand Remington rifles, five hundred machetes, and an artillery corps that had made its own cannons out of aqueduct pipes—could have stood up on an equal footing to twelve thousand government soldiers who had allowed themselves the luxury of wearing brand-new uniforms intended for the day the revolution was defeated. GOVERNMENT ROUT IN PERALONSO STOP URIBE DURÁN HERRERA MARCH TRIUMPHANT TOWARD PAMPLONA said the telegram, and nobody believed it could be true. General Benjamín Herrera took a bullet in the thigh and won the battle from a stretcher; he was four years my senior but could already call himself a war hero. That was at Christmas; and on January 1, Colón awoke to find the world still in its place. The French Curse had expired. And I, Eloísa dear, felt that my apolitical house was an invincible fortress.

I felt it with total conviction. The simple force of my will, I thought, had managed to keep the Angel of History far away and marginalized. The war, in this country of windbags, was something that happened in telegrams, in letters exchanged by generals, in the capitulations that were being signed from one end of the Republic to the other. After Peralonso, the revolutionary General Vargas Santos was proclaimed "Provisional President of the Republic." Mere words (and excessively optimistic ones). From the Panamanian city of David, the revolutionary General Belisario Porras protested before the Conservative government for the "acts of banditry" committed by government soldiers. Mere words. The Liberal command complained of the "flagellations" and "tortures" inflicted on prisoners captured "in their houses" and without "weapons in their hands."

Mere words, mere words, mere words.

I concede, however, that the words made their sounds from closer and closer. (Words pursue, they can wound, they're dangerous; words, in spite of being the empty kind of words that Colombians tend to pronounce, can sometimes explode in our mouths, and we mustn't underestimate them.) The war had now landed in Panama, and in Colón the sound of nearby gunshots reached us and also news of them, the agitation of the prisons crammed with political prisoners and rumors of mistreatment, the smell of the dead that began to be left scattered over the Isthmus, from Chiriquí to Aguadulce. But in my Schizophrenic City, the neighborhood of Christophe Colomb remained firmly installed in a parallel world. Christophe Colomb was a ghost town, and was, to be specific, a French ghost town: What good could a place like that be to a Colombian civil war? As long as we didn't leave it—I remember having thought—my two women and I would be safe. . . . But maybe (as I've implied elsewhere using other words but finding the exact formula is the writer's task) my enthusiasm was premature. For at the same time, in the distance, the ill-fated department of Santander, cradle of the war, was flooded with blood, and that battle mysteriously set in motion the hypocritical and backstabbing mechanisms of politics. In other words, a conspiracy was set in motion by which the Gorgon and the Angel of History prepared to invade, in collaboration and without any consideration whatsoever, the paradise of the Altamirano-Madinier household.

It happened in a place called Palonegro. Barely recovered from the bullet wound to his thigh, General Herrera had advanced northward as part of the revolutionary vanguard. In Bucaramanga he took the opportunity to toss out a new crop of words: "Injustice is an everlasting seed of rebellion," and things like that. But there was no rhetoric worthy of May 11, when eight thousand revolutionaries found themselves up against twenty thousand government troops, and what followed . . . How to explain what followed? No, the numbers are of no use to me (those old standbys so beloved of journalists like my father), and statistics, though they travel so well by telegraph, are of no use either. I can say that the combat lasted fourteen hours; I can talk of the seven thousand dead. But numbers don't decompose, nor are statistics a breeding ground for pestilence. For fourteen days the air of Palonegro filled with the fetid stench of rotting eyes, and the vultures had time to peck open the cloth of the uniforms, and the field became covered in pale naked corpses, with broken bellies and spilled entrails staining the green of the meadow. For fourteen days the smell of death penetrated the nostrils of men too young to recognize it or to know why their mucous membranes were stinging or why it wouldn't go away even when they rubbed gunpowder into their mustaches. Wounded revolutionaries fled down the Torcoroma trail and collapsed like milestones along the escape route, so one could have kept track of their fate simply by observing the flight paths of the vultures.

The fate of the escaped generals was immediate exile: Vargas Santos and Uribe Uribe left Riohacha for Caracas; General Herrera fled by way of Ecuador, managing to escape the government troops but not the willful, stubborn words. In a message that pursued him until it caught up with him, Vargas Santos entrusted him with directing the war in the departments of Cauca and Panama.

From Panama it was possible to win the war.

In Panama the liberation of the country would begin.

General Herrera agreed, as was to be expected. In a matter of weeks he had put together an expeditionary army—three hundred Liberals who'd been defeated in the battles of the south and of the Pacific coast anxious for an opportunity to avenge themselves and avenge their dead—but they lacked a ship to get them to the Isthmus. At that moment the deus ex machina (so at home in the theater of history) brought him good news: idly anchored in the port of Guayaquil was a ship called the *Iris*, full of cattle and destined for El Salvador. Herrera inspected the vessel and discovered the most important technical attribute: the owner, the firm of Benjamin Bloom & Co., had put it up for sale. Without delay, the General gave his word, signed promissory contracts of sale, toasted the business with a glass of *agua de panela* with lemon while the Salvadoran Captain and his first mate raised recurrent glasses of *aguardiente de caña*. At the beginning of October, filled with as many young revolutionary soldiers as cows, each of whose four stomachs seemed to come to an agreement to suffer simultaneously from diarrhea, the *Iris* set sail from Guayaquil.

One of the soldiers interests us in particular: the camera approaches, laboriously avoiding one or two cows' backs, passes under a soft, freckled udder, and avoids the whip of a treacherous tail, and its gray image shows us the immaculate, frightened (and hidden among the cow pies) face of a certain Anatolio Calderón. Anatolio would have his nineteenth birthday flanked by the cows of the *Iris*, as the ship passed the coast of Tumaco, but his shyness wouldn't allow anyone to find out. He'd been born on a hacienda in Zipaquirá, son of an Indian servant who died giving birth to him and the owner of the property, Don Felipe de Roux, rebellious bourgeois and socialist dilettante. Don Felipe had sold the family estates and set sail for Paris before his illegitimate son reached puberty, but not without leaving him enough money to study whatever he wanted in any university in the country. Anatolio enrolled in the Externado University to study law, although deep down he would rather have read literature at the University of Rosario and followed in the footsteps of Julio Flórez, the Divine Poet. When General Herrera went through Bogotá, after the Battle of Peralonso, and was received as a hero by the young Liberals, Anatolio was among those, blazing with patriotic fervor, who leaned out of the windows of the university. He saluted the General, and the General singled him out from among all the students to return his salute (or at least so it seemed to him). When the parade had finished, Anatolio went down to the street and found, among the paving stones, a lost Liberal horseshoe. The find struck him as a sign of good luck. Anatolio cleaned the mud and dried shit off the horseshoe and put it in his pocket.

But war is not always as orderly as it seems when narrated, and young Anatolio did not join up with General Herrera's revolutionary army at that moment. He carried on with his studies, determined to change the country by way of the very laws the Conservative governments had trampled on. But on July 31, 1900, one of those same Conservatives visited the quasi-nonagenarian Don Manuel Sanclemente's tropical retreat, and in less decent words than mine told him that a useless old man mustn't hold the reins of the nation, and then and there declared him removed from Bolívar's throne. The coup d'état was perpetrated in a matter of hours; and before the week was out, six law students had left the university, packed their things, and gone in search of the first Liberal battalion prepared to enlist them. Of the six students, three died in the Battle of Popayán, one was taken prisoner and transferred back to the Panóptico Prison in Bogotá, and two escaped to the south, went round the Galeras volcano to avoid the Conservative troops, and made it to Ecuador. One of those was Anatolio. After wandering the battle-fields for so many months, Anatolio had nothing but one rusty horse-shoe, a leather canteen, and a Julio Flórez book whose brown covers had become impregnated with sweat. The day the commanding officer of the Cauca battalion, Colonel Clodomiro Arias, notified him that the battalion would be incorporated into General Benjamín Herrera's army,

Anatolio was reading and rereading the lines of "Everything Comes to Us Late."

> *And glory, that nymph of fate,*
> *dances only on sepulchers.*
> *Everything comes to us late*
> *. . . even death!*

Suddenly, he began to feel an itching in his eyes. He read the lines, realized he felt like crying, and wondered if the most terrible thing had happened, if war had turned him into a coward. Days later, hiding among the cows of the *Iris* for fear that someone—Sergeant Major Latorre, for example—might look him in the eye and notice the cowardice that had settled in there, Anatolio thought of the mother he never knew, cursed the day he'd considered joining the revolutionary army, and felt a violent urge to go home and eat a hot meal. And instead here he was, smelling the vapors of cow dung, breathing the saline humidity of the Pacific, but most of all scared to death of what awaited him in Panama.

The *Iris* arrived in El Salvador on October 20. General Herrera met the ship's owners in Acajutla and signed a sales agreement that was more like a bond: if the revolution was successful, the Liberal government would pay the gentlemen of Bloom & Co. the sum of sixteen thousand pounds sterling; if they lost, the ship would form part of the "contingencies of war." There, in the Salvadoran port, General Herrera had them disembark in a strict order—cattle, soldiers, crew—and climbed up on a wooden crate so everyone could hear as he ceremoniously rechristened the ship. The *Iris* would henceforth be called the *Almirante Padilla*. Anatolio took note of the change but also noted that he was still scared. He thought of José Prudencio Padilla, Guajiran martyr of Colombian independence, and said to himself that he didn't want to be a martyr to absolutely anything, that he wasn't interested in dying in order to be honored by decree, and much less so for some half-mad military man who would name a ship after him. In December, after putting into port at Tumaco to pick up a contingent of fifteen hundred soldiers, a hundred and fifteen cases of ammunition, and nine hundred and ninety-seven projectiles for the cannon mounted on the prow, the *Almirante Padilla* put into port in Panama. It was Christmas Eve and the heat was dry and pleasant. The soldiers had not even disembarked when the news reached them: the Liberal forces had been destroyed across the entire Isthmus. While up on deck they recited the novena; Anatolio stayed hidden in the bowels of the ship and wept with fear.

With the arrival of Herrera's troops in the Isthmus, the war began to take on a different aspect. Under the orders of Colonel Clodomiro Arias, Anatolio participated in the taking of Tonosí, disembarked in Anton, and liberated the forces of the Indian Victoriano Lorenzo from the siege of La Negrita, but in none of those places did he stop considering desertion. Anatolio took part in the Battle of Aguadulce; one night when the moon was full, while General Belisario Porras's revolutionary forces took the Vigia hill and advanced toward Pocri, those of the Indian Victoriano Lorenzo destroyed the government battalions guarding the city, the Sanchez and the Farias. At noon the next day, the enemy started to send emissaries to request ceasefires in order to bury their dead, to negotiate more or less honorable capitulations. Anatolio was part of this historical date in which the balance appeared to shift to the revolutionary side, during which for a few hours the revolutionaries believed in that pipe dream: definitive triumph. The Cauca battalion buried eighty-nine of their men, and Anatolio took personal charge of several bodies; but what he would remember forever did not come from his side but from the government side: the smell of roasting flesh that invaded the air when the medic of the Farias battalion began to incinerate, one at a time, the hundred and sixty-seven Conservative corpses he preferred not to bury.

The smell stayed with him all the way to Panama City, Herrera's army's next objective. It soon seemed to him that even the pages of Julio Flórez's book were impregnated with the stench of Conservatives reduced to ashes, and if he read a line like "Why do you fill the air I breathe?" the air would immediately fill with incinerated nerves, muscles, and fat. But the battalion kept advancing, indifferent; no one sensed the hell that was overwhelming Anatolio, no one looked him in the eye and discovered the cowardice lurking there. Less than fifty kilometers from Panama City, Colonel Clodomiro Arias divided his battalion: some carried on with him toward the capital, planning to camp at a prudent distance and wait for the arrival of the reinforcements the *Almirante Padilla* would deposit east of Chame; the others, including Anatolio, would carry on northward under the orders of Sergeant Major Latorre. Their mission was to get to the railway at Las Cascadas and guard the line against any attempt to obstruct the free circulation of trains. General Herrera wanted to send a clear message to the marines waiting in the North American steamships—the *Iowa* off the coast of Panama City, the *Marietta* off Colón—like a ghostly presence: there was no need for them to disembark, because the Liberal army would ensure that neither the railway nor the Canal works were in any danger. Anatolio, part of this placation strategy, pitched his tent in the place chosen by Sergeant Major Latorre. That night, he was awakened by three shots. The sentinel had mistaken the frenetic movements of a wildcat for a governmental counterattack and had fired three times in the air. It was a false alarm; but Anatolio, sitting on top of his only blanket, felt a new warmth

between his thighs and realized he'd wet himself. By the time the camp
had calmed down and his tent mates had gone back to sleep, Anatolio
had already wrapped the horseshoe and the Julio Flórez book in a dirty
shirt, and begun to do—under the protection of the shadows—what he
should have done a long time earlier. Before the birds started to wake up
in the dense treetops, Anatolio had already become a deserter.

Meanwhile, General Herrera received the first news of the executions.
Aristides Fernández, Minister of War, had ordered Tomás Lawson, Juan
Vidal, Benjamín Mañozca, and fourteen more generals of the revolution
to face the firing squad. That wasn't all: on board the *Almirante Padilla*
and in the Aguadulce camp, the general staff of the Liberal army received
the circular that the Minister had printed and sent to all the governmental
commanding officers, all the Conservative mayors and governors, ordering them to shoot without trial any and all armed revolutionaries they
captured. But Anatolio never found out: he had already gone into the
jungle, he'd already descended the Central Cordillera on his own, making short-lived fires to frighten off the poisonous snakes and mosquitoes,
eating monkeys that he hunted with his army-issue rifle or threatening
the Indians of La Chorrera in order to get boiled yucca or coconut milk.

The war, very much in spite of its deserters, continued its course. In
Panama City everyone was talking about the letter that General Herrera had written to the provincial governor, complaining again of the
"treatment inflicted on the Liberal prisoners" who had been "tortured
as much in the flesh as had their dignity and spirits been ill-treated";
but Anatolio knew nothing of the letter, or of the disdain with which
the provincial governor redirected it to Aristides Fernández, or of the
Minister of War's reply, which consisted of seven selective executions in
the same plaza where the Canal Company's office had stood, and where
the Grand Hotel still stood, converted into government barracks and ad

hoc dungeon. Like a one-man expedition (like Stanley penetrating the Congo), Anatolio had discovered Lake Gatún. He started round it with the vague notion that he'd eventually arrive at the Atlantic, but soon realized that he'd have to use the train if he wanted to get there before the month was out. He had got it into his head—his head obscured by the phantoms of cowardice—that from Colón, that Caribbean Gomorrah, he'd be able to find a ship willing to get him out of the country, a captain willing to look the other way as he disembarked in Kingston or Martinique, in Havana or Puerto Cabello, and he would finally be able to start a new life far away from war, that place where normal, ordinary men—good sons, good fathers, good friends—wet their trousers. The port of Colón, he thought, was the place where nobody notices anybody, where with a little bit of luck he would go unnoticed. To arrive without being discovered, find a steamer or a sailing ship, no matter what the cargo or flag: nothing else mattered.

Colón had been in the hands of government forces for almost a year. The defeats of San Pablo and Buena Vista had left General De la Rosa's Liberal battalions seriously decimated and the city unprotected. When the gunboat *Próspero Pinzón* appeared in the waters of the bay, full of enemy troops, De la Rosa knew he'd lost the city. General Ignacio Foliaco, in command of the gunboat, threatened to bombard the city as well as the French hamlet of Christophe Colomb, which was even more within range. De la Rosa rejected the threat. "From my side not a shot will be fired," he sent word. "You'll see how you look entering the city after having flattened it with cannonballs." But before Foliaco could carry out his threat, De la Rosa received a visit from four captains— two North Americans, one English, and one French—who had assumed the role of mediators to avoid possible damage to the railway system. The captains brought a proposal for dialogue; De la Rosa accepted. The

British cruiser *Tribune* served as the meeting place and negotiation table for Foliaco and De la Rosa; five days later, De la Rosa met on board the *Marietta* with General Albán, that leader of the government forces in the Isthmus who was called "the madman" and not in jest. In the presence of the ship's Captain, Francis Delano, and Thomas Perry, commander of the cruiser *Iowa*, General De la Rosa signed the surrender. Before evening fell, the troops of the *Próspero Pinzón* had disembarked in Puerto Cristóbal, occupied the Mayor's office, and distributed government proclamations. Eleven months later, Anatolio Calderón headed for this occupied city.

Anatolio got to the railway shortly before midnight. Between La Chorrera and the first bridge over the waters of Lake Gatún he'd found a little hamlet of ten or twelve huts whose straw roofs touched the ground, and with his loaded rifle pointed in the face of a woman, managed to get her husband (supposing it was her husband) to hand over a cotton shirt that seemed to be his single belonging, and put it on instead of the black jacket with nine buttons that was his soldier's uniform. Dressed like that, he waited for the morning train before the bridge, hidden behind the carcass of an abandoned dredger; when he saw the locomotive pass, he leapt aboard the last freight car, and the first thing he did was throw his felt hat into the water so it wouldn't give him away. Lying on his back on top of three hundred bunches of bananas, Anatolio watched the sky of the Isthmus pass by above his head, the invading branches of the *guácimo* trees, the *cocobolos* filled with colorful birds; and the warm breeze of a day without rain messed his straight hair and slipped inside his shirt, the friendly clatter of the train rocked and didn't threaten him; and during those three hours of the journey he felt so calm, so unpredictably relaxed, that he fell asleep and forgot for an instant the stabbings of fear. The grinding of the carriages as the train switched gears woke him. They were stopping, he thought, they were arriving some-where. He peeked over the side of the car and the luminous image of the bay, the reflection of the afternoon sun on the water of the Caribbean, hurt his eyes but also made him feel briefly happy. Anatolio grabbed his bundle, leaned with difficulty on the squashed bananas, and jumped. When he landed, his body rolled and Anatolio hurt himself with the horseshoe, tore the shirt on invisible pebbles, and pierced the thumb of his left hand on a thorn, but none of that mattered to him, because he'd finally arrived at his destination. Now it was just a question of finding somewhere to spend the night, and in the morning, as a legitimate pas-senger or as a stowaway, his new life would have begun.

He was at the foot of Mount Hope. Although he might not have known, he was at that moment very close to the four thousand graves of the railway workers who'd died in the first months of the construc-tion, half a century before. Anatolio thought of waiting until dark before approaching the city, but the six o'clock mosquitoes forced him to get ahead of himself. As the sun set he'd already begun to advance toward the north, between the remains of the French Canal, on his right, and Limón Bay, on his left. These were genuine wastelands, and Anatolio felt sure he wouldn't be seen as long as he stayed there, because no govern-ment soldier would venture into those quagmires—the rain had loos-ened the earth from the former trench—unless he'd received a direct order. After the distance he'd traveled, the leather of his boots had started to smell, and the swamps weren't helping matters. Anatolio began to feel a pressing need to find a dry place to take them off and clean the insides with a cloth, because he could feel the skin between his toes riddled with fungus. His shirt smelled of bananas and moss, of its original owner's sweat, and of the wet ground he'd rolled down. And his gray-and-black-checked trousers, those trousers that had earned him the mockery of his comrades in arms, began to reek unbearably, as if it had been a furious wildcat and not a poor student who pissed in them. Anatolio had become distracted by the impertinent festival of his own smells when he suddenly found himself surrounded by darkened houses.

His first instinct was to jump under the closest veranda and hide behind the posts, but he soon realized that the place—it looked like a neighborhood of Colón, but it wasn't: Colón was farther north—was abandoned. He stood up straight again. Anatolio began to walk casually down the single muddy street, chose a dark house at random, and went inside. He felt his way along the walls, went all around, but he didn't find any food, didn't find any drinking water, didn't find any blankets or clothes at all; instead he did hear something moving across the floorboards that could have been a rat, and his head filled with other possible images, snakes or scorpions that would attack him while he slept. Then, as he went back outside again, he saw light shining out of a window, ten or so houses along. He looked up: yes, there were the poles and cables; the glow was coming from electric lights, which incredibly were still working. Anatolio felt apprehensive but also relieved. One house, at least, was inhabited. His hand closed over his rifle. He climbed the porch steps (saw a hammock hanging empty), found the door open, and pushed the screen door. He saw the luxurious furniture, shelves with books and some newspapers and a cupboard with glass doors full of clean crystal, and then he heard a woman's voice, two voices talking amid the sounds of fine china. He followed the voices to the kitchen and discovered that he'd been mistaken: it wasn't two women, it was just one (white but dressed in a black woman's clothes) who was singing in an incomprehensible language. Seeing him come in, the woman dropped the saucepan, which crashed to the floor spitting out potatoes, vegetables, and pieces of stewed fish that splashed Anatolio. At first she didn't move; she stayed still, her black eyes fixed on him, without saying a word. Anatolio explained that he didn't want to hurt her, but that he was going to spend the night in her house and that he needed clothes, food, and all the money she had. She nodded, as if she perfectly understood those needs, and it seemed that everything was going to be fine, until Anatolio took his eye off her for a second, and when he looked back, he saw her gathering up her dress in both hands, with a movement that revealed her pale calves, and take off running for the door. Anatolio managed to feel pity, a fleeting pity, but he thought inevitably of the firing squad that awaited him if he was captured. He raised his rifle and fired, and the bullet pierced the woman near her liver and ended up lodged in the living room cabinet.

Anatolio didn't know where he was and could not have known that the abandoned houses (all except one) of Christophe Colomb were barely a hundred paces from the port, that more than five military vessels of four different nationalities were anchored in the bay, among them the *Próspero Pinzón*, and that—as is at the very least logical—thirty government sentries of the Mompox and Granaderos battalions were patrolling the wharf. Not a single one of them did not hear the shot. Following the orders of Sergeant Major Gilberto Durán Salazar, they divided into two groups to enter Christophe Colomb and encircle the enemy, and it didn't take them long to find the only light on the street and follow it like a squadron of moths. They had not finished surrounding the house when a window opened and an armed silhouette leaned out. Then some of them swept the side wall of the house with bullets and others entered knocking down the screen door and also opening fire indiscriminately, wounding the enemy in both legs but taking him alive. They dragged him to the middle of the street, there where years before all the belongings of an engineer who'd died of yellow fever had been burned in a bonfire, sat him in a chair taken from the same house, on a velvet cushion, and tied his hands behind the wicker back. They formed a firing squad, the Sergeant Major gave the order, and the squad fired. Then one of the soldiers discovered another body in the house, that of the woman, and took her outside to leave her there, so everyone would know the fate of those who gave shelter to Liberals, not to mention cowards. And there, leaning against the chair like a rag doll, her clothes dirty with the executed deserter's blood, Eloísa and I found her, having spent the afternoon in Colón watching the performance of a Haitian fire-eater, a black man with bulging eyes who claimed to be invulnerable to burns by the grace of the spirits.

VIII

The Lesson of Great Events

Pain has no history, or rather, pain is outside history, because it situates its victim in a parallel reality where nothing else exists. Pain doesn't have political commitments; pain is not Conservative, it's not Liberal; it's not Catholic or Federalist or Centralist or Masonic. Pain wipes everything out. Nothing else exists, I've said; and it's true that for me—I can insist without grandiloquence—nothing else existed in those days: the image of that rag doll, found in front of my invaded house, that empty doll, broken on the inside, began to haunt me at night. I can't call it Charlotte, I can't, because that wasn't Charlotte, because Charlotte had left that bullet-ridden body. I began to be frightened: concrete fear (of the armies that would return one day to finish the job and murder my daughter) and abstract, intangible fear as well (of the dark, of noises that might be a rat or a rotten mango falling off a tree in the next street, but that gave rise in my terrorized imagination to the silhouettes of uniformed men, of hands pointing rifles). I couldn't sleep. I spent the nocturnal hours listening to Eloísa cry in the next room, and left her to her weeping, to her own bewildered pain; I refused to console her. Nothing would have been easier than to take the ten steps to her room and her bed, to hug her and weep with her, but I didn't do it. We were alone: we suddenly felt irrevocably alone. And nothing would have been easier for me than to ease my solitude at the same time as consoling my daughter. But I didn't do it; I left her alone, so she would find her own way to comprehend what the violent death of a loved one means, that black pit that opens in the world. How can I justify myself? I was afraid Eloísa would ask for explanations I wouldn't be able to supply. "We're at war," I would have said, aware of the poverty, the futility of that answer, "and these things happen in wars." Of course, that explanation didn't convince me either. But something inside me went on believing that refusing to offer those slight comforts to my daughter, refusing to search out her company (and perhaps her involuntary protection), would eventually expose the cruel joke of which we were the object, and one of these days the heartless joker would appear at the door and reveal Charlotte's actual whereabouts, regretting that his cruel joke hadn't had the desired effect.

It was during those days that I began to spend the nights walking to the port, sometimes getting as far as the Railroad Company, and later the Freight House, that Company warehouse from which I'd have been evicted at gunpoint had I been discovered. Colón, in those wartime nights, was a cold, blue city; walking around it alone, defying tacit or declared curfews depending on the day and the vicissitudes of the war, a civilian (though a lost and desperate civilian) running countless risks. I was too much of a coward to take my tired head's suicidal pursuits seriously, but I can confess that several times I went so far as to imagine a scenario in which I'd fling myself bare-chested with knife in hand at the men of the Mompox battalion, shouting "Long Live the Liberal Party!" and force them to receive my onslaught with bullets or bayonets. I never did, of course, never did anything of the sort. My act of greatest daring, during those dazed nights, was to visit the side streets of Colón the Widow of the Canal had visited, according to legend, and once I was sure I saw Charlotte turn a corner in the company of an African man in a hat, and ran after the specter until I realized I'd lost a shoe between the cobblestones and my scraped heel was bleeding.

I changed. Pain alters us; it's the agent of slight but terrifying disruptions. After several weeks during which I grew gradually familiar with the night, I allowed myself the private exoticism of visiting the Europeans' brothels, and more than once made use of their women (relics in their forties from de Lesseps's times, in some cases heirs of these relics, girls with surnames like Michaud or Henrion who didn't know who Napoleon Bonaparte was or why the French Canal had failed). Later, back in that house where Charlotte survived in a thousand phantasmagorical ways, in her clothes that Eloísa had begun to wear or in the destruction still visible if you looked closely at the glass door of the cabinet, something I can only call shame would descend upon me. At those moments I felt incapable of looking Eloísa in the face, and she, out of some kind of last respect she held for me, was incapable of formulating a single one of the questions that were (clearly) crowding the tip of her tongue. I sensed that my actions were destroying the affection between us, that my behavior was tearing down the bridges that united us. But I accepted it. Life had accustomed me to the idea of collateral victims. Charlotte was one. My relationship with my daughter, one more. We are at war, I thought. In war these things happen.

I attributed to the war, then, the obvious fracture of the bridges, the gap that opened between my daughter and myself from that time on like

some sort of biblical sea. The school suspended services with shameless frequency, and Eloísa, who learned to battle with the absence of her
mother with much more talent than I did, began to have free time and
to enjoy it in ways that didn't involve me. She didn't make me part of her
life (I don't blame her: my sadness, the bottomless pit of my grief, was a
rebuff to any invitation), or rather, her life evolved in directions I didn't
understand. And in rare moments of lucidity—nights of mourning and
fear can be rich in revelations—I managed to glimpse that something
more concrete than Charlotte's death had come into play. But I didn't
manage to give it a name. Busy as I was with the memory of my shred-
ded happiness, with attempts to accept the reality of the devastation, to
process the information of my shattered life and dominate the anguish
of nocturnal solitude, I didn't manage to name it. . . . And I realized this:
in the long Colón nights, on my long walks, sweaty and smelly, through
streets that just a little while ago I'd strolled well dressed and fragrant,
names of things were disappearing. Insomnia gradually takes away
the memory of things: I forgot to wash, forgot to clean my teeth, and I
remembered (that is, remembered that I'd forgotten) when it was already
too late; the Chinese butcher, the Gringo soldier at the station, the man
who sold sugar cane on Sundays from his beach stall, raised their hands
instinctively to their faces at the blast of the breath of my greeting, or
took a step back as if pushed when I opened my mouth. . . . I lived outside of conscience; I also lived outside the tangible world around me: I
experienced my being a widower like exile, but without ever figuring out
where I'd been expelled from, where I was forbidden to return. On better days I could glimpse a slight hope: just as I'd forgotten the most basic
rules of urban life, maybe the despair itself was forgettable.

And that was how the Political Gorgon finally invaded the
Altamirano-Madinier household. That was how History, incarnate in

the particular destiny of a cowardly and confused soldier, dashed my pretensions to neutrality, my attempts at separation, my eagerness for studied apathy. The lesson I learned from Great Events was clear and easy: you won't escape, they told me, it's impossible for you to escape. It was a real show of strength, as well, for at the same time the Gorgon ruined my illusory plans for earthly happiness, it also ruined those of my country. Now I could go into detail about those days of disorientation and despair, about the anguish painted on Eloísa's face when she looked straight at me, about my lack of interest in remedying that anguish. Were we talking about shipwrecks? That was when mine happened. But now, after the painful lessons the Gorgon and the Angel have taught me, how can I attend to those banalities? How can I talk about my pain and that of my daughter, of the nights of apolitical tears, of the outside-of-history solitude that overtook me, heavy as a wet poncho? The death of Charlotte—my lifesaver, my last resort—at the hands of the War of a Thousand Days was a memorandum in which someone reminded me of the hierarchies that must be respected. Someone, Angel or Gorgon, reminded me that beside the Republic of Colombia and its vicissitudes my minuscule life was a grain of salt, a frivolous and unimportant matter, the tale the idiot tells, the sound, the fury, and so on. Someone called me to order to make me realize that in Colombia more important things than my thwarted happiness were happening.

An essentially Colombian paradox: after a brilliant campaign by which he managed to recapture almost the entire Isthmus of Panama, the revolutionary General Benjamín Herrera found himself suddenly forced to sign a peace treaty in which his army and his party came out the losers from every angle. What had happened? I thought of the words my father had said to me on a certain day in 1885: when Colón was destroyed by fire and war and yet the Canal—that unfinished

Canal—was spared, I told him we'd had good luck and he said no, we'd had Gringo ships. Well then, the War of a Thousand Days was special for several reasons (for its hundred thousand dead, for having left the National Treasury in complete ruin, for having humiliated half the population of Colombia and turned the other half into voluntary humiliators); but it was also special for less conspicuous and, another paradox, more serious circumstances. No more beating about the bush: the War of a Thousand Days, which actually lasted one thousand one hundred and twenty-eight, was special for having been resolved from start to finish in the bowels of foreign ships. Generals Foliaco and De la Rosa did not negotiate aboard the *Próspero Pinzón* but on the HMS *Tribune*; Generals Foliaco and Albán did not negotiate on the *Cartagena*, which arrived around the same time in Colón, but on the USS *Marietta*. After the surrender of my Schizophrenic City, where did they arrange the prisoner swaps? Not on the *Almirante Padilla*, but on the *Philadelphia*. And last but not least: after the various peace proposals made by Benjamín Herrera and his isthmian revolutionaries, after the radical refusal of those proposals on the part of the stubborn Conservative government, where was the negotiation table that led to the Treaty? Where did they sign the little piece of paper that put an end to the one thousand one hundred and twenty-eight days of relentless slaughter? It was not on board the Liberal *Cauca*, or on the Conservative *Boyaca*: it was on the USS *Wisconsin*, which was neither one nor the other but was much more. . . . We Colombians were taken by the hand of our big brothers, the Grown-up Countries. Our fate was played for on the gaming tables of other houses. In those poker games that resolved the most important issues of our history, we Colombians, Readers of the Jury, just sat there like statues.

November 12, 1902. The postcard that commemorates that disastrous date is well known (everyone's inherited the image from their victorious or defeated fathers or grandfathers; there's no one in Colombia who doesn't have a copy of that memento mori on a nationwide scale). Mine was printed by Maduro & Sons, Panama, and measures fourteen by ten centimeters. Along the bottom edge in red letters appear the names of the participants. From left to right and from Conservative to Liberal: General Victor Salazar. General Alfredo Vásquez Cobo. Doctor Eusebio Morales. General Lucas Caballero. General Benjamín Herrera. But then we remember (those who have the postcard) that there is among these figures—the Conservatives with mustaches, the others bearded— a notable absence, a kind of emptiness that opens in the middle of the image. For Admiral Silas Casey, the great architect of the *Wisconsin* Treaty, the one in charge of talking to those on the right and convincing them to meet with those on the left, is not in it. He's not there. Nevertheless, his northerly presence is felt in every corner of the yellowing image, in each of its silver cells. The dark and vaguely baroque tablecloth is the property of Silas Casey; on the table are piled, as if this has nothing to do with them, the untidy papers of the Treaty that will change forever the history of Colombia, will change forever what it means to be Colombian, and it is Silas Casey who put them there just a few minutes before. And now I'll concentrate on the rest of the scene. General Herrera appears to be separated from the table, as if the bigger boys won't let him play; General Caballero, in the name of the revolutionaries, is signing. And I say, Bring me a movie camera! Because I need to fly over the scene, enter the *Wisconsin* through the skylight, and float above the table with its baroque cloth, and read that preamble, in which the signatories establish, with perfectly straight faces, that they have gathered there to "put an end to the bloodshed," to "procure the reestablishment of peace in the Republic," and above all so that the Republic of Colombia "can bring to a satisfactory conclusion the negotiations pending on the Panama Canal."

Four words, Readers of the Jury, just four words: *Negotiations. Pending. Panama. Canal.* On paper, of course, they seem inoffensive; but there is a newly made bomb in them, a charge of nitroglycerine from which there is now no possible escape. In 1902, while José Altamirano, a little man without historical importance, fought tooth and nail for the recuperation of his tiny life, while he, an insignificant father of a daughter, forced himself to ford the river of shit his life as a widower (and his motherless daughter's) had become, the negotiations that had been going on between the United States and the Republic of Colombia had already claimed the health of two ambassadors in Washington; my country began by putting Carlos Martínez Silva in charge, and months later Martínez Silva was retired from the post, without having advanced matters in the slightest, and died of physical exhaustion, pale, haggard, and gray, so tired he even gave up talking in his final days. His replacement was José Vicente Concha, former Minister of War, an unsubtle and rather brutal man who faced up to the negotiations with an iron will and was steelily defeated in a few months; subject to great nervous excitement, Concha suffered a violent crisis before leaving for Bogotá, and the port authorities in New York were forced to restrain him in a straitjacket while he shouted at the top of his lungs words that no one understood: *Soberanía, Imperio, Colonialismo.* Concha died a short time later, in his bed in Bogotá, ill and hallucinating, occasionally cursing in languages he didn't know (and the lack of knowledge of which had been one of his main problems as a negotiator of international treaties). His wife said he spent his final days talking of the Mallarino-Bidlack Treaty of 1846, or arguing over articles and conditions with an invisible interlocutor who was sometimes President Roosevelt and at others an anonymous man who in his delirium he called Boss and whose identity has never been, nor will it ever be, established.

"Sovereignty," shouted poor Concha without being understood by anyone. "Empire. Colonialism."

On November 23, the ink not yet dry on the *Wisconsin* Treaty, came the turn of Tomás Herrán, chargé d'affaires of the Colombian legation in Washington and destined to go down in history as the Last of the Negotiators. And while there, in Caribbean America, Eloísa and I began, after enormous efforts, to find our way through the labyrinths of sorrow, in icy North America, Don Tomás Herrán, a sad-looking, reserved sixty-year-old who spoke four languages and was equally indecisive in all of them, was trying to do the same through the labyrinths of the Treaty. That's how Christmas went by in Colón: for Panamanians, the signing of the Treaty was a matter of life or death, and during the last days of 1902, when they hadn't yet replaced the telegraph wires destroyed by the war, it didn't seem unusual for me to leave the house at six in the morning (I could rarely sleep) and find myself in the port waiting with the crowds for the first steamers and their cargo of U.S. papers (the French were no longer news). That was an especially dry and hot season, and before the first roosters crowed, the heat had already driven me out of bed. My daybreak ritual consisted of a cup of coffee, a spoonful of quinine, and a cold shower, which I depended on to exorcise the night's demons, the recurring image of Charlotte sitting dead beside an executed deserter, the memory of the appalling silence Eloísa kept at the sight of her mother's body, the memory of the pressure of her hand on mine, the memory of her crying and shaking, the memory of . . . Dear reader, my private exorcisms were not always successful. Then I'd reach for the extreme remedy of whiskey, and more than a few times managed to get the stabbings of fear to stop with the first seethings of alcohol in the pit of my stomach.

In January celebrations burst out in the streets of Colón. After doubts and reticence, after bloodless tugs and slackenings, the U.S. Secretary of State John Hay issued an ultimatum that seemed to come from the mouth of President Roosevelt: "If this isn't signed now," he said, "we'll build the Canal in Nicaragua." A hasty order came from Bogotá. Forty-eight hours later, in the middle of the night, Tomás Herrán wrapped himself up in a black woolen cloak and, defying the biting winter wind, walked to Hay's house.

The Treaty was signed in the first fifteen minutes of his visit, between glasses of brandy. The Canal Company was authorized to sell to the United States the rights and concessions relating to the works. Colombia guaranteed the United States complete control of a ten-kilometer-wide zone between Colón and Panama City. The cession was for a space of one hundred years. In exchange, the United States would pay ten million dollars. The protection of the Canal would be Colombia's responsibility; but if Colombia was unable to do so effectively, the United States reserved the right to intervene . . .

Et cetera. Et cetera. A long et cetera.

Three days later, the arrival of the papers that carried the news was celebrated as if the times of Ferdinand de Lesseps were back for the Isthmus. Paper lanterns adorned the streets, tropical orchestras spontaneously emerged to fill the air with the metallic sound of their trombones and tubas and trumpets. Eloísa, who at sixteen years of age was already wiser than me, dragged me forcibly to Front Street, where people were drinking toasts with whatever was at hand. In front of the great stone arch of the railway offices people were dancing and waving the flags of the two signatory nations: yes, the air was again impregnated with patriotism, and yes, I had difficulties breathing again. And then, as we walked between the offices and the sleeping carriages, Eloísa turned around and said to me, "Grandfather would have enjoyed this."

"What do you know?" I barked at her. "You hardly even knew him."

Yes, that's what I said. It was a cruel retort; Eloísa withstood it unblinkingly, perhaps because she understood better than I the complexity of what I was feeling at that moment, perhaps because she was starting to become sadly resigned to my tormented-widower's reactions. I looked at her: she had turned into a living portrait of Charlotte (her small breasts, her tone of voice); she'd had enough presence of mind to cut her hair short like a boy, trying to reduce as much as possible the resemblance that tormented me; however, at that moment I felt a gap opening up between us (a Darien Jungle) or that an insuperable obstruction (a Sierra Nevada) arose between us. She was turning into someone else: the woman she was becoming was colonizing her territory, appropriating the city in ways that I, an incomer, could not imagine. Of course, Eloísa was right: Miguel Altamirano would have liked to have witnessed that night, written about it even if no one would publish the article, left a record of the Great Event for the benefit of future generations. That's what I was thinking all night, in the 4th of July saloon, while I drank half a bottle of whiskey with a banker from San Francisco and his lover, next to the statue of Columbus, where the Haitian fire-eater was still performing his spectacle. And as we walked back home, along the shore of Limón Bay, seeing the lights of the ships flickering in the distance like fireflies over the black sheet of the night, I felt for the first time at the back of my mouth the bitter taste of resentment.

Eloísa was walking with both hands clasped around my arm, like when she was a little girl; our feet were stepping on the same ground where the deserter Anatolio Calderón had stepped, but neither of us spoke of that disgrace that was still with us, that would never, never leave us alone, that would sleep in our house like a pet until the end of time. But as we crossed the dark street of the ghost town of Christophe Colomb, it was as if all the ghosts of my past came out to meet me. I didn't think the word, but as I climbed the porch steps the notion of revenge had already installed itself in my mind. Not only would I not flee from the Angel of History again, not only would I not seek a submissive distance from the Gorgon of Politics, but I would make them my slaves: I would burn the wings of one, decapitate the other. There, lying in the hammock at midnight on January 24, I declared war on them.

And while this was happening in the tropical heat, up there, in the frigid fog of perfidious Albion, Joseph Conrad was having a little tantrum.

He'd been invited to London to meet an American (a banker, just like the man in the 4th of July: the correspondence is insignificant but no less deserving of mention). The banker says he's a great admirer of the maritime novels: he recites the beginning of *Almayer's Folly* from memory, feels like a close friend of Lord Jim although the novel had struck him as "dense and tedious." In the middle of dinner, the banker asks Conrad "when he'd spin some more yarns about the sea," and Conrad explodes: he's sick of being seen as a writer of little adventures, a Jules Verne of the Southern Seas. He protests and complains, explains himself too much undoubtedly, but at the end of the argument the banker, who can smell the need for money the way dogs can smell fear, offers him a deal: Conrad will write a commissioned novel of around one hundred thousand words with a maritime setting; the banker, as well as paying him, will arrange for publication by *Harper's Magazine*. Conrad accepts (the tantrum has reached its end), mostly because he already has the subject for the novel, and has even written a few notes for it.

These are not easy days. For months now, Conrad and Ford Madox Ford have been writing a four-handed, romantic, adventure novel, the most obvious object of which is to make (quick, immediate) money to alleviate both their financial difficulties. But the collaboration has not gone well: it's taken much longer than they planned, and has created situations of tension between the friends and their wives that little by little have poisoned the cordial atmosphere between them. Complaints and apologies, accusations and alibis, go back and forth. "I'm doing my damnedest," writes Conrad. *Blackwood's*, the magazine that was to publish the novel, has now turned it down; debts pile up on his desk and represent, to Conrad, a real threat against his family. Tormented by the guilt of his neglected responsibilities, he sees his wife as a widow and his sons as orphans; they depend on him and he has nothing to give them. His health does not make matters any easier: he has one attack of gout after another, and when it's not gout it's dysentery, and when it's not dysentery it's rheumatism. As if that weren't enough, nostalgia for the sea overwhelms him more and more each day, and during those days he has seriously considered the possibility of looking for a captain's post and returning to his old life. "What I wouldn't give for a cutter and the River Fatshan," he writes, "or that magnificent dilapidated ship between the Mozambique Canal and Zanzibar!" In these conditions, the banker's commission is a cause for gratitude.

The idea has been growing gradually in his head. It started as a short story, something about the length of "Youth," maybe, or "Amy Foster" at most, but Conrad misjudged the elements (or perhaps he was aware that short stories don't sell well) and the original concept swelled as the days and months went by, going from twenty-five thousand to eighty thousand words, going from a single setting to two or three, and all that before he'd started actually writing it. During those days the project disappears from Conrad's letters and conversations. At the time of the proposal, Conrad knows little about it, but one of the things he does know is that the story will be a hundred thousand words long, and that its protagonists will be a group of Italians. His memory has returned to the admired figure of Dominic Cervoni, the Ulysses of Corsica; his memory goes back to 1876, the year of his travels to the ports of the Caribbean, the year of his experiences as a gunrunner in Panama, the year of experiences that led him to the (secret and never confessed) suicide attempt. In those initial notes, Cervoni has been transformed into a *capataz* of *cargadores* who has ended up working in a Caribbean port. His name is Gian Battista, and his surname is Nostromo. Around that time Conrad reads the maritime memoirs of a certain Benton Williams, and finds there the story of a man who has stolen a shipment of silver. That story and the image of Cervoni blend in his head. . . . Maybe (he thinks) his Nostromo doesn't need to be a thief; maybe circumstances have led him to the booty by chance, and he takes advantage of them. But what circumstances? In what situation can a decent man find himself forced to steal a shipment of silver? Conrad doesn't know. He closes his eyes and tries to imagine motives, construct scenes, assemble psychologies. But he fails.

In March 1902, Conrad had written: "*Nostromo* shall be a first-rate story." Months later his enthusiasm had declined: "There is no help and no hope; there is only the duty to try, to try everlastingly with no regard for success." One day, in the middle of an unusual burst of optimism and shortly after the conversation with the banker, he takes out a blank sheet of paper, puts the number 1 on the top right-hand corner, and in capital letters writes: "NOSTROMO. PART FIRST. THE ISABELS." But nothing more happens; the words do not come to him. Conrad immediately notices something is wrong. He crosses out "THE ISABELS" and writes: "THE SILVER OF THE MINE." And then, for reasons that are inexplicable, the images and memories, the oranges he saw in Puerto Cabello and the stories of galleons he heard when they put into port at Cartagena, the waters of Limón Bay, its mirror-like stillness and islands that are really the Mulatas crowd into his head. It's that moment again: the book has begun. Conrad experiences it with excitement, but he knows the excitement will not last, that soon it'll be replaced by the most assiduous visitors to his desk: his linguistic uncertainties, architectural anguish, and financial anxieties. This novel must succeed, thinks Conrad; otherwise, bankruptcy awaits him.

I've lost track of the nights I've spent imagining, like a man obsessed, the writing of the novel; and once, I confess, I imagined that Conrad's desk caught fire again like it caught fire while he was writing *Romance* (or maybe it was *The Mirror of the Sea*, who can remember?), taking with it a good part of the manuscript; but I imagined that this time it was the story of *Nostromo*, the good silver thief, that was lost to the flames. I close my eyes, I picture the scene, the desk that belonged to Ford Madox Ford's father, the paraffin lamp exploding and the flammable paper burning to cinders in seconds, consuming the sentences of exquisite calligraphy but halting grammar. I also imagine the presence of Jessie Conrad (who comes in with a cup of tea for the patient), or little Borys, whose unbearable crying slows down the already problematic writing of the novel. I close my eyes again. There's Conrad, sitting in front of a smudged page that has not been burned, remembering the things he saw in Colón, on the railway lines, in Panama City. There he is, transforming the little he knows or remembers about Colombia, or, rather, transforming Colombia into a fictional country, a country whose history Conrad can invent with impunity. There he is, marveling at the course events in the book have taken from the starting point of those distant memories. He writes to his friend Cunninghame Graham (May 9): "I want to talk to you of the work I am engaged on now. I hardly dare avow my audacity—but I am placing it in South America in a Republic I call Costaguana. However, the book is mostly about Italians." Conrad, astute eliminator of his own footprints, makes no mention of Colombia, the original convulsive Republic disguised behind the Costaguanan speculations. A little while later he insists on the suffering Colombia/Costaguana is causing him (July 8): "I am dying over the curst *Nostromo* thing. All my memories of Central America seem to slip away." And even more: "I just had a glimpse twenty-five years ago—a short glance. That is not enough *pour bâtir un roman dessus*." If *Nostromo* is a building, the architect Conrad needs to find a new supplier of raw material. London, luckily for him, is full of Costaguanans. Will it be necessary to resort to those men, exiles like him, men—like him— whose place in the world is roving and vague?

As the days pass and the written pages pile up on the desk, he realizes that the story of Nostromo, the Italian sailor, has lost its direction: its foundations are weak, its plot banal. Summer arrives, a fainthearted, bland summer, and Conrad devotes it to voracious, desperate reading, in an attempt to season his paltry memories. Will you allow me an inventory? He reads the Caribbean maritime memoirs of Frederick Benton Williams and the Paraguayan terrestrial memoirs of George Frederick Masterman. He reads Cunninghame Graham's books (*Hernando de Soto*, *Vanished Arcadia*), and books that Cunninghame Graham recommends: *Wild Scenes in South America*, by Ramón Páez, and *Down the Orinoco in a Canoe*, by Santiago Pérez Triana. His memories and his readings intermingle: Conrad no longer knows what he lived and what he has read. At night, nights when the threat of depression turns into deep and dark oceans of insomnia, he tries to establish the difference (and fails); by day, he fights tooth and nail with the fiendish English language. And all the time he wonders: What is it, what's it like, this Republic whose story I'm trying to tell? What is Costaguana? What the devil is Colombia?

At the beginning of September, Conrad receives a visit from an old enemy: gout, that aristocratic affliction that, like his surnames, is inherited from his family. The cause of that particular crisis, which for Conrad is one of the most terrible in his long history as victim of the disease, lies in the tale he's working on, in the anguish and fears and ghosts provoked by the unmanageable material he is confronting. Conrad spends ten whole days in bed, devastated by the pain in his joints, by the irrefutable conviction that his right foot is in flames and the big toe of that foot the epicenter of the blaze. For those ten days he requires the company of Miss Hallowes, the selfless woman who acts as his secretary so Conrad can dictate the pages he can't write by hand. Miss Hallowes puts up with the incomprehensible irascibility of this haughty man; the secretary doesn't know it, but what Conrad dictates to her from his bed, what he dictates with his feet uncovered in spite of the cold—they hurt him so much he can't even bear the weight of the covers on them—provokes hitherto unknown levels of nervous tension, pressure, and depression in the novelist. "I feel like I'm walking a tightrope," he writes at the time. "If I falter I am lost." With the arrival of autumn he has the increasingly frequent feeling of losing his balance, that the rope is about to snap.

And then he asks for help.

He writes to Cunninghame Graham and asks after Pérez Triana.

He writes to his editor at Heinemann and asks after Pérez Triana.

Little by little we begin to draw nearer.

The United States Senate took less than two months to ratify the Herrán–Hay Treaty: there were newspapers arriving in the bay again, long parties in the streets of Colón-Aspinwall again, and for a few moments it seemed that its ratification by the Colombian Congress, the only remaining formality, would happen almost automatically. But taking a step back and watching events with a tiny degree of coolness (as I regarded them from the house in Christophe Colomb; I will not use the word *cynicism*, nor will I object to others using it) was all that was needed to notice, in these festive and jubilant streets, at the railway crossings or on the walls of every public building, the same geological faults that had divided Colombians since Colombians could recall. The Conservatives supported the Treaty unconditionally; the Liberals, ever the wet blankets, dared to raise the strangest ideas, like that the payment was small and the length of the concession was large, and to the most audacious it seemed a tiny bit confusing, but just a tiny bit, that the famous ten-kilometer strip should be governed by U.S. law.

"Sovereignty," José Vicente Concha, that crazy old man, shouted absurdly from somewhere. "Colonialism."

Readers of the Jury, allow me to tell you a secret: beneath colored lamps and the music of hastily gathered bands (beneath the drunken enthusiasm reigning in Colón-Gomorrah), the pure and deep divisions of the War of a Thousand One Hundred and Twenty-eight Days continued to shudder like tectonic plates. But—a curious thing—only we cynics could detect this; only those of us who'd been vaccinated against any sort of reconciliation or camaraderie, only those of us who dared in silence to profane the Sacred Word of the *Wisconsin* received the true revelation: the war, in Panama, was far from over. It remained active in underground ways; at some point—I thought prophetically—that clandestine or submerged war would surface like a cursed white whale, to take some air or look for food or kill fictional captains, and the result would be invariably disastrous.

So, in the middle of May, the whale surfaced. The Indian Victoriano

Lorenzo, who had fought for the Liberals in the war and trained guerrillas who drove the government troops mad, had escaped from his prison on board the *Bogotá*. He had received some terrible news: the victors all over the Isthmus, and especially those of his native land, were expecting him to be tried for war crimes. Lorenzo decided not to sit and bide his time until a trial he knew would be corrupt, and spent a week waiting for an opportune night. One Friday, as evening fell, a vicious thunderstorm bucketed down over Panama; Victoriano Lorenzo decided there would be no better moment, and in the middle of the cloudy night dived through the curtains of rainwater (those heavy drops that hurt your head) into the sea, swam to the port and hid out in General Domingo González's Panama City house. But refugee life didn't last long: not twenty-four hours had passed when the stubborn government forces were already knocking down the door of the house.

Victoriano Lorenzo did not return to the cells of the *Bogotá* but was taken to an airtight vault and chained up there until the arrival in the city of General Pedro Sicard Briceño, military commander of Panama. Unusual demonstrations of efficiency on the part of General Sicard: on May 13, during the night, he decided that the Indian Victoriano Lorenzo would be tried by verbal court-martial; by noon on the fourteenth, posters were up informing the general public; on the fifteenth, at five in the afternoon, Lorenzo was killed by thirty-six bullets shot from a distance of ten paces by a firing squad. Usual demonstrations of cunning on the part of the same General: the defense was put under the charge of a sixteen-year-old trainee; no witnesses were allowed to speak in favor of the accused; the sentence of capital punishment was carried out with deliberate haste, to prevent the President from having time to receive the telegrams pleading for mercy that the Panamanian authorities from both parties sent. For the Liberals of Colón the whole trial had a certain stale (or rather rotten) taste, and the fact that a firing squad enacted the sentence did not prevent many from recalling the crossbeam set up across the railway lines and Pedro Prestán's hanging body, his hat still on his head.

The Panama newspapers, gagged (for a change) by a Conservative decree, at first kept an obliging silence. But on July 23 all of Colón awoke papered. I walked down the quagmires we had for streets, skirted the cargo docks, and darted through the fruit stalls in the market, I even visited the hospital, and everywhere saw the same thing: on the telegraph poles, a poster announced the imminent publication, in the Liberal newspaper *El Lápiz* (number 85, special eight-page edition), of an article on the murder of Victoriano Lorenzo. The advertisement caused two immediate responses (which did not appear posted anywhere). Secretary of Government Aristides Arjona decreed resolution number 127A, declaring that the description of a sentence issued by a military tribunal as "murder" to be in contravention of the 6th ordinance of the 4th article of the legislative decree of January 26. And while the resolution provided for a caution to be issued against the publisher of the newspaper as set out in the 1st ordinance of the 7th article of the same decree, and by virtue of that caution publication of the newspaper was suspended until further notice, Colonel Carlos Fajardo and General José María Restrepo Briceño, much more expeditious, visited Pacífico Vega's printing press, recognized the publisher of the newspaper, and beat the hell out of him with their boots, swords, and batons, not before spilling and stamping on the type, destroying the presses, and publicly burning the existing stocks of *El Lápiz* (number 85, special eight-page edition). The newspaper was subversive and must be punished. So ordered.

And that was the straw that broke the camel's back. As time goes by it seems increasingly clear to me that it was at that moment, at nine-fifteen on that July evening, that the map of the Republic began to crack. All earthquakes have an epicenter, don't they? Well then, this is the one that interests me. The Liberal newspapers, indignant over the execution of the Indian Victoriano Lorenzo, took the aggression of the military boot (and sword, and baton) very badly; but nothing had prepared us for the words that appeared in *El Istmeño* the following Saturday, and that arrived in Colón on the morning's first train. I'm not going to inflict on my tolerant readers the entire contents of that new explosive charge; it's enough to know that they harked back to the times of the Spanish Empire, when the name of Colombia "resounded in human ears with incomparable fame," and Panama, seeking "a golden future," did not hesitate to join that nation. The rest of the text (published between an advertisement for a herbal remedy for gaining weight and another for a manual on learning hypnotism) was a long declaration of regret; and after wondering like a resentful lover if Colombia had reciprocated the affection Panama had lavished upon it, the shameless author—who with every phrase gave new meaning to the word *corny*—wondered if the Isthmus of Panama was happy belonging to Colombia. "Would it not be more content separate from the Republic and constituting itself as a sovereign and independent Republic of its own?" Immediate reply: Secretary of Government Aristides Arjona decreed resolution number 35 of the year of Our Lord 1903, declaring that those questions expressed "subversive ideas contrary to national integrity" and violated the 1st ordinance of the 4th article of decree 84 of the same year. Therefore *El Istmeño* had earned the corresponding sanctions, and publication was suspended for a period of six months. So ordered.

In spite of the sanctions, fines, and suspensions, there was no longer anything to be done: the idea was left floating in the air like an observation balloon. In the Darien Jungle, I swear, though I've not seen it, the land began to open (geology receiving orders from politics), and Central America began to float free toward the ocean; in Colón, I swear, with full knowledge of proceedings, it was like a new word had entered the citizens' lexicon.... One walked among the ruckus and smells of Front Street and could hear it in all the accents of Spanish, from the Caribbean Spanish of Cartagena to the purest *bogotáno*, from the Cuban to the Costa Rican. "Separation?" people asked each other on the street. "Independence?" These words, still abstract, still uncut, made their way up north as well; weeks later the steamship *New Hampshire* arrived in Colón, with a particular edition of *New York World* in its hold. A long article about the question of the Canal contained, among other explosive charges, the following:

> *Information has reached this city that the State of Panama, which embraces all the proposed Canal Zone, stands ready to secede from Colombia and enter into a Canal Treaty with the United States. The State of Panama will secede if the Colombian Congress fails to ratify the Canal Treaty.*

The anonymous text was widely read in Bogotá, and very soon came to form part of the government's worst nightmares. "What the Gringos want is to frighten us," said one of those battle-hardened congressmen. "And we're not going to give them that pleasure." On August 17, those nightmares leapt from the unconscious to reality: on a day of unbearably strong wind, a wind that made the deputies' hats fly from their heads, that forced open the finest umbrellas and inconsiderately ruined the ladies' hairstyles—and made one or two suffer a wee bit of embarrassment—the Colombian Congress unanimously rejected the Herrán-Hay Treaty. Neither of the two representatives from the

Isthmus was present for the vote, but no one seemed to care too much. Washington trembled with fury. "Those contemptible little creatures in Bogotá ought to understand how much they are jeopardizing things and imperiling their own future," said President Roosevelt, and days later added: "We may have to give a lesson to those jackrabbits."

On August 18, Colón awoke in mourning. The deserted streets seemed to be preparing for a state funeral (which was not all that far from the truth); days later, one of the few Liberal newspapers that had survived Aristides Arjona's purges published a cartoon I still have; in fact, I have it here, in front of me, while I write. It has several scenes and is not terribly clear. In the background is the capital of Colombia; a little lower down, a coffin on a funeral carriage, and on the coffin the words: HERRÁN-HAY TREATY. Sitting on a rock, a man wearing a Colombian peasant hat weeps disconsolately, and standing next to him, leaning on his cane, Uncle Sam looks at a woman pointing the way to Nicaragua. . . . If I have described it in detail, it's not, dear readers, on a whim. In the weeks after August 17, those weeks that, seeing what they presaged, passed almost masochistically slowly, in all of Panama people talked of the Treaty's death or demise, never of its rejection or failure to be approved. The Treaty was an old friend and had died of a sudden heart attack, and in Colón the rich paid for Masses to lament its passing from the world of the living, and some paid more so the priest would include in his words the promise of resurrection. Those days—when the Canal in our heads turned into some sort of Jesus Christ the Savior, capable of miracles, dead at the hands of impious men and who would rise from the dead—have remained associated with the cartoon in my memory.

I could swear that the cartoon was in my pocket that morning, at the end of October, when I arrived at the Railroad Company docks, having spent the night wandering the tolerant streets and fallen asleep on the veranda of my house (on the wooden floorboards, not in the hammock, so I wouldn't wake Eloísa with the creaking sound the beams made whenever someone lay down in it). It hadn't been, I must confess, an easy night: after Charlotte's death, the days of greatest pain had passed by then, or seemed to have passed, and it seemed possible again that a certain normality, a normal and shared grief, could be established between my daughter and myself; but when I got home, after dark in Christophe Colomb, I heard a too-familiar humming, a music that Charlotte used to sing on her happiest days (those days when she did not regret her decision to stay in Panama). It was a childish tune, the words of which I never knew, because Charlotte didn't remember them; it was a tune that to me always seemed too sad for its ostensible aim of getting an unruly child to sleep. And when my footsteps followed the humming, on arriving at Eloísa's room, I came across the frightful image of my wife, who had returned from the dead and was more beautiful than ever, and it took me a second to discern Eloísa's features beneath her makeup, Eloísa's adolescent body beneath a long African dress, Eloísa's hair beneath a green African scarf: Eloísa playing dress-up in her dead mother's clothes. I can barely imagine my little girl's dismay when she saw me leap toward her (perhaps she thought I was going to embrace her) and slap her across the face, not too hard, but enough to knock one end of the scarf off her head so it lay over her right shoulder like a lock of hair out of place.

The sun was already making itself felt when I began to wait, with the salty wind hitting me in the chest, for the first North American steamer to dock. It turned out to be the *Yucatán*, en route from New York. And there I was, regretting what had happened with Eloísa, thinking without wanting to think of Charlotte, breathing that warm air while the dockers brought the bundles of the foreign newspapers down to the port, when

Dr. Manuel Amador came down off the ship. I wish I'd never seen him, wish I'd never noticed him, wish, having noticed him, that I hadn't been able to deduce what I deduced.

What I must now tell is painful. Who can blame me for looking away, for trying to postpone the suffering as I'm going to do. Yes, I know: I should follow the chronological order of events, but nothing forbids me from taking a leap into the immediate future. . . . Barely a week after that chance meeting with Manuel Amador (a dreadful week), I found myself on my way to London. What forbids me this conjuring trick that hides or defers the least pleasant days in my memory? In fact, is there some contract that obliges me to tell them? Does every individual not reserve the right not to testify against himself? After all, it wouldn't be the first time I hid, I pretended to forget, those troublesome events. I have already spoken of my arrival in London and my meeting with Santiago Pérez Triana. Well, the story I've told up to now is the story I told Pérez Triana over the course of that afternoon in November 1903. The story I told Pérez Triana went this far. Here it stops, here it ends. No one forced me to tell him the rest, nothing suggested that doing so could be beneficial to me. The story Pérez Triana knew ended on this line, with this word.

Santiago Pérez Triana listened to my censored story during lunch, coffee, and an almost four-hour stroll that took us from Regent's Park to Cleopatra's Needle, crossing St. John's Wood and into Hyde Park, with a detour to see the daring people ice skating along the edges of the Serpentine. This was the story; and Pérez Triana found it so interesting, that, at the end of that afternoon, insisting that all exiles were brothers, that voluntary expatriates and banished refugees were of the same species, offered to put me up in his house indefinitely: I could help him with secretarial tasks while I got myself settled in London, although he was very careful not to go into any detail about the tasks he'd entrust to me.

Then he accompanied me to Trenton's, where he paid for the night I'd spent in the hotel and also paid for the night that was beginning. "Get some rest," he said, "get your things in order, as I shall mine. Unfortunately, neither my house nor my wife is well disposed to receiving guests at such short notice. I'll make all the necessary arrangements to have someone come and collect your things. That will be in the late morning. And you, dear friend, I'll expect tomorrow afternoon at five o'clock sharp. By then I'll have arranged what needs to be arranged. And you shall join my household as if you'd been raised in it."

What happened until five the next day has no importance; the world didn't exist until five in the afternoon. Arrival at the hotel in the nocturnal fog. Emotional exhaustion: eleven hours of sleep. Awaken slowly. Late, light lunch. Leave, omnibus, Baker Street, park just about to be illuminated by the gaseous light of the street lamps. A couple strolls by, arm in arm. It has begun to drizzle.

At five o'clock I was in front of 45 Avenue Road. The housekeeper showed me in; she did not speak to me, and I didn't manage to figure out if she was Colombian as well. I had to wait half an hour before my host came down to greet me. I imagine what he must have seen: a man not much younger than himself but from whom he was separated by several layers of hierarchy—he, a famous paradigm of the ruling class; I, an outcast—sitting in the reading chair, with a round hat on his lap and a copy of *Down the Orinoco in a Canoe* in his hand. Pérez Triana saw me reading without any spectacles and told me he envied me. I was wearing . . . What was I wearing that day? I was dressed like a young man: a short-collared shirt, boots so shiny the light from outside drew a silver line on the leather, a pompous, exaggerated knot in my tie. At that time I had started to grow a sparse and still blond beard, darker on the chin and sideburns, almost invisible over my bulging cheeks.

When I saw Pérez Triana come in, I jumped to my feet and returned the book to the pile of three on the side table, apologizing for having picked it up. "That's what it's there for," he said. "But I should change it for something more recent, shouldn't I? Have you read Boylesve's latest? George Gissing's?" He didn't wait for an answer; he kept talking as if he were alone. "Yes, I really must. I mustn't inflict my clumsy amateur attempts at writing on every visitor, and much less when that clumsiness was perpetrated months ago." And thus, as gently as one accompanies a convalescent, he took me by the arm and led me to another smaller room, at the back of the house. Standing next to the bookshelves, a man with weathered skin, a thick, dark beard and pointed mustache, looked over the titles on the leather spines with his left hand in the pocket of his checked jacket. He turned round as he heard us come in, held his right hand out to me, and in the handshake he gave me I felt the calloused hand of a man of experience, the firm grip of that hand that knew the elegance of calligraphy as well as it did eighty-nine ways to knot a rope, and I felt that the contact of our two hands was like the collision of two planets.

"My name is Joseph Conrad," the man introduced himself. "I'd like to ask you some questions."

IX

The Confessions
of José Altamirano

I talked. You better believe I talked. I talked without stopping, desperately: I told him everything, the whole history of my country, the whole story of its violent people and their pacific victims (the history, I mean, of its convulsions). That November night in 1903, while the temperature plummeted precipitously in Regent's Park and the trees obeyed autumn's alopecic tendencies, and while Santiago Pérez Triana watched us, a cup of tea in his hand—steaming up his glasses every time he took a sip—marveling at the twists of fate that had made him a witness of that meeting, that night, no one could have shut me up. Then and there I knew my place in the world. Pérez Triana's sitting room, a place made out of the accumulated remains of Colombian politics, of its games and disloyalties, of its infinite and never well-pondered cruelty, was the scene of my epiphany.

Readers of the Jury, Eloísa dear: at some imprecise moment of that autumn night, the figure of Joseph Conrad—a man who asks me questions and will use my answers to write the history of Colombia, or the history of Costaguana, or the history of Colombia-Costaguana, or the history of Costaguana-Colombia—began to acquire for me an unexpected importance. I have often tried to locate that moment in the chronology of my own life, and recording it, I would very much like to use one of my solemn phrases of a Great Events Participant: "While in Russia the Party of the Workers divided into Bolsheviks and Mensheviks, in London I opened my heart to a Polish writer." Or: "Cuba leased the base at Guantánamo to the United States, and at the same time José Altamirano presented the history of Colombia to Joseph Conrad." But I can't do it. Writing these sentences is impossible, because I don't know at what moment I opened my heart to him, nor when I handed over the history of my Republic. As the *bogotáno* biscuits Pérez Triana's servant had baked were served? Maybe, but maybe not. As a faint-hearted sleet began to fall on the porch and the London sky prepared to drop the year's first snowfall on the living and the dead? I don't know, I couldn't say. But that doesn't matter; what matters is the intuition I had. And it was this: there, at 45 Avenue Road, under the auspices of Santiago Pérez Triana, I would answer Conrad's questions, satisfy his curiosity; I'd tell him what I knew, all that I'd seen and all that I'd done, and in exchange he (faithfully, nobly) would tell my life story. And then . . . then the things that happen when one's life is written in golden letters on the notice board of destiny would happen.

History will absolve me, I thought, or I believe I thought (the phrase was not an original one). But I actually meant: "Joseph Conrad, absolve me." Because it was in his hands. I was in his hands.

And now, finally, the moment has come. There is no sense in putting it off: I must speak of this guilt. "I could tell you episodes of the separatist revolution that would astound you," says a character in the Damn Con-radian Book. Well then, I can do that, too, I plan to do that, too. And so I return to the image of the *Yucatán*. I return to Manuel Amador.

I had met him, alongside my father, at the banquets Panama City offered years before for Ferdinand de Lesseps. How old was Don Manuel Amador? Seventy? Seventy-five? What had he been doing in New York, this man who was famous for his hatred of foreign travel? Why had no one come to meet him? Why was he in such a hurry and so reluctant to talk, why did he seem tense, why was he determined to be on the first train leaving for Panama City? Then I noticed that he wasn't alone: one person had come to meet him, and had even boarded the *Yucatán* to accompany him (in view of his age, no doubt). It was Herbert Prescott, assistant superintendent of the Railroad Company. Prescott worked in the Railroad offices in Panama City, but it didn't strike me as odd that he should have crossed the whole Isthmus to come and meet an old friend; Prescott, furthermore, knew me well (my father had been the Com-pany's prime publicist for several years) but nevertheless kept walking when I approached to say hello to Manuel Amador. I thought nothing of it; I concentrated on the Doctor. He looked so haggard I instinc-tively stretched out a hand to help him with the briefcase that looked too heavy for him, but Amador snatched the case out of my reach and I didn't insist. It took me several years to understand what happened that day on the Company dock. I had to wait a long time to find out the historical contents of that briefcase, but it took only a couple of days to understand what was happening in my schizophrenic city.

There are good readers and bad readers of reality; there are men able to hear the secret murmur of events better than others. . . . From the moment I saw him flee from the Company dock, I didn't stop thinking about Dr. Amador. His nerves had been clearly legible, as had his haste to get to Panama City; also the company of Herbert Prescott, who a few days later (on October 31 or November 1, I don't know precisely) would return briefly, accompanied by four engine drivers, to take all the idle rolling stock from Colón station to Panama City. Everyone saw the empty trains leave, but no one thought for a second that it was anything other than some routine maintenance procedure. Anyway, the Gringos had always stood out for their rather strange ways of behaving, and I suppose even the witnesses had forgotten about it in a matter of hours. But the trains had gone. Colón was left without trains.

By November 2, however, it was no longer possible to avoid the force of events. While I was at the port waiting for my newspapers to arrive in some passenger steamer, what showed up on the horizon was something else entirely: a gunboat with a U.S. flag. It was the *Nashville*, which had arrived in record time from Kingston, and hadn't yet been announced in the port of Colón (the *Nashville* became one more event, an event anchored innocently in the bay, ready to be interpreted). To me, an obsessive observer, the text of the story was completed the following morning: before the first glimmers of dawn, the lights of the *Cartagena*, battleship, and the *Alexander Bixio*, merchant steamer, were visible from the port; both, of course, were as Colombian as Panama. Before lunch— it was a sunny day, the still waters of Limón Bay sparkled pacifically, and I was planning to pick up Eloísa from school and share a grilled *mojarra* fish while we watched the ships—I guessed what the cargo was. It wasn't very difficult to find out that those two ships, veterans of the War of a Thousand One Hundred and Twenty-eight Days, were bring- ing five hundred government soldiers under the command of Generals Juan B. Tovar and Ramón Amaya to Panamanian soil.

I didn't say anything to Eloísa. Before falling asleep I had associ- ated the hasty and almost clandestine presence of the five hundred soldiers with the trains that Prescott had taken to Panama City. And before dawn broke the certainty that a revolution would take place in Panama City that very day woke me. Before night falls, I thought, the Isthmus of Panama—that place where my father had lived his heyday and his decline, the place where I'd met my father, fallen in love, and had a daughter—before night falls, I said to myself, the Isthmus will have declared its independence from Colombia. The idea of a fractured map frightened me, of course, and imagining the blood and death every revolution brings with it frightened me. . . . It was no later than seven when I threw on a cotton shirt and a felt hat and began to walk toward the Railroad Company. I confess: I wasn't very sure of my intentions, if I even had in mind anything as complex as an intention. But I knew at that moment there was no better place in the world than the Company offices, there was nowhere I would rather have found myself on that November morning.

When I arrived at the offices, in that stone building resembling a colonial prison, I found them deserted. This, moreover, was logical: if there were no trains in the terminus station, why should there be any engine drivers, mechanics or ticket collectors, or any passengers? But I didn't leave, I didn't go looking for anyone, because in some obscure way I had guessed something would happen in this place. I was still formulating these absurd deliberations when three figures came in through the stone arches: Generals Tovar and Amaya were walking together, their pace almost synchronized, and the uniforms they wore seemed about to succumb to the bristling weight of belts, epaulettes, medals, and swords. The third man was Colonel James Shaler, superintendent of the Railroad Company, one of the most popular and respected Gringos in the whole Isthmus and an old acquaintance of my father's. It was obvious from his greeting, halfway between affectionate and concerned, that Colonel

Shaler wasn't expecting to see me there. But I wasn't prepared to move: I ignored the hints and brush-offs, and went as far as to raise one hand to my forehead to salute the governmental generals. Just then, on the other side of the building, the tapping of the telegraph began. I don't know if I've mentioned this yet, but the Railroad Company had the only means of communication between Colón and Panama City. Colonel Shaler found himself obliged to answer the incoming message. Reluctantly, he left me alone with the generals. We were in the entrance hall of the building, barely protected from the killing heat that by then, just after eight in the morning, was beginning to come in through the wide door. None of us spoke: we all feared revealing too much. The generals arched their eyebrows the way children do when they suspect a salesman is trying to trick them. And at that moment I understood.

I understood that Colonel James Shaler and assistant superintendent Herbert Prescott were party to the conspiracy; I understood that Dr. Manuel Amador was one of its leaders. I understood that the conspirators had received news of the imminent arrival of government troops on board the *Cartagena* and the *Alexander Bixio*, and I understood that they'd requested help (I didn't know who from), and the unexpected arrival of the gunboat *Nashville* was that help or part of that help. I understood that the success or failure of the revolution that was just then beginning in Panama City depended on the five hundred soldiers of the Tiradores battalion, under the command of Generals Tovar and Amaya, being able to board a train and cross the Isthmus to put it down before it was too late, and I understood that the Panama City conspirators had understood that, too. I understood that Herbert Prescott had moved the empty trains out of Colón for the same reason that now, after receiving a telegram the contents of which were not difficult to imagine, Colonel Shaler was trying to convince Tovar and Amaya to board on their own, without their troops, the only available train, a single coach and locomotive, and calmly proceed to Panama City. "Your troops will catch up with you as soon as I can get a train, I promise," Colonel Shaler was saying to General Tovar, "but meanwhile, with this heat, there's no reason for you gentlemen to stay here." Yes, that's what he said, and I understood why he said it. And at exactly half past nine in the morning, when Generals Tovar and Amaya fell into the trap and climbed aboard the superintendent's private coach, along with fifteen of their adjutants, subordinates, and messengers, I understood that there, in the railway station, history was about to perpetrate the separation of the Isthmus of Panama and at the same time the disgrace, the profound and irreparable disgrace, of the Republic of Colombia. Readers of the Jury, Eloísa dear, the time for my proud and guilty confession has arrived: I understood all that, I understood that a word of mine could have given the conspirators away and avoided the revolution, and nevertheless I remained silent, I kept quiet with the most silent of silences that had ever been, the most damaging and most malicious. Because Colombia had ruined my life, because I wanted revenge on my country and its meddling, despotic, murderous history.

I had more than one chance to speak. Today I have to ask myself: Would General Tovar have believed me if I, a complete stranger, had told him that the shortage of trains was a revolutionary strategy, that the promise to send the battalion in the first available trains was false, and that by separating from their five hundred men the generals were submitting to the revolution and losing the Isthmus out of pure naïveté? Would he have believed me? Well, the question is merely rhetorical, for this was never my intention. And I remember the moment when I saw them all (General Tovar, General Amaya, and their men) sitting in Colonel Shaler's luxurious carriage, basking in the privileged treatment, receiving complimentary glasses of juice and plates of bite-sized pieces of papaya while waiting for departure time, satisfied at finally having earned the Americans' respect. Dear readers, it was not out of cynicism or sadism or simple egotism that I climbed aboard the coach and insisted on shaking hands with the two government generals. I was moved by something less comprehensible and decidedly less explicable: the proximity to the Great Event and, of course, *my participation in it*, my silent role in Panama's independence or, to be more precise and also more honest, in Colombia's disgrace. To have the chance to speak again, even the horrible temptation to speak, and not to do so: my historical and political destiny was then reduced, and would be forever reduced, to that delicate, catastrophic, and vengeful silence.

Colonel James Shaler's private train began to spit out steam seconds later. The whistle blew a couple of hoarse notes; I was still on board, amazed at the cosmic ironies of which I was the victim, when the landscape outside the window began to move backward. I said a hurried farewell, wished the generals luck, and leapt down onto Front Street. The carriage began to take the generals away; behind, waving the most hypocritical handkerchief in the history of humanity, was Colonel Shaler. I stood beside him as we both engaged in that strange revolutionary task: seeing off a train. The back door of the carriage grew smaller and smaller until there was just a black dot above the rails, then a cloud of gray smoke, and finally not even that: the lines of iron converging, stubborn and determined on the green horizon. Without looking at me, as if not speaking to me, Colonel Shaler said, "I've heard a lot about your father, Altamirano."

"Yes, Colonel."

"It's a shame what happened to him, because the man was on the right side. We're living in complicated times. Besides, I don't know much about journalism."

"Yes, Colonel."

"He wanted what we all want. He wanted progress."

"Yes, Colonel."

"If he had lived to see independence, his sympathies would have been with it."

I was grateful that he wasn't attempting fictions, or half-truths, or concealment strategies. I was grateful he respected my talents (my talents as a reader of the real, as an interpreter of immediate reality).

I said, "His sympathies would have been with those who made the Canal, Colonel."

"Altamirano," said Shaler, "can I ask you a question?"

"Ask away, Colonel."

"You know this is serious, right?"

"I don't understand."

"You know people are risking their lives, don't you?"

I didn't answer.

"I'll make it easy for you. Either you're with us, with independence and progress, or you're against us. It would be best if you decided right now. This Colombia of yours is a backward country. . . ."

"It's not my Colombia, Colonel."

"Does it seem fair to keep the rest behind? Does it seem fair that all these people should be screwed just because that congress of crooks hasn't managed to get their own slice of the Canal?"

"It doesn't seem fair, Colonel."

"It's really not fair, is it?"

"It's really not fair."

"Good. I'm glad we agree on this, Altamirano. Your father was a good man. He would have done whatever it took to see this Canal. Mark my words, Altamirano, mark my words: the Canal will be built and we're the ones who'll build it."

"You'll build it, Colonel."

"But we'll need your help. The patriots, no, the heroes of Panama City will need your help. Are you going to lend us a hand, Altamirano? Can we or can we not count on you?"

I think my head moved, I think I nodded. In any case, Shaler's satisfaction at my consent was reflected in his voice and in his face, and at the back of my mind my thirst for revenge was quenched, the organ of the lowest instincts was satisfied again.

A tired old mule went by pulling a cart. On the back a child with a dirty face and bare feet sat with his legs hanging over the edge. He waved good-bye to us. But Colonel Shaler didn't see, because he'd already left.

And after that, there was no going back. Colonel Shaler must have had magic powers, because with those few words he had magnetized me, turned me into a satellite. During the hours that followed I found myself touched, much to my chagrin, by the waters of the revolution, and there was nothing I could do about it. My will, I seem to recall now, did not have much to do with it: the whirlwind—no, the vortex—of events involved me irremediably. The ingenuous generals went to Panama City; the Tiradores battalion remained in Colón under the command of Colonel Eliseo Torres, a small man with an insolent voice who still looked baby-faced despite the mustache that cast a shadow on both sides of his serpent's mouth. Readers of the Jury: allow me to show you the sound, faint but very evident, of the least noisy revolution in the history of humanity, a march marked by the inevitable rhythm of the clock. And you'll have to be witnesses to that unbearable mechanism.

At 9:35 on the morning of November 3, Herbert Prescott receives in Panama City the telegram that says GENERALS LEFT WITHOUT BAT-TALION STOP ARRIVING 11 AM STOP TAKE AGREED ACTIONS. At 10:30,

Dr. Manuel Amador visits the Liberals Carlos Mendoza and Eusebio Morales, in charge of composing the Declaration of Independence and the Manifesto of the Junta of the Provisional Government. At 11:00: Generals Tovar and Amaya are met with profuse, cordial greetings by Domingo Díaz, the provincial governor, and seven illustrious citizens. At 3:00 p.m., General Tovar receives an anonymous letter telling him to trust no one. Rumors of revolutionary meetings in Panama City proliferate, and the General goes to see Governor Díaz to ask him to order the superintendents of the Railroad to transport the Tiradores battalion immediately to Panama City. At 3:15: Tovar receives the reply to his request. From Colón, Colonel James Shaler refuses to allow his trains to be used to transport the Tiradores battalion, arguing that the government owes large sums of money to the Railroad Company. Tovar, a man with a subtle though perhaps slow sense of smell, begins to get a whiff of something strange, heads for the Chiriquí barracks, headquarters of the National Guard, for detailed discussions of the situation with General Esteban Huertas, commander of the guard.

At 5:00, Generals Tovar, Amaya, and Huertas have sat down on a pine bench outside the barracks, a few steps from the oak door. Tovar and Amaya, concerned by the rumors, begin to discuss military solutions that can be carried out without the support of the Tiradores battalion, captive of the debts. At this, Huertas stands up, gives some excuse, and leaves. Suddenly, a small contingent of eight soldiers bearing Grass rifles arrives. The generals suspect nothing. In the barracks, meanwhile, Huertas orders Captain Marco Salazar to arrest Generals Tovar and Amaya. Salazar, in turn, orders the soldiers to carry out the arrest. The generals suspect something. And at that moment, the eight Grass rifles swing through the air and aim at Tovar's and Amaya's heads. "I think something's gone wrong," says Tovar, or maybe Amaya. "Traitors!

Turncoats!" shouts Amaya, or maybe it's Tovar. According to some versions, that's when they both say in unison: "I suspected as much."

At 6:05, revolutionary demonstrations begin to occupy the streets of Panama City. Collective shouts go up: "*Viva Panamá Libre!* Long live General Huertas! Long live President Roosevelt!" And most of all: "Long live the Canal!" The governmental military, in fear, load their weapons. One of them, General Francisco de Paula Castro, is discovered hidden in a stinking latrine. He has his breeches up, all the buttons of his uniform well fixed in their buttonholes, so the excuse offered (which makes reference to certain intestinal upset) loses validity; nevertheless, this Francisco would go down in history as the General Who Was Scared Shitless. At 8:07: Colonel Jorge Martinez, in command of the cruiser *Bogotá* anchored in the revolutionary city's bay, receives news of the occurrences on land and sends Dr. Manuel Amador, leader of the insurgents, the following message: "Either you hand the generals over to me or I'll bomb Panama City." Amador, excited by the revolution, loses his composure and replies: "Do whatever the hell you want, if you've got the balls." At 8:38: Colonel Martinez examines his balls and finds them full of fifteen-pound shells. He approaches the shore, loads his cannons, and fires nine times. The first shell lands in El Chorrillo neighborhood, on Sun Hao Wah (Chinese, killed on impact) and a few meters from Octavio Preciado (Panamanian, killed by heart attack provoked by the fright). Shell number two destroys the house of Ignacio Molino (Panamanian, absent at the time) and number three hits a building on West Twelfth Street, killing Babieca (Panamanian, percheron horse). Shells number four through nine do not cause any damage whatsoever.

At 9:01: the Revolutionary Junta, meeting in the Panama City's Hotel Central, presents the flag of the future Republic. It has been designed by Dr. Manuel Amador's son (applause) and sewn by Dr. Manuel Amador's wife (applause and gazes of admiration). At 9:03: explanation of the symbols. The red square represents the Liberal Party. The blue square represents the Conservative Party. The stars, well, the stars will be something like peace between the parties, or the eternal concord of the new Republic, or some pretty little idea along those lines—they'd have to come to an agreement or put it to a vote. At 9:33: Dr. Manuel Amador reveals details of his trip to New York in search of North American support for the secession of Panama to those who don't know about it. He speaks of a Frenchman, a certain Philippe Bunau-Varilla, who advised him on all the practical details of the revolution, and even supplied him with a briefcase with the following contents: a declaration of independence, a model constitution for new countries, and some military instructions. The audience applauds with admiration. Those French sure know how to do things, damn it. At 9:45: the Revolutionary Junta proposes they send a telegram to his Excellency the President of the United States with the following text: SEPARATION MOVEMENT PANAMA REST OF COLOMBIA HOPES RECOGNITION YOUR GOVERNMENT FOR OUR CAUSE. But the conspirators' joy was premature. The revolution was not yet sealed. It still needed my intervention, which was lateral and superfluous and in any case dispensable, as also had been my treasonous silence, but it nevertheless stained me forever, contaminated me as cholera contaminates water. It was the moment when my crucified country (or maybe it was the new resurrected country?) chose me as evangelist.

"You shall testify," I was told. And that's what I'm doing.

Dawn was cloudy on November 4. Before seven I left without saying good-bye to you, dear Eloísa, who was sleeping faceup; I leaned down to give you a kiss on the forehead, and saw the first sign of the day's stifling, humid heat in your damp hair, a few locks sticking to the white skin of your neck. Later I would learn that at that very moment Colonel Eliseo

Torres, delegated commander of the Tiradores battalion, was urinating under a chestnut tree, and it was there, with one hand leaning on the trunk, that he found out about the generals' detention in Panama City. He went immediately to the Railroad Company offices; indignant, he demanded Colonel Shaler assign a train to take the Tiradores battalion across the Isthmus. Colonel Shaler could have invoked the Mallarino-Bidlack Treaty—as he in fact later did—and his obligation, established in that text, to maintain neutrality in any political conflict, but he did not. The only answer he gave was that the Colombian government had still not paid him the money it owed, and furthermore, to be honest, Colonel Shaler did not like to be spoken to in that tone of voice. "I'm sorry, but I cannot help you," said Colonel Shaler at the same time as I leaned down to kiss my little girl (careful not to wake her), and it's not impossible that as I did so, I would have thought of Charlotte and the happiness that had been snatched away from us by the Colombian war. Eloísa dear, my face close to yours, I smelled your breath and pitied your motherlessness and wondered if it was my fault in some obscure way. All events, I've learned over time, are connected: everything is a consequence of everything else.

The telephone rang at seven in the Company offices. While I was walking slowly through the streets of Christophe Colomb, taking my time, breathing the heavy morning air, and wondering what face my schizophrenic city would be wearing the day after the beginning of the revolution, from the Panama City station three of the conspirators were speaking to Colonel Eliseo Torres to suggest that he lay down his weapons. "Surrender to the revolution, but also to the evidence," one of them told him. "The oppression of the central government has been defeated." But Colonel Torres was not prepared to bow to the pressures of the separatists. He threatened to attack Panama City; he threatened to torch Colón as Pedro Prestán had done. José Agustín Arango, who was the conspirators' spokesman at that moment, informed him that Panama City had already embarked on the path to liberty and did not fear confrontation. "Your aggression will be repelled with the might of a just cause," he said (Colombians have always been good at grand phrases for precise moments). The call ended abruptly, with Colonel Eliseo Torres throwing the telephone with such force that it chipped the wood of the desk. The echo of the blow resounded through the high-ceilinged hallways of the Company and reached my ears (I was at the port, twenty meters from the Company entrance), but I didn't know, I couldn't have known, what it was about. Did I even wonder? I don't think so; I think at that moment I was distracted or rather absorbed by the color the Caribbean takes on overcast days. Limón Bay was not part of the immensity of the Atlantic, but a greenish-gray mirror, and on that mirror floated, in the distance, the silhouette of what looked like a toy model of the battleship *Nashville*. You could hear only a few seagulls, only the lapping of the waves against the breakwaters and the deserted docks.

Colón resembled a besieged city. In a way it was, of course, and would continue to be as long as the soldiers of the Tiradores carried on patrolling the muddy streets. Besides, the revolutionaries in Panama City were well aware that independence was only illusory while government troops remained on isthmian territory, and that was the reason for the phone calls and frenetic telegrams that went back and forth between the two cities. "As long as Torres remains in Colón," José Agustín Arango said to Colonel Shaler, "there is no republic in Panama." Around half past seven, at the time I was casually approaching a man selling bananas, Arango was dictating a telegraphic message for Porfirio Meléndez, leader of the separatist revolution in Colón. I asked the man if he knew what was going on in the Isthmus, and he shook his head. "Panama is seceding from Colombia," I told him.

His skin was leathery, his voice worn out, his decaying breath hit me in a dense wave: "I've been selling fruit at the railway for fifty years, boss," he said to me. "As long as there are Gringos with money, I couldn't care less about the rest."

A few meters from us, Porfirio Meléndez was receiving this telegram: AS SOON AS TORRES AND TIRADORES BATTALION LEAVE COLÓN PROCLAIM REPUBLIC OF PANAMA. Inside the Railroad Company offices the air was filled with bells and clatter and tense voices and heels on wooden floorboards. José Gabriel Duque, publisher and editor of the *Star & Herald*, had contributed a thousand dollars in cash to be used for the Colón chapter of the Revolution, and Porfirio Meléndez received it shortly before the following text made its way through the Company's machines: CONTACT COLONEL TORRES STOP TELL HIM REVOLUTIONARY JUNTA OFFERS TROOPS MONEY AND PASSAGE TO BARRANQUILLA STOP ONLY CONDITION COMPLETE ABANDONMENT OF ARMS AND SWEAR NOT TO TAKE UP ARMED STRUGGLE AGAIN.

"He'll never accept," said Meléndez. And he was right.

Torres had made camp in the middle of the street. The word *camp*, of course, was a bit grand for those tents set up on top of the broken or missing paving stones of Front Street. Across the road from the 4th of July saloon and Maggs & Oates pawnshop were the five hundred soldiers, and what was stranger still, the wives of the higher-ranking officers. They could be seen leaving before dawn and returning with saucepans full of river water; they were seen chatting among themselves with their legs tightly crossed under their petticoats, covering their mouths with a hand when they laughed. Anyway, two messengers from Porfirio Meléndez arrived at this makeshift camp, two smooth-chested young men in rope-soled sandals who had to fix their eyes on the horse shit on the ground to keep from staring at the officers' wives. Colonel Eliseo Torres received from their tiny hands a letter hurriedly composed at the Railroad Company. "The Panamanian revolution wants to avoid unnecessary bloodshed," read Colonel Torres, "and in this spirit of reconciliation and future peace, we invite you, Honorable Colonel, to surrender your weapons with no injury whatsoever to your dignity."

Colonel Torres returned the open letter to the younger of the two messengers (his greasy fingerprints remained on the edge of the page). "Tell that traitor he can stick his revolution up his ass," he replied. But then he thought better of it. "No, wait. Tell him that I, Colonel Eliseo Torres, send word that he has two hours to liberate the generals detained in Panama City. That if he does not, the Tiradores battalion will not only burn Colón to the ground but will also shoot every Gringo we can find, including women and children." Readers of the Jury: by the time this ultimatum reached the Railroad Company, by the time the most barbaric message he'd ever had to hear reached the ears of Colonel Shaler, I had already finished my conversation with the banana seller, finished my stroll through the port, I had already seen the silvery flash of the dead fish floating on their sides, washing up on the beach, crossed the railway lines stepping on the rails with the arch of my foot with an infantile delight, like that of children sucking their thumbs, and was walking toward Front Street, breathing the air of the deserted besieged city, the air of days that change history.

Colonel James Shaler, for his part, had summoned Mr. Jessie Hyatt, U.S. Vice Consul in Colón, and between the two of them they were deciding whether Colonel Torres's threats should be believed or treated as the impetuous flailing of a man in dire political straits. It was not a difficult decision (the image of children slaughtered and women raped by Colombian soldiers came to mind). So seconds later, when I passed the front door of the offices—still not knowing what was happening within—Vice Consul Hyatt had already given the order, and a secretary who spoke no Spanish in spite of having spent twenty-five months in Panama was climbing the stairs to wave a red, white, and blue flag from the roof. Now I think that if I'd looked up at that moment I probably could have seen it. But that doesn't matter: the flag, without my witnessing, waved in the humid air; and immediately, while Colonel Shaler ordered that the most prominent U.S. citizens be taken to the Freight House, the battleship *Nashville* docked with great noises from its boilers, huge displacement of Caribbean water, in the port of Colón, and seventy-five marines in impeccable white uniforms—knee-high boots, rifles tilted over their chests—disembarked in perfect order and occupied Freight House, positioning themselves on top of the goods wagons, under the arches of the railway entrance, ready to defend U.S. citizens from any attack. On the other side of the Isthmus there were immediate reactions: when he found out about the landing, Dr. Manuel Amador met with General Huertas, the man who had arrested the generals, and they were preparing to send revolutionary troops to Colón with the sole mission of helping the marines. It was not yet nine in the morning and already Colón-Aspinwall-Gomorrah, that schizophrenic city, was a powder keg ready to explode. It didn't explode at ten. It didn't explode at eleven. But at twenty past twelve, or thereabouts, Colonel Eliseo Torres arrived at Front Street and, as the bugle sounded, ordered the Tiradores battalion to fall in and line up in battle formation. He was preparing to eliminate the *Nashville* marines, to take by force the few available trains in the station and cross the Isthmus to put down the rebellion by the traitors to the nation.

Colonel Torres had gone deaf; the clock, faithful to its habits, continued its impassive ticking; at around one o'clock, General Alejandro Ortiz came from headquarters to dissuade him, but there was no getting through to him; General Orondaste Martinez tried at one-thirty, but Torres remained installed in a parallel reality where neither reason nor prudence could reach him.

"The Gringos are already under protection," General Martinez told him.

"Well, they won't be under mine," said Torres.

"The women and children have gone aboard a neutral ship," said Martinez, "which is anchored in the harbor. You're making a fool of yourself, Colonel Torres, and I've come to prevent your reputation from sinking any lower." Martinez explained that the *Nashville* had loaded its cannons and had them aimed at the Tiradores battalion's encampment. "The *Cartagena* scampered off like a rabbit, Colonel," he said. "You and your men have been left alone. Colonel Torres, do the sensible thing, please. Fall out of this ridiculous formation, save the lives of your men and let us invite you for a drink."

Those preliminary negotiations—carried out in the dense midday heat, in an atmosphere that seemed to dehydrate the soldiers like pieces of fruit left out in the sun—lasted five minutes. In this space of time, Colonel Torres accepted a summit meeting (in the summit of the Hotel Suizo, just across Front Street), and in the hotel restaurant drank three glasses of papaya juice and ate a sliced watermelon, and still had time to threaten to blow Martinez's unpatriotic brains out. The bugler serving as his aide, however, didn't eat anything, because no one offered him anything and his position prevented him from speaking unless his superior officer gave him permission. Then General Alejandro Ortiz joined the delegation. He explained the situation to Colonel Torres: the Tiradores battalion was decapitated; Generals Tovar and Amaya were still prisoners in Panama City, where the revolution was triumphing; all resistance against the independence movement was futile, since it implied confronting the army of the United States as well as the three hundred thousand dollars the Roosevelt government had offered to the cause of the new Republic; Colonel Torres could assume the reality of events or embark on a quixotic crusade that even his own government had given up for lost. By the time of the fourth glass of papaya juice, Colonel Torres began to weaken; by three o'clock in the afternoon he consented to meet Colonel James Shaler at the Railroad Company, and before five he'd agreed to withdraw his troops (the powder in the powder keg) from Front Street and set up camp outside the city. The chosen place was the abandoned hamlet of Christophe Colomb, where just one man lived with his daughter.

Eloísa and I were taking our siestas when the Tiradores battalion arrived, and the noise woke us both up at once. We saw them come into our street, five hundred soldiers, their faces stifled with the heat of their uniforms, necks swollen and tense, sweat running down their sideburns. They carried their rifles halfheartedly (bayonets pointing to the ground) and dragged their boots as if every step were a whole campaign. On the other side of the Isthmus, the separatists launched their manifesto. The Isthmus of Panama had been governed by Colombia "by the narrow criteria that long ago the European nations applied to their colonies," in view of which it decided "to reclaim its sovereignty," "create its own fate," and "fulfil the role the situation of its territory demands." Meanwhile, our little ghost town filled with the sounds of canteens and cooking pots, the clatter of bayonets being dismantled and rifles being cleaned with great care. The hamlet where my father had lived, where Charlotte and the engineer Madinier had lived, the place where the Colombian civil war had arrived to kill Charlotte and along the way give me a valuable lesson on the might of Great Events, now became again one of history's stages. The air was permeated with the smell of unwashed bodies, of clothing showing signs of the weight of the days; the more modest soldiers went behind the pillars to defecate out of view, but during that November evening it was more common to see them walk around the house, drop their trousers facing the street, find a comfortable spot under a palm tree, and crouch down with a defiant look on their faces. The smell of human shit floated through Christophe Colomb with the same shameless intensity as had French perfume years before.

"How long are they going to stay?" asked Eloísa.

"Until the Gringos kick them out," I said.

"They're armed," said Eloísa.

That they were: the danger had not passed; the powder keg had not yet been defused. Colonel Eliseo Torres, suspecting or foreseeing that the whole matter—his confinement to an abandoned neighborhood of old houses, bordered by the bay on three sides and Colón on the other—was nothing but an ambush, had posted ten guards to patrol round the whole hamlet. So that night we had to endure the noise of their caged beasts' footsteps passing by our veranda at regular intervals. Over the course of that night Eloísa and I spent besieged by the Colombian military, and beyond them by the separatist revolution, it occurred to me that perhaps, just perhaps, my life in the Isthmus had finished, that perhaps my life, as I'd known it, no longer existed. Colombia had taken everything from me; the last remnant of my previous life, of what could have been and was not, was this seventeen-year-old woman who looked at me with a terrified expression each time a soldier's shout reached our ears, at each hostile and paranoid *Who goes there?* followed by a shot fired in the air, a shot (I thought Eloísa must be thinking) like the one that had killed her mother. "I'm scared, *Papá*," Eloísa said. And that night she slept with me, like when she was a little girl. And to me Eloísa, in spite of the shapes filling out her nightgown, was a little girl, Readers of the Jury, was still my little girl.

I couldn't sleep a wink. I was talking to Charlotte's memory, asking her what I should do, but I got no answer: Charlotte's memory had turned inscrutable and unfriendly, looked away when she heard my voice, refused to advise me. Panama, meanwhile, shifted beneath my feet. Panama had once been said to be "flesh of Colombian flesh, blood of Colombian blood," and for me it was impossible not to think of my Eloísa, who slept at my side now unafraid (falsely convinced that I could protect her from anything), when remembering the flesh of the Isthmus that was about to be amputated a few kilometers from our shared bed. You were flesh of my flesh and blood of my blood, Eloísa; that's what I was thinking as I lay beside you, head resting on my elbow, and looked closely at you, closer than we'd been since you were a babe in arms, recently recovered from the risks of your extreme prematurity. . . . And I think that's when I realized.

I realized that you were also flesh of the flesh of your land, I realized that you belonged to this country the way an animal belongs to its particular landscape (made for certain colors, certain temperatures, certain fruit or prey). You were Colónian as I never was, Eloísa dear: your mannerisms, your accent, your different appetites reminded me with the insistence and fanaticism of a nun. Each of your movements said to me: I am from here. And seeing you up close, seeing your eyelids vibrating like the wings of a dragonfly, at first I thought I envied you, that I envied your instinctive rootedness—because it hadn't been a decision, because you'd been born with it the way one is born with a mole or one eye a different color from the other—then, seeing how placidly you slept in this land of Colón that seemed to blend with your body, I thought I would have liked to ask you about your dreams, and finally thought again of Charlotte, who never belonged to Colón or to the province of Panama or much less to the convulsive Republic of Colombia, the country that had exterminated her family. . . . And I thought of what had happened at the bottom of the Chagres River that afternoon when she decided it was worthwhile to go on living. Charlotte had taken that secret to the grave, or the grave had come looking for her before she'd had time to reveal it to me, but it had always made me happy (briefly, secretly happy) to think that I had something to do with that deep decision in the depths. Thinking of that I laid my head on your chest, Eloísa, and the scent of your naked underarm reached me, and I felt so calm for a moment, so deceitfully and artificially calm, that I ended up falling asleep.

The martial maneuvers that, according to Eloísa, the Tiradores battalion carried out in front of our house did not wake me up. I slept dreamlessly, without any notion of time; and then Panamanian reality came flooding in. At about noon, Colonel Shaler was standing on my front porch, beside the hammock that had belonged to my father, pounding on the screen door so hard he might have knocked it off its hinges. Before starting to wonder where Eloísa had gone on this exceptional day when all the schools were closed, the smell of the fish stew she was cooking in the kitchen reached my nose. I barely had time to pull on a pair of boots and a decent shirt and answer the door. Behind Shaler, far enough back not to be able to hear his words, was Colonel Eliseo Torres, duly accompanied by his bugler.

Shaler said: "Lend us your table, Altamirano, and serve us some coffee, for the love of God. You won't regret it, I swear. At this table history is going to be made."

It was a heavy oak table, with round legs and a drawer with iron rings on each of the longest edges. Shaler and Torres sat on opposite sides, each in front of a drawer, and I sat at the head of the table where I always sat; the bugler stood out on the porch looking at the street occupied by the Tiradores soldiers, as if the battalion still expected a treacherous attack from the revolutionaries or the marines. So we were sitting, and were still settling into the heavy chairs, when Colonel Shaler put both hands, like gigantic water spiders, on the table and began to speak with his tongue tangled by the stubbornness of his accent but with the persuasive powers of a hypnotist.

"Honorable Colonel Torres, allow me to speak frankly: yours is a lost cause."

"What?"

"The independence of Panama is a fait accompli."

Torres leapt to his feet, his eyebrows arched indignantly, and attempted an unconvincing protest: "I haven't come here to—" But Shaler cut him off.

"Sit down, man, don't be foolish," he said. "You have come here to listen to offers. And I have a very good one, Colonel."

Colonel Torres tried to interrupt him—his hand went up, his throat emitted a snarl—but Shaler, consummate hypnotist, shut him up with his gaze. Before the day was out, he explained, the battleships *Dixie* and *Maryland* would appear in Limón Bay, full to the gunnels with U.S. Marines. The *Cartagena* had fled at the slightest sign of confrontation, and that should give him an idea of the central government's position. On the other hand, nobody could shout about independence as long as the Tiradores remained physically present on the Isthmus, and the *Cartagena* was the battalion's only means of transport. "But this morning things have changed, Colonel Torres," said Shaler. "If you look out toward the port, you'll see anchored in the distance a steamship with a Colombian flag. It's the *Orinoco*, a passenger ship." Colonel Shaler steadied his spider-like hands on the dark wood of the oak table, on each side of a coffee served in French porcelain, and said that the *Orinoco* would be sailing for Barranquilla at half past seven that evening. "Colonel Torres: I've been authorized to offer you the sum of eight thousand U.S. dollars if you and your men can be on board by then."

"But this is a bribe," said Torres.

"Certainly not," said Shaler. "That money is for rations for your troops, who well deserve it."

And at that moment, like a punctual extra in a theater play—and we already know, Readers of the Jury, who was angelically directing ours—the revolutionaries' agent in Colón, Porfirio Meléndez, appeared on my front porch. He was accompanied by a *cargador* from the Freight House carrying a chest on his shoulders, like he would a small child (as if the *cargador* was a proud father and the leather chest his son who wanted to see the parade).

"Is this it?" asked Shaler.

"This is it," said Meléndez.

"Lunch is almost ready," said Eloísa.

"I'll let you know," I told her.

The *cargador* dropped the chest on the table and the cups jumped in their saucers, splashing the coffee left in them and coming perilously close to getting chipped. Colonel Shaler explained that inside were eight thousand dollars removed from the coffers of the Panama Railroad Company under the guarantee of the Brandon Bank of Panama City. Colonel Torres stood up, walked to the porch, and said something to his bugler, who immediately disappeared. Then he returned to the negotiating table (to my dining-room table, awaiting a fish stew and finding itself involuntarily transformed into a negotiating table). He did not say a single word, but Shaler the hypnotist didn't need words at that moment. He understood. He understood perfectly.

Porfirio Meléndez opened the chest.

"Count it," he said to Torres. But Torres had folded his arms and did not move.

"Altamirano," said Shaler, "you're the host of this meeting. You represent neutrality, you're the judge. Count the money, please."

Readers of the Jury: the Angel of History's sense of humor, that sublime comedian, was confirmed for the umpteenth time on that fifth of November 1903, between one and four in the afternoon, in the Altamirano-Madinier house in the Christophe Colomb neighborhood of the future Republic of Panama. During those hours I, evangelist of the crucifixion of Colombia, handled a greater quantity of U.S. dollars than I had ever in my life seen in one place. The acrid, metallic smell of the dollars stuck to my hands, these clumsy hands that were not used to touching what they held that afternoon. My hands don't know—have never known—how to shuffle cards for poker; imagine how they felt faced with what fate brought before them that day. . . . Eloísa, who had stopped in the frame of the kitchen door with a wooden spoon in her hand, ready to give me a taste of the stew, witnessed my quasi-notarial labor. And something happened at that moment, because I was unable to look her in the eye. *I am flesh of Colón flesh.* Eloísa did not remind me out loud, but she didn't have to: she didn't have to pronounce those words for me to hear them. *I am blood of Panamanian blood.* We did not share that, Eloísa dear, that's what separated us. In the middle of the revolution that would carry off Panama, I realized that you, too, could be dragged far away from me; the Isthmus was detaching itself from the continent and beginning to distance itself from Colombia, floating in the Caribbean Sea like an abandoned lighter, and carrying off my daughter, my daughter who had fallen asleep inside, under the palm leaves, on top of the cases of coffee covered in ox hides like my stepfather used to use in happier times, when he traded up and down the Magdalena River. . . . My hands moved, passing worn bills and pil-ing up silver coins, but I could have paused to tell her to go ahead and eat her lunch, or given her a complicit or perhaps cheerful glance so we understood each other, but none of that happened. I kept count-ing with my head bowed, like a medieval thief about to be decapitated, and after a certain point the movements became so automatic that my mind could occupy itself with the other thoughts pushing and shoving their way in. I wondered if my mother had died in pain, what my father would have thought if he'd seen me at this juncture. . . . I thought of the dead engineer, of his dead son, of the profound irony that yellow fever should have given me the only love I'd ever known. . . . All the images were ways of avoiding the limitless humiliation that was overwhelming me. And then, at some moment, my humiliated voice began to give out figures almost of its own accord. Seven thousand nine hundred and ninety-seven. Seven thousand nine hundred and ninety-eight. Seven thousand nine hundred and ninety-nine. The end.

Colonel Shaler left as soon as Torres declared himself satisfied with the receipt of his money for rationing his troops; before leaving, he said to Torres: "Send one of your men to the Company offices before six to collect the tickets. Tell him to ask for me, I'll be expecting him." Then he said good-bye to me with a rather casual salute. "Altamirano, you've been of great service to us," he said. "The Republic of Panama is grateful." He turned toward Eloísa and clicked his heels. "Señorita, a pleasure," he said, and she nodded, still with the wooden spoon in hand, and soon went back into the kitchen to serve lunch, because life had to go on.

Now you can understand, Eloísa: it was the most bitter fish stew I've ever eaten. The yucca and the *arracacha* tasted like much-handled coins. The flesh of the fish did not smell of onion or coriander but of dirty dollar bills. Eloísa and I lunched as the street filled with soldiers' movements, the laborious drive of the battalion taking down their tents and packing up their equipment and beginning to depart Christophe Colomb for the Railroad Company wharf, to leave the way open for the revolution. Later the sky cleared and a merciless sunlight fell over Colón like a herald of the dry season. Eloísa, I remember perfectly the expression of serenity, of complete confidence, with which you went to your room, picking up the copy of *María* you were reading, and lay down in your hammock. "Wake me up when it gets dark," you said. And in a matter of minutes you'd fallen asleep, with your index finger stuck between the pages of the novel, looking like the Virgin receiving the Annunciation.

Eloísa dear: God knows, if he exists, that I did all I could to let you catch me in the act. My body, my hands, took on a deliberate slowness in the process of taking out of the utility room (which in the houses on stilts of Christophe Colomb was barely a corner in the kitchen) the smallest trunk, one I could carry without help. I dragged it instead of picking it up, perhaps intending that the noise might wake you, and when I dropped it onto the bed, I didn't worry about the creaking of the wood. Eloísa, I even allowed myself time to choose certain outfits, discard some, carefully fold the others . . . all to try to give you time to wake up. I looked on the desk that had belonged to Miguel Altamirano for a leather bookmark; you didn't notice when I took the book out of your hands taking care not to lose your place. And there, standing next to your sleeping body that did not sway in your hammock, beside your breathing so quiet that the movements of your chest and shoulders were not visible at first glance, I looked through the novel for the letter in which María confesses to Efraín that she is ill, that she is slowly dying. He, from London, comes to believe that only his return can save her and sets off immediately; a short time later he passes through Panama, crosses the Isthmus, and boards the schooner *Emilia López* that takes him to Buenaventura. At that moment, on the brink of doing what I was planning to do, I felt for Efraín the most intense sympathy I've ever felt for anyone in my life, because I seemed to see in his fictional destiny an inverted and distorted version of my real destiny. By way of Panama, he returns from London to find his beloved; from Panama, I was beginning to flee, leaving behind that budding woman who was my entire life, and London was one of my probable destinations.

I set the book on top of you and walked down the porch steps. It was six o'clock in the evening, the sun had sunk into Lake Gatún, and the *Orinoco*, that shitty ship, was beginning to fill with shitty soldiers from a shitty battalion, and in one of its compartments was a shipment of enough dollars to break a continent in two, open geological faults, and disrupt borders, not to mention lives. I stayed on deck until the port of Colón was out of sight, until the lights of the Cunas that Korzeniowski had seen years before, as he approached our shores, had disappeared from sight. The landscape I'd been part of for more than a quarter of a century disappeared suddenly, devoured by the distance and the mists of the night, and with it disappeared the life I led there. Yes, Readers of the Jury, I know very well it was my ship that was moving; but there, on the deck of the *Orinoco*, I could have sworn that before my eyes the Isthmus of Panama had separated from the continent and was beginning to float away, like a lighter, and I knew inside that adrift lighter was my daughter. I confess it willingly: I don't know what I would have done, Eloísa, if I had seen you, if you had woken up in time and, understanding everything in a flash of lucidity or clairvoyance, had rushed to the port to beg me with your hands or eyes not to go, not to leave you, my only daughter, who still needed me.

After taking from the Isthmus the last fallback of Colombian central power, after guaranteeing with its departure that Panamanian independence was definitive and irrevocable, the *Orinoco* put into port at Cartagena and stopped there for a few hours. I remember the spotty face of a corporal who gambled away his last paycheck on a game of poker dice. I remember the scene kicked up by a lieutenant's wife in the dining room (according to some, there was another woman involved). I remember

Colonel Torres ordering a subordinate to spend thirty days in the brig for suggesting there was money somewhere on board, American money that had been paid in exchange for that desertion, and that the soldiers were owed a share of it.

The next morning, with the first light on the pink horizon, the *Orinoco* arrived in Barranquilla.

By the afternoon of November 6, the government of President Theodore Roosevelt had granted the Republic of Panama its first formal recognition, and the *Marblehead*, the *Wyoming*, and the *Concord*, of the U.S. Pacific fleet, headed for the Isthmus to protect the nascent Republic from Colombian restoration efforts. Meanwhile, I found a ticket for the passenger steamer *Hood*, of the Royal Mail, that plied the Barranquilla–London route, from the mouth of the Magdalena to the belly of the Thames, and prepared to embark on that journey which did not include my daughter. How could I condemn Eloísa to exile and uprootedness, too? No, my broken country had broken me inside, but she, seventeen years old, had the right to a life free of that rupture, free of the voluntary ostracism and phantoms of exile (for she, flesh of my flesh, was also flesh of Colón flesh, as I was not). And I, of course, could no longer give her that life. My adored Eloísa: if you are reading these lines, if you have read those that precede them, you've witnessed all the forces that overcame us, and perhaps you've understood the extreme acts a man must carry out to defeat them. You've heard me talk of Angels and Gorgons, of the desperate battles I fought against them for the control of my own minuscule and banal life, and you can perhaps testify to the honesty of my private war and can forgive the cruelties this war has led me to commit. And you can especially understand that there was no longer a place for me in the wastelands I was able to escape, those cannibal lands where I no longer recognized myself, that no longer belonged to me the way a homeland belongs to a satisfied man, to a clean conscience.

Later came the arrival, the encounter with Santiago Pérez Triana, those events I have put, as meticulously as I was able, before the reader. . . . Joseph Conrad left the house at 45 Avenue Road at about six in the morning, after spending a sleepless night listening to my story. Over the years I have reconstructed the days that followed: I knew that after seeing me, he had gone not to his residence at Pent Farm but to a London flat near Kensington High Street, a cheap and dark place he and his wife had rented and where he habitually met Ford Madox Ford to write, in collaboration (and effortlessly), the adventure novels that might pull them out of poverty. By the time he arrived at the flat, Joseph Conrad already knew that *Nostromo*, that problematic novel, was no longer the simple story of Italians in the Caribbean it had been up till then, and would rather examine up close the traumatic birth of a new country in traumatized Latin America, which he'd just been told about in doubtless hyperbolic terms, doubtless contaminated by tropical magic, by the tendency to mythologizing that oppresses those poor people who don't understand politics. Jessie received him in tears: Borys had a fever of thirty-nine degrees, the doctor hadn't arrived, Borys wouldn't eat or drink, London was a city of uncaring, distant people. But Conrad didn't listen to her complaints: he went straight to that desk that wasn't his and, seeing that dawn was slow in breaking, lit that lamp that wasn't his, and began to take notes on what he'd heard over the course of the night. The next day, after a breakfast he ate but didn't taste, he began to incorporate the new material into the manuscript. He was very excited; like Poland, like the Poland of his childhood, the Poland his parents had died for, this little land of Panama, this little province transformed into a republic by inscrutable arts, was a pawn on the board of world politics, a victim of forces that exceeded it. . . . "And apropos, what do you think of the Yankee Conquistadores in Panama?" he wrote to Cunninghame Graham just before Christmas. "Pretty, isn't it?"

The first installment of *Nostromo* appeared in *T.P.'s Weekly* in January 1904, more or less at the same time that the Panama Canal Company sold all its properties to the United States, without a single Colombian representative even allowed to participate in the negotiations, and twenty days after my desperate country had made the Panamanians this humiliating proposal: Panama City would be the new capital of Colombia if the Isthmus rejoined Colombian territory. While Panama refused outright like a spurned lover (batting eyelashes, listing past grievances, arms akimbo and fists on hips), Santiago Pérez Triana gave me directions to the nearest newsagent and forced me to look through my pocket for those coins whose confusing denominations I still hadn't mastered and separate out, into another pocket, the exact cost of the *Weekly*. Then he sent me outside with an affectionate pat on the back. "My esteemed Altamirano, don't come back without that magazine," he said. And then, more seriously: "I congratulate you. You are now part of the memory of mankind."

But that's not how it went.

I was not part of mankind's memory.

I remember the slanted, blinding light on the street when I found the place, that winter light that cast no shadows yet dazzled me, reflecting off the paper of the magazines on sale and, depending on the angle, the glass of the recently cleaned windows. I remember the mix of excitement and terror (a mute, cold terror, terror of the new) as I went back outside after paying. I remember the misty and a little unreal quality that the rest of the objects in the world took on for me, the passersby, the lampposts, the occasional carriages, the park's threatening railings.

However, I don't remember the reasons I postponed reading, I don't remember having guessed that the contents of the magazine would not be what I was expecting, I don't remember having had any reasons to allow that implausible intuition into my head, I don't remember suspicion or persecution accompanying me during that long circular walk around Regent's Park.... Yes, that's right: I carried the magazine in my pocket all day, patting my side occasionally to make sure it was still there, as if the one I'd bought was the only copy in the world, as if the dangerous nature of its contents would be neutralized if I kept it in my power. But what had to happen (everyone knows it) ended up happening. Nothing can be delayed forever. No one can find reasons to put off forever something as innocent, as peaceful, as inoffensive, as the reading of a book.

So at about four, when the sky was already beginning to darken, I sat down on one of the park benches at the same time as an incipient snowfall began over London and perhaps over all of Imperial England. I opened the magazine, I read that word that will pursue me till the end of my days. *Nostromo*: three bland syllables, one repeated and insistent vowel like an eye that keeps watch on us.... I carried on, between oranges and galleons, between sunken rocks and mountains that sink their heads in the clouds, and began to wander like a sleepwalker through the story of that fictitious republic, and I traveled through descriptions and events that I knew and at the same time did not know, that seemed my own and alien at the same time, and I saw the Colombian wars, the Colombian dead, the landscape of Colón and Santa Marta, the sea and its color and the mountain and its dangers, and there it was, at last, the discord that had always been.... But there was something missing in that tale: an absence was more visible than all those presences. I remember my desperate search, the frenzy of my eyes going over each page of the magazine, the heat I felt in my armpits and whiskers as I entered into that painful truth.

Then I knew.

I knew I would see Conrad again.

I knew there would be a second encounter.

I knew this encounter could not be postponed.

In a matter of minutes I had arrived at Kensington High Street, and a newspaper seller directed me to Gordon Place, where the novelist lived. There was hardly any light left (an old man was going along with a ladder, climbing up and down the movable steps, lighting the street lamps) when I knocked on his door. I didn't reply to the questions the unsuspecting woman who answered the door asked me; I brushed against her apron as I passed, I ran up the steps as fast as my legs could carry me. I don't remember what ideas, what indignation went through my head while I opened doors and crossed hallways, but I know for certain that nothing had prepared me for what I found.

There were two dark rooms, or they'd gone dark in the premature January dusk. A door connected them, and that door was open at the moment of my arrival, but it was obvious that its function was to remain stubbornly, constantly, and inevitably closed most of the time. In the back room, contained by the door frame, there was a desk of dark wood, and on top of the desk a pile of papers and a paraffin lamp; in the other room, the one I'd just burst into, a little boy with long brown hair slept on a miserable-looking cot (he was breathing laboriously, snoring a little), and the other bed in view was occupied by a woman in street clothes, a woman with an inelegant and chubby-cheeked face who was not lying down but reclining against a backrest, and who had some sort of board across her lap that after a couple of seconds (after my eyes adjusted to the interior lighting) turned into a portable desk. From her closed hand emerged a black-tipped pen, and it was as I focused on her and the ink-covered pages that I heard the voice.

"What are you doing here?"

Joseph Conrad was standing in the corner of the room; he was wearing leather slippers and a housecoat of dark silk; he was wearing, most of all, an expression of intense, almost inhuman concentration. In my head the pieces fell into place: I had interrupted him. To be more precise: I had interrupted his dictation. To be even more precise: while the first scenes of *Nostromo* were getting wrinkled in my pocket, in that room Conrad was dictating the last ones. And his wife, Jessie, was in charge of putting the story—the story of José Altamirano—onto the blank pages.

"You," I said, "owe me an explanation."

"I owe you nothing," said Conrad. "Leave immediately. I'll call someone, I'm warning you."

I took the copy of the *Weekly* out of my pocket. "This is false. This is not what I told you."

"This, my dear sir, is a novel."

"It's not my story. It's not the story of my country."

"Of course not," said Conrad. "It's the story of my country. It's the story of Costaguana."

Jessie watched us. Her expression was one of attentive confusion, like one who's arrived late to the theater. She started to speak, and her voice was weaker than I'd expected: "Who . . . ?" But she didn't finish the question. She tried to move, and a grimace of pain exploded across her face, as if a cord had broken inside her body.

Conrad then invited me into the backroom; the door was closed, and through the wood we could hear the woman's sobs.

"She's had an accident," said Conrad. "Both knees. Both knees dislocated. It's serious."

"It was my life," I said. "I entrusted it to you, I trusted you."

"A fall. She was out shopping, she'd gone to Barker's, she slipped. Seems silly, doesn't it? That's why we are in London," said Conrad. "She must be examined every day, the doctors come every day. We do not know if she'll need surgery."

It was as if he'd stopped listening to me, this man who'd spent a whole night doing nothing else. "You've eliminated me from my own life," I said. "You, Joseph Conrad, have robbed me." I waved the *Weekly* in the air again, and then threw it down on his desk. "Here," I whispered, my back to the thief, "I do not exist."

It was true. In the Republic of Costaguana, José Altamirano did not exist. My tale lived there, the tale of my life and my land, but the land was another, it had another name, and I had been removed from it, erased like an unmentionable sin, obliterated without pity like a dangerous witness. Joseph Conrad told me of the terrible effort of dictating the story under the present conditions, and dictating it to Jessie, whose pain prevented her from working with due concentration. "I could dictate a thousand words an hour," he told me. "It's easy. The novel is easy. But Jessie gets distracted. She cries. I wonder if she'll be left an invalid, if she'll have to use crutches for the rest of her life. I'll soon be forced to hire a secretary. The boy is ill. Debts pile up on my desk, and I must submit this manuscript on time to avoid greater disasters. And then you came along, answered a number of questions, told me a number of more or less useful things, and I have used them as my intuition and knowledge of this trade dictated. Think of this, Altamirano, and tell me: Do you really believe your little sensitivities have the slightest importance? Do you really think so?" In the other room the bed boards creaked, and it was presumably Jessie who emitted those timid groans of pain as genuine as they were selfless. "Do you really believe your pathetic life has anything to do with this book?"

I approached his desk. I noticed then that there wasn't one pile of papers but two: one of them consisted of marked-up pages, with crossings out, marginal notes, dark arrows, wavy lines eliminating whole paragraphs; the other was a stack of typed pages that had been corrected several times. *My corrected life*, I thought. And also: *My misappropriated life*. "Stop it," I said to Conrad.

"That's impossible."

"You can do it. Stop it all." I picked up the manuscript. My hands moved with an impulse that seemed beyond my control. "I'll burn it," I said. In two steps I was at the window; with a hand on the catch, I said, "I'll throw it out."

Conrad crossed his arms behind his back. "My tale is now on its way, dear friend. It is already on the street. Right now, as you and I speak, there are people reading the story of the wars and revolutions of that country, the story of that province that secedes over a silver mine, the history of the South American Republic that does not exist. And there is nothing you can do about it."

"But the republic does exist," I said, or rather beseeched him. "The province does exist. But the silver mine is really a canal, a canal between two oceans. I know because I know it. I was born in that republic, I lived in that province. I am guilty of its misfortunes."

Conrad didn't answer. I returned the manuscript to his desk, and doing so was like a concession, like the laying down of weapons by a warrior chief. At what moment does a man concede defeat? What happens in his head to convince him to give up? I would have liked to ask those things.

Instead, I asked: "How does it all end?"

"Pardon?"

"How does the history of Costaguana end?"

"I'm afraid you already know that, my dear Altamirano," said Conrad. "It's all here, in this chapter, and it might not be what you're expecting. But there is nothing, absolutely nothing that you don't know." He paused and added: "I can read it to you, if you like."

I went over to the window, which by then was a darkened square. And I don't know why, but there, looking out toward the street, refusing like a child what was going on behind my back, I felt safe. It was a false sensation, of course, but I didn't care. I couldn't have cared.

"Read," I said. "I'm ready."

Life out on the street began to die down. The intense cold was reflected in the faces of passersby. My eyes and mind were distracted by the image of a little girl playing with her dog on the icy pavement—dark red coat, a scarf that looked thin from the distance—and while that confident voice began to speak to me of the destiny of those characters (and obliged me to some extent to attend the revelation of my own destiny), the snow fell in dense flakes on the pavement and melted immediately, forming little stars of damp that vanished straightaway. Then I thought of you, Eloísa, and of what I'd done to us; without asking permission I opened the window, leaned outside, and looked up so the falling snow would wet my eyes, so the snow would camouflage my tears, so Santiago Pérez Triana would not notice I'd been crying when he saw me. Suddenly, only you mattered; I realized, not without some terror, that only you would ever matter. And I knew: there, among gusts of icy wind, I knew what my punishment was. I knew that, many years later, when time had left behind my conversation with Joseph Conrad, I would go on remembering that afternoon when I disappeared from history by magic, I would go on being aware of the magnitude of my loss but also of the irreparable damage the events of my life had caused us, and most of all I would go on waking up in the middle of the night wondering, as I'm wondering now, where you might be, Eloísa, what kind of life you will have had, what place you will have occupied in the unfortunate history of Costaguana.

AUTHOR'S NOTE

It's possible *The Secret History of Costaguana* arose from *Nostromo*, which I read for the first time in Francis and Suzanne Laurenty's house (Xhoris, Belgium) during the summer of 1998; it's possible that it came from the essay "El *Nostromo* de Joseph Conrad," which Malcolm Deas included in his book *Del poder y la gramatica*, which I read in Barcelona at the beginning of the year 2000; and it's possible that it came from an informative article that Alejandro Gaviria published in the Colombian journal *El Malpensante* in December 2001. But it is also possible (and this is my preferred possibility) that the first hunch of the novel came into being in the year 2003, while I was writing, for my friend Conrado Zuluaga, a brief biography of Joseph Conrad. The opportune commission obliged me to revise, out of rigor or curiosity, Conrad's letters and novels, as well as Deas's and Gaviria's texts and many others, and at some point it struck me as implausible that this novel had not been written before, which is undoubtedly the best reason someone can have for writing a novel. Among the fifty or so books I read in order to write this one, it would be dishonest not to mention *Joseph Conrad: The Three Lives* by Frederick Karl, *The Path Between the Seas* by David McCullough, *Conrad in the Nineteenth Century* by Ian Watt, *History of Fifty Years of Misrule* by José Avellanos, and *1903: Adiós, Panama* by Enrique Santos Molano. It would be unjust to forget certain phrases that accompanied the writing of the novel as guides or as tutors and that would have been epigraphs if it hadn't seemed to me, in a capricious and rather untenable way, that they would break the chronological autonomy of my tale. From the story "Guayaquil" by Borges: "It may be that one cannot speak about the Caribbean republic without echoing, however remotely, the monumental style of its most famous historian, Captain Józef Korzeniowski." From *A History of the World in 10½ Chapters* by Julian Barnes: "We make up a story to cover the facts we don't know or can't accept, we keep a few true facts and spin a new story round them. Our panic and our pain are only eased by soothing fabulation; we call it history." From *Artificial Respiration* by Ricardo Piglia: "The only things that are mine are things whose history I know." Joyce's "History is a nightmare from which I am trying to awake" was useless to me; it's fine for Stephen Dedalus, but José Altamirano, I think, would feel closer to notions of farce or vaudeville.

Be that as it may, the first pages of the novel were written in January 2004. Over the course of the more or less two years that passed until the definitive version, many people got involved in its composition, voluntarily or involuntarily, directly or (very) indirectly, facilitating the writing on some occasions and life on others and on rare occasions both, and here I would like to record my gratitude and acknowledgments. They are, in the first place, Hernán Montoya and Socorro de Montoya, whose generosity can never be repaid with these couple of lines. And then Enrique de Hériz and Yolanda Cespedosa, Fanny Velandia,

Justin Webster and Assumpta Ayuso, Alfredo Vásquez, Amaya Elezcano, Alfredo Bryce Echenique, Mercedes Casanovas, María Lynch, Gerardo Marín, Juan Villoro, Pilar Reyes and Mario Jursich, Mathias Enard, Rodrigo Fresán, Pere Sureda and Antonia González, Héctor Abad Faciolince, Ramón González and Magda Anglès, Ximena Godoy, Ignacio Martínez de Pisón, Camila Loew, and Israel Vela.

This book owes something to all these people, and at the same time owes everything (as do I) to Mariana.

J.G.V.

A NOTE ON THE AUTHOR

Juan Gabriel Vásquez is the critically acclaimed, award-winning Colombian author of *The Informers*. He has translated works by E. M. Forster, Victor Hugo, and John Dos Passos, among others, into Spanish. His fiction has been translated into fourteen languages.

Educated in Colombia, and in Paris at the Sorbonne, he now teaches in Barcelona, where he lives with his wife and twin daughters.

A NOTE ON THE TRANSLATOR

Anne McLean has translated Latin American and Spanish novels, short stories, memoirs, and other writings by authors including Julio Cortázar, Ignacio Martínez de Pisón, Héctor Abad, Enrique Vila-Matas, and Tomás Eloy Martínez. Two of her translations have been awarded the *Independent* Foreign Fiction Prize: *Soldiers of Salamis* by Javier Cercas, in 2004, and Evelio Rosero's *The Armies*, in 2009.